ORION SIX

By DAN KLASING

Publisher, Copyright, and Additional Information

Orion Six
Copyright © 2025 by Dan Klasing

ISBNs:
979-8-9881498-6-6
Cover design and interior design by Rafael Andres

CHAPTER ONE

The cold rain that soaked Upper Austria during the night finally stopped, leaving behind soggy fields and muddy roads under a thick blanket of low-hanging clouds. On Gusen II's otherwise empty parade ground, bored guards shoved and kicked the unlucky prisoners chosen for the day's work party into two ragged lines. Moments later, a piercing whistle blown by the lead sergeant signaled the beginning of their short march to the Nazi's secret tunnel complex. Huddled together for warmth and support, the laborers hid injuries and fought the overwhelming fatigue of starvation as they struggled to place one foot in front of the other. They moved like robots, knowing that every painful step brought them closer to what might well be their last hour on earth.

The only female in the group, Rachel Cohen, followed a few steps behind the men. She kept her head down, short black hair falling over dark eyes, both arms wrapped tightly around an impossibly slim frame.

Rachel didn't know the two prisoners limping along just ahead of her. One man walked with his hand on the other's shoulder as they shuffled through the mud side by side, heads almost touching. She could see they were engaged in a hushed but intense conversation about something important. Intrigued, and with the guards somewhere up ahead preoccupied with shouting and cursing at other prisoners, she picked up her pace so she could hear what the two men were saying.

"Yes. The carpenter from C barracks, Goldman or something, told me he heard it straight from the fat, sweaty corporal who gets drunk every night."

"Do you believe him?" the other man asked. "Isn't that the same ugly bastard that claimed the Americans would be coming soon? I have not seen any of these Americans."

The first man looked around before answering.

"The Nazi pigs have been on edge. They are worried about something. But who really knows?"

Rumors shot through the camp faster than the winter wind sliced through the thin walls of the camp's barracks. And Rachel knew that gossip couldn't conjure up steaming loaves of bread or make the barbed wire fences disappear. Still, any tidbit of news could feed the last thing any of the prisoners possessed – hope.

Stepping forward, Rachel screwed up her courage and tapped one of the men on the back.

The man who claimed to know the carpenter turned around. Rachel looked up into a near-skeletal face framed by a filthy blanket draped over a bald head. Sunken, bloodshot eyes met hers with a look of disgust.

"What?" he snarled.

"I...I wanted to know what the carpenter heard," Rachel replied, unable to meet the man's steely gaze.

"You shouldn't be eavesdropping on conversations between men, little girl. And, why should I tell one of the Nazi's favorites anything?"

"But, I'm..."

"You work for them. You follow the work crews every morning. Most of us don't come back. You do. They give you clothes and shoes. You will run to them if I tell you anything."

Rachel plucked at the sides of the dark blue smock she wore over a threadbare prison dress and looked down at the crude wooden clogs that raised painful blisters on her bare feet. But she pressed on, desperately needing something she could cling to.

"I have no choice. They make me translate technical documents in one of their laboratories. And this," Rachel said, crumpling the front of the blue smock in her fist. "All this means is that the guards aren't allowed to pull me into their beds whenever they please."

The man's eyes softened a bit. "How old are you, child?"

"Eighteen."

"Well, since this shitty day will probably be my last, I'll tell you. The carpenter said that Hitler killed himself in Berlin a week ago. Now you know. May you live for many good days."

***

A few minutes later, the tunnel entrance loomed in the distance.

On either side of the wide rectangular opening, two giant eagles molded into massive steel doors faced each other, their wings spread and beaks open as if screaming at each other. Rachel had passed through the same doors every day for almost a year, but the dark void beyond still reminded her of the entrance to Hades, the realm of the dead from Homer's Odyssey. As a child, her father, a professor of history, had regaled her and her brother with fanciful tales of the ancient Greek underworld. But she had never expected to find herself walking into such a place under the Upper Austrian countryside.

Once inside, the guards marched the prisoners along a smooth concrete road next to two railroad tracks. Further on, a convoy of covered trucks waited to be loaded with wooden crates piled high on a concrete loading dock. As each vehicle backed up to the raised platform, soldiers shouted obscenities at the men loading the cargo, often punctuating their demands to work faster with pointless and savage kicks and blows from their rifles.

A few minutes later, one of the guards pushed Rachel out of line. Taking a separate tunnel leading down and to the left, she soon stood outside a long wooden structure built against the tunnel wall. At one end, a single door between two windows led into the office where she worked. The rest of the building stretched out to Rachel's left. The 30-yard-long windowless space contained one of the complex's research laboratories. That part of the building frightened her the most. She had heard that German scientists conducted high-altitude testing inside the lab. To what end, she had no idea. But a steady stream of prisoners had disappeared into that part of the building, never to return.

Rachel took a deep breath to steady her nerves before stepping through the open door. When she first came to the Gusen camp almost a year earlier, the laboratory office was ordered and efficient. But over the past several weeks, she had noticed the Germans growing increasingly tense. Now, she would be walking into near chaos. Smoke curled out the open door and windows from intense fires rising from several old oil drums. As clerical workers dumped armloads of papers into the barrels, the flames would subside, only to shoot back up toward the ceiling as the newly added documents ignited.

The Nazis apparently decided they couldn't, or perhaps shouldn't, save every bit of research generated in the underground laboratories.

"Get to the back," an officer Rachel barely recognized ordered as she stepped into the room. "There are piles of notebooks in English and French for you to sort. Keep anything related to aircraft or rocket technology. Burn everything else. Do you understand?"

Rachel stood a moment too long, unnerved by the man's wide, bloodshot eyes, sweat-covered forehead, and trembling lips.

"Go! Now!" the officer shouted, brutally slapping the Jewish girl across the face.

Rachel moved away quickly, rubbing her cheek and scurrying past the harried clerks and soldiers. A moment later, she slipped gratefully behind the small wooden table, tucked behind several filing cabinets in a back corner, where she translated English, French, and sometimes Italian documents into German.

Rachel got right to work, opening one notebook or set of documents after another. Her father had raised his children to speak and read several languages, but translating technical documents had proved challenging. Her skills had improved over the nearly five years she had been in the camps. But as she worked, she couldn't help but fear that her usefulness to the Germans was going up in flames along with the documents and records feeding the fires.

Rachel tried to overcome the sense of dread building quickly in her gut by concentrating on her task. Absorbed by her work, she wouldn't have noticed what happened next if she hadn't needed to deposit an armload of heavy notebooks into the burn box.

As she stood, a frighteningly tall soldier dressed in a black uniform stepped confidently through the open door and strode through the smoky office. The major that had slapped her earlier followed closely behind, like a dog obeying its cruel master. Rachel had never seen the black-uniformed officer wearing the rank of full colonel. But she knew *what* he was – SS.

Almost reflexively, Rachel took a step backward. The silver skull and crossbones on the officer's hat gleamed in the firelight, and his light blue eyes swept ominously across the entire space. Rachel gasped involuntarily at the harshness of the man's face and the long scar that bisected his left cheek from ear to jaw. For a brief moment, the SS officer's gaze fell directly on her.

Rachel froze, barely able to breathe. When the SS appeared, death always followed.

Somehow, Rachel managed to squirm backward into her chair and lower her eyes. When she glanced up again, the tall officer was motioning for someone to enter the building. All around, the work never stopped. The panicky clerks and soldiers in the office paid the SS colonel's sudden appearance little heed – or perhaps acted like they didn't notice.

But Rachel had to see what would happen next.

A moment later, two more SS men came through the door, followed by a shorter figure wrapped in a camel-hair overcoat and wearing a black fedora. This person walked upright but somewhat unsteadily, his chin peeking over the collar of his greatcoat. Small dark eyes peered out from under the brim of his hat, flitting back and forth as if expecting an imminent attack. Without a word, he followed the tall SS officer through the double doors leading into the now-empty laboratory.

Rachel had only observed the man for a few seconds as he walked between the flaming document barrels, and it took a moment for her mind to fully accept who she had just seen. When she did, the Jewish girl began trembling uncontrollably and tried not to scream.

No. Please, God. No. Do not let this be.

After a minute, Rachel forced herself to take one deep breath. And then another. Slowly, she stopped shaking and sat up straight in her chair. When she looked back toward the laboratory, her brow knitted together, and her hands balled into fists.

Rachel got back to work but kept one eye on the laboratory entrance. She watched for hours, but neither the man in the camel-hair coat nor the SS officer reappeared.

Rachel had no doubt about who she saw.

The carpenter's story was a lie.

But who would believe her?

Who could she tell?

CHAPTER TWO

Near Abwinden, Austria
The same day

As dawn began to chase away the low clouds hanging over the Austrian countryside, two monstrous half-track personnel carriers ground to a slow halt, leaving long chewed-up furrows in the muddy road. Ahead, the lonely farm track ended abruptly at the edge of a thick pine forest.

Second Lieutenant Cy Jacobson grabbed the lead vehicle's cold metal windshield frame and pulled himself out of his seat. His lips tightened into a thin line, and his eyes widened as the freshly commissioned West Point graduate tried to understand where he had gone wrong.

"Corporal, shut it off while I take a look around," Jacobson ordered.

"Yes, sir, Lieutenant, sir," the rather amused corporal sitting behind the steering wheel responded, tossing a mocking salute at the platoon's new commanding officer.

Jacobson rummaged in a canvas bag and pulled out a detailed map of the area before swinging the door open and jumping to the ground, landing less than gracefully on his hands and knees in the sticky muck.

As Jacobson climbed to his feet and wiped his hands on the trousers of his fresh combat fatigues, he could hear barely concealed laughter and snide comments from the grizzled combat veterans that filled the back of both vehicles.

"Awe, now that's just a shame. He got his nice new clothes dirty."

"Yeah, he ain't going to look very pretty if he ever does find this town or bridge or whatever."

"Not much chance of that. We've been riding around in circles for hours. Wake me up if the college boy ever figures out how to find his ass with both hands."

Bristling at the stinging remarks but more concerned about locating their objective, Jacobson snatched his map off the ground and spread it over the truck's fender.

Looking at his watch, Jacobson shook his head in disgust. His first mission should have been simple. Secure the small village of Abwinden and its crucial bridge over the Danube River. But the town was still nowhere in sight, and the hands of his watch seemed to taunt him with how far behind schedule they had fallen.

With the sun finally breaking through the overcast and illuminating the pastures and farmland of Upper Austria, Jacobson held onto the map with one hand as he desperately scanned the area for any landmark he could use to pinpoint their current position. He had spent the last four years training for this moment at West Point, the world's premier military academy. But with the Allies taking Berlin and the papers reporting Hitler's death, Jacobson knew this assignment might be his only chance to prove he could lead men in combat. And he was failing.

Consumed with getting his bearings, the lieutenant didn't notice Sergeant Fred Tucker stroll up and look over his shoulder. Standing at nearly six-foot-four, Tucker towered over Jacobson. The sergeant's wrists stuck out from sleeves far too short for his long arms, and a shock of straight red hair peeked out from under his cap. An impressive Adam's apple bobbed up and down over his collar when he spoke. The sergeant's sheer size and how he carried a submachine gun like an extension of his tattooed right arm intimidated Jacobson from the moment they met just the day before.

"Excuse me, *sir*," Tucker said in a thick southern accent dripping with sarcasm. "May I be of assistance, *sir*?"

Jacobson did his best not to show any reaction to Tucker's tone. He might have made a mess of the mission, but his training demanded he maintain an air of authority.

And it didn't hurt that he finally knew where they were.

"Abwinden is less than a mile ahead on the other side of those trees," Jacobson replied as confidently as possible, pointing south. "Headquarters doesn't anticipate much enemy resistance, but there have also been reports of die-hard true believers who refuse to throw in the towel. I don't want to take any chances, so I'm considering sending a small patrol ahead to scout out the area before committing the entire platoon. But I want your opinion. You've done this before. I haven't."

Tucker leaned over and studied the map for himself before standing upright, sticking a thick cigar in his mouth, and scanning their surroundings.

The dirt road where they stopped ran between two abandoned wheat fields. Ahead, the dense woods blocked any view of the town and prevented the half-tracks from continuing in that direction. They could find another way around, but they were already seriously behind schedule, and moving the loud vehicles closer could attract unwanted attention. After a moment, Tucker had to agree with Jacobson. The fact that the green kid came up with a decent plan and had the good sense to ask for his opinion were the first two things the lieutenant got right.

Maybe this baby-faced officer isn't going to get us all killed just before we get to go home after all. Maybe.

"Yep. Looks like we got to where we're supposed to be. I can take a couple of guys through those trees and report back by walkie-talkie," Tucker responded, dropping the condescending tone.

"Sounds good," Jacobson replied, refolding his map. "I'll go too."

"Uh, that's not necessary, sir," Tucker replied quickly. "We can go take a gander and be back here in no time."

"I know what you're thinking, Sergeant. But I can take care of myself."

Tucker had to clamp his teeth down on the cigar to keep from laughing out loud.

***

Tucker chose two less-than-eager men from the back of the personnel carrier and headed into the woods. Jacobson followed close behind, but before long, he was out of breath and struggling to keep up. He couldn't believe how quickly and quietly Tucker and his men could move through a forest.

Suddenly, Jacobson stumbled over a tree root, barely managing to stay on his feet.

Tucker turned and scowled but kept moving.

Jacobson could only put his head down and pick up his pace. After less than a mile, they arrived at the far edge of the trees. Ahead lay a newly plowed field. A hundred yards further on, the windows of several houses overlooked the open ground. Even Jacobson could see the windows provided perfect cover for snipers or machine-gun emplacements.

"I don't see any movement in the windows or streets. Looks quiet to me," Corporal Anthony Pernell reported softly from behind a pair of field binoculars. "Just another damn Kraut town."

"Jeez, Pernell, we've been in Austria for weeks. Krauts are *Germans*," Private Bill "Downtown" Downton chided. "You know that."

"Yeah, yeah. So, what do I care? They say the Krauts in Berlin and all over Germany are giving up. Why do they have us all the way out here in Australia, or Austria, or whatever, sticking our necks out?" Pernell groused in a thick Brooklyn accent.

"Yeah, how come, Sarge?" Downtown asked.

"Because I told you to. That's why. Now shut your mouths and open..."

Before Tucker could finish his sentence, a single shot rang out from the town, smacking into a tree trunk just above their heads.

Tucker, Pernell, and Downtown dove to the ground while Jacobson just froze in place.

In an instant, Tucker launched himself off the forest floor and tackled the stunned officer. As the big sergeant rolled them behind a sturdy pine, all hell seemed to break loose. Bullets buzzed through the woods. Bits of branches, leaves, and bark fell all around, severed from the trees by hundreds of rounds fired from the nearby houses. Jacobson could hear the sharp staccato of at least one machine gun interspersed with single cracks and pops from a variety of other small arms. The enemy had them pinned down.

"Damnit, Lieutenant, are you tryin' to get yourself killed?" Tucker shouted. "Stay down."

Jacobson, finally realizing that someone was trying to kill him, tried to make himself as small as possible. He would have melted into the ground if he could. He knew he should do something. Issue an order. Make a decision. But his brain seemed to be locked in a vicelike grip of terror and simply refused to cooperate.

Then he saw Tucker.

The big Tennessean sat with his back resting comfortably against the tree's trunk, casually checking his submachine gun and chewing absently on the now-mashed end of his cigar.

"Well, now. Somebody didn't get the word the war's over," Tucker said loudly enough for Jacobson to hear. "You think maybe we should call in a little artillery?"

Jacobson's eyes were as wide as dinner plates, but he managed to nod.

Tucker winked and made a signal for him to stay put.

"Downtown! The lieutenant wants you to call in a fire mission. Artillery support 100 yards west of our position. In the field," Tucker shouted.

Jacobson thanked the big sergeant with a second nod.

While the sporadic and inaccurate small-arms fire tore through the trees, the Americans waited, pressed themselves flat into the forest floor, and covered their ears.

The barrage took less than two minutes to arrive. Twenty 105mm artillery shells whistled overhead before slamming into the field, throwing massive plumes of dark earth into the sky. In the town, windows blew inward, and whole houses shook violently in the concussive blasts. Even nearly a hundred yards away, dirt and debris fell through the trees, splattering over the Americans.

The message had been sent loud and clear – surrender or the entire town disappears.

The Austrians' reaction came sooner than expected. As the smoke slowly drifted away from the field, Jacobson could make out a small white flag waving from a second-story window.

"What do you think, Sarge?" Pernell called.

"One way to find out, I suppose," Tucker replied loudly. "Coming, Lieutenant?"

Jacobson jumped to his feet, drew his Colt pistol with a shaky hand, and walked as steadily as he could manage next to Tucker out into the open. Downtown and Pernell followed on either side, their M-1 rifles up and looking for targets.

CHAPTER THREE

At first, they saw nothing. But soon, several soldiers appeared at the edge of the town with hands raised high over their heads. More emerged tentatively from houses and walked toward Jacobson and his men through wisps of smoke still rising from the newly created shell craters. Tucker waved them forward, aiming his Tommy Gun menacingly from his hip.

"Okay, boys, step right up! *Komm her*!" he shouted in bad German.

Jacobson counted fifteen men approaching. As they got closer, he was relieved to see they were mostly old men and one young boy – all wearing tattered, poorly-fitting infantry uniforms. He had heard the enemy was running short on manpower, but these men could hardly be called soldiers.

"They look like a bunch of shopkeepers and farmers," Downtown commented as the Austrian locals began to kneel in the field and place their hands behind their heads. "And they're all shaking in their boots for some reason."

"Yeah, like we're going to execute them on the spot. Something's fishy here," Pernell added.

Suddenly, one of the prisoners at the front of the group pointed backward and shouted, "SS! SS!"

The next instant, an enemy soldier hanging behind the others whipped open his long overcoat, revealing a hidden submachine gun.

Jacobson's head snapped around toward where the kneeling prisoner was pointing and tried to raise his pistol. But even as he did, he knew he was too late. Time seemed to slow down. The German's weapon rose directly at him, and Jacobson could see the murderous snarl on the SS soldier's face.

He was about to die.

Then, without warning, a sharp blast of gunfire exploded from behind Jacobson's head. The German stumbled backward, throwing his weapon in the air, before landing on his back.

"Nice shooting, Sarge!" Pernell blurted.

Jacobson stood speechless for a moment before turning to Tucker.

"Thank you, Sergeant," Jacobson said in a voice barely above a whisper.

Tucker wasn't at all surprised when his new lieutenant suddenly turned away and vomited.

After witnessing the SS officer's death, the rest of the Austrians began begging for mercy. The one young boy just cried openly.

"Damn, I hate it when they do that," Pernell huffed.

"Downtown, check the dead guy for papers," Tucker ordered. "You know the drill."

Downtown walked over to the corpse and opened the old gray coat the SS corporal wore to cover his black uniform. Rifling through the dead man's clothes, he retrieved an identity card and a single sheet of paper.

"What you got there?" Tucker asked.

"Well, this guy's name was Eric ... uh, something or other I can't pronounce. This paper looks like orders of some kind, but it's all in

Kraut," Downtown responded. "Maybe one of these jokers speaks English."

One of the prisoners slowly raised his hand. "I do not need to read the paper. I know what is written there," he offered hesitantly.

Tucker shrugged. "Okay then, what's it say?"

The prisoner stood and removed his cap, clutching it nervously in front of his crotch.

"He is ordered to die for the Führer and to force the local auxiliary detachment, us, to do the same," the man explained. "We did not want to fight. He forced us to shoot. He said he would kill our families if we disobeyed."

"That don't make any sense. If that's true, why did you surrender?" Tucker asked suspiciously.

"It is what he ordered us to do. He wanted to die killing Americans, not by, uh, the bombs," the prisoner responded, pointing to the shell holes all over the field.

"Are there any more soldiers?" Tucker asked, pointing the barrel of his weapon at the town.

"No! No! No more soldiers! Only our families! Please, sir, the town belongs to you now. I swear it on my life!"

"Well, then. I guess you better be telling the truth," Tucker responded threateningly.

Jacobson walked hesitantly over to look at the dead German. He had never seen a member of the SS. He'd heard stories about the extreme fanaticism and cruelty of Hitler's elite paramilitary force. But, somehow, stories of black-uniformed supermen with silver skulls on their uniforms had seemed too fantastic to believe. Not anymore. This one had almost killed him.

Tucker noticed Jacobson examining the body and walked over.

"You think this guy really thought he could kill us all?" Jacobson asked, confused at the insanity of the German's hopeless assault.

"Not really. The stupid SOB probably wanted to die in a glorious last stand for his Führer. He's SS. They're all brainwashed or somethin' and take a personal oath to Hitler himself. They'll do anything for Hitler and the Nazis. Kill anyone. Women. Children. Old people. Most of the time, they just murder for fun. Every last one is crazy as hell and highly trained. And that makes them especially dangerous," Tucker explained.

"What now, Sarge?" Downtown asked, ending Tucker's lesson.

"How do I know? How about it, Lieutenant? It looks like we already captured the town, the bridge, and this sorry bunch. So, what's next?" Tucker asked.

Jacobson had to pull himself together before answering. In the last thirty minutes, Tucker had saved his life not once but twice. To make matters worse, he had nearly failed to find the town at all – and then puked his guts up at the first sight of blood. He had to step up his game.

Jacobson responded, trying to sound like he knew what he was talking about.

"Once the rest of the platoon catches up with the vehicles, you guys secure the town and the bridge. Make sure it's clear. Another detachment will take over here in a day or so. Maybe sooner. After that, Tucker, you take the platoon and head over to a town called Gusen. The captain wanted me to run up to Linz for more orders and a company staff meeting if we finished this operation in time. I'll meet you in Gusen on Sunday. We're supposed to occupy and administer the town."

"What's that mean, sir?" Pernell asked. "Nobody ever ordered us to administer or occupy nothing before."

"Not sure myself, Pernell," Jacobson replied. "I guess we'll start with setting up camp and making sure the locals know who won the war."

"Anything important in, what did you call it? Gusen?" Tucker asked.

Jacobson pulled a set of orders out of his top pocket and scanned through the paperwork.

"This says there's an underground airplane plant and some sort of work camp. My orders call it a 'concentration camp.' I guess I'll find out more when I see the captain."

CHAPTER FOUR

Late that afternoon, Jacobson arrived at company headquarters for his first meaningful meeting with his commanding officer, Captain John Feilding. Jacobson had only met Feilding briefly when he arrived in Austria and didn't know what to expect. The captain turned out to be a West Point graduate, like himself.

Jacobson stood in front of the captain's desk and described the action in Abwinden earlier in the day.

"So, it wasn't a complete cakewalk after all. Nice job, Lieutenant. Securing that bridge was crucial," Feilding said, offering his hand to Jacobson and pointing to a chair.

"Mostly just badly equipped locals who didn't know what they were doing. The problem turned out to be an SS corporal who wanted to die for the fatherland and force the townspeople to do the same. To be truthful, sir, Sergeant Tucker saved my butt on that mission," Jacobson responded while taking a seat.

"Yeah? Well, that's his job. Utilizing your experienced non-coms is precisely how you should have handled that, Cy. That was your first time out in the field. Don't beat yourself up," Feilding replied, pulling a sheet of paper off the top of a stack of orders. "Let's see. You got the Gusen area. The fighting is over in that sector, and we've had no other reports of Hitler fanatics causing trouble. The Austrians appear to be satisfied with surrendering quietly as long as it's not to the Russians. So, I don't see you having any trouble over there. Just make sure the locals stay in line. Our job now is to occupy this country until the politicians figure out what to do next. Your platoon will set up camp in the village of Gusen. Administering a town is like being a mayor. A bunch of paperwork and listening to complaints. Probably a lot of complaints. Are you holding any prisoners of war that need dealing with?"

Jacobson had come prepared. "We have the fourteen from Abwinden. But, as I said, they're just old men and one kid, mostly armed with rifles from the last war."

"Fine, fine. Check them out to be sure some big-wig Nazi isn't posing as a private, then let them go home. We don't have the man-power or resources to feed and house prisoners," Feilding replied almost dismissively.

"Yes, sir. Have there really been high-ranking Nazis disguised as regular troops?" Jacobson asked, a little surprised.

"Not around here. Division picked up a couple of generals dressed as common soldiers and hiding like rats among regular enlisted personnel. I don't expect you'll find any Nazis trying to escape like that way out here. But I'll have my clerk give you a list with pictures just in case."

"Yes, sir."

"There's more. I've also got a special job for you while you sit on the townspeople. Your records show you studied military law and law enforcement at the Academy. We're going to put that education to the test. There's a giant network of tunnels hiding an underground aircraft manufacturing and testing facility under the hills near the town. We think that's where the Germans developed that Messerschmitt jet fighter. Maybe even more advanced stuff. It's no big secret the Germans were well ahead of us in developing new aircraft. We need to know just how far ahead and the full extent of what they were doing in those tunnels. We want you to get into that facility as soon as possible and gather any available intelligence from what the Nazis left behind. But be careful. We don't know for sure whether the Germans have fully evacuated the place. The Army will eventually send along engineers and scientists, but that won't happen for a while. Take a good look inside and secure whatever you find."

"Yes, sir. If this tunnel complex is big enough to hide an entire airplane factory, I may need some help finding my way around. Did Division round up any Germans who worked there? They might be a big help."

"Unfortunately, no. But good thinking. Maybe someone in the labor camp can act as a guide."

"I saw something about a camp in my orders, but I don't have any details," Jacobson said.

"Yeah. You'll see when you get there. The people in the camp will be in rough shape. Do what you can for them. Use any resources you find in town. But your first priority is uncovering any secrets those tunnels hold. I got brass breathing down my neck on this one. So, I'll expect your initial report in five days. When do you expect to get your platoon to Gusen?"

"Day after tomorrow at the latest. I have Tucker setting up security in Abwinden and at the bridge. As soon as relief arrives, he'll move the platoon into Gusen. I'll get started on inspecting the tunnels after I meet up with them in town."

Jacobson had no idea what he would find in the tunnels or at the camp, but it wouldn't be what he expected.

CHAPTER FIVE

After rushing the man in the camel-hair coat through the chaotic offices, SS Colonel Otto Skorzeny closed the door to the laboratory and posted one of his five SS guards nearby with orders to prevent anyone from entering.

Inside the lab, dim lighting from a single overhead surgical-style lamp revealed white-tiled walls that arched high above their heads, creating a long subway-like space that receded into darkness. Rows of abandoned stainless steel work tables stretched from one end of the lab to the other. The Germans had been thorough. Nothing remained of what had been one of the Reich's primary aeronautical research facilities except a strong disinfectant odor still lingering in the air.

Skorzeny shrugged out of the black leather overcoat he wore over his muscular shoulders, folded it carefully, and placed it on one of the tables. While his eyes took in every detail of the laboratory, he slowly pulled off matching black gloves one finger at a time. The SS officer removed his cap, placed it on top of his coat, and ran one hand over a head of closely cropped gray hair. With a square jawline and standing over six-foot-two-inches tall, the colonel embodied the perfect version of the Nazi's supposed 'master race.' But Skorzeny was no poster boy. The Iron Cross with Oak Leaves medal hanging from the second button of his form-fitting black tunic testified to his valor. The Führer himself had placed the Iron Cross around his neck for combat operations in Russia, and the oak leaf cluster was added for his daring rescue of the Italian dictator, Mussolini, after the fall of his fascist regime.

"Make our special guest comfortable," Skorzeny ordered.

Skorzeny's men led the man in the camel-hair coat to a worn leather couch where he sat stiffly upright, silent, and unmoving. As soon as the figure was settled, a doctor sat down at his side and began a detailed examination.

Skorzeny watched the doctor fuss over the man, checking vital signs, shining a light into his pupils, and testing his reflexes with a little rubber hammer. While he knew the examinations were necessary, the constant medical care had caused significant, sometimes dangerous, delays as Skorzeny's team secreted the doctor's patient out of Berlin, through Germany, and into Austria.

It had been no easy feat to covertly escort the most recognizable man in the world through enemy-held territory. They had barely stayed ahead of advancing Allied occupation forces before arriving at the relative safety of the underground tunnel complex. But they could not stay. The last report he received predicted that advance American units would arrive in the town of Gusen, just a mile from the entrance to the complex, as early as that same day.

Skorzeny tried to be patient while the doctor wrapped up his exam. When he finally placed his stethoscope and other tools back in his bag, Skorzeny called him over for a full report.

"He is physically stable, and his vital signs are strong. As you saw from our hurried entry, he is fully capable of walking," the nervous doctor reported.

"Does he know where he is?" Skorzeny asked.

"No. Not specifically. I prepared a special pharmaceutical therapy that induces and maintains a mild hallucinogenic state. He is not fully conscious but maintains enough cognition to walk and follow simple directions. This, as you know, I thought necessary to spare him at least some of the stress of our journey. At the moment, he is fatigued and slightly dehydrated, as we all are. I recommend at least a day of rest before we continue."

Skorzeny bristled at the doctor's clipped, overly complex explanation but decided to let it pass. He needed the doctor's expertise to keep the man they called 'Subject A' moving. Maintaining the delicate balance between Subject A's health and the demands of their escape route had proven to be a constant struggle.

"I'm afraid a day of rest is out of the question. We will be leaving in less than six hours," Skorzeny said, glancing at his watch. "It is your responsibility to ensure he is ready at that time. Do I make myself clear?"

Only a fool would challenge an order given by Otto Skorzeny, leaving the other man with but one response.

"Yes, Colonel. He will be prepared."

***

For the next several hours, Skorzeny paced around the laboratory, trying not to look at his watch. Since arriving in the Messerschmitt tunnels, the dark interior had robbed him of any sense of time. And time meant everything. Every hour, every minute they remained hidden underground, more Americans poured into the surrounding area, cutting off potential avenues of escape. The enemy could even now be standing just outside the tunnel entrance.

As Skorzeny turned to make another lap of the laboratory, Major Schumer, the army officer in charge of evacuating the tunnel complex, knocked at the laboratory door.

"Let him in," Skorzeny ordered.

Skorzeny noted the officer's crumpled, stained uniform and sweat-soaked hair.

"Colonel, the evacuation of the complex is complete. The last of my men boarded transport vehicles a few minutes ago. All sensitive documents have been moved or destroyed. The last of the technical equipment left hours ago. I must report that the Americans now hold all roads and villages north of the Danube, including Gusen. And they have seized control of the bridge at Abwinden."

Skorzeny hadn't noticed the departure of the office personnel outside the laboratory.

"Excellent work, Major. And you are the last to leave?" Skorzeny asked.

"Yes, Colonel," the major replied, glancing at the man on the couch. "It would be an honor if you would allow me to place myself under your command."

Leaving the major standing stiffly at attention, Skorzeny turned slightly to the right while drawing a long, thin dagger from its sheath.

"Your loyalty and attention to duty are impressive, Major," Skorzeny replied.

The compliment made Schumer stand a bit taller.

"Thank you, sir! To personally serve the Fuh –"

Before the major could finish his sentence, the SS Colonel turned and plunged the razor-sharp weapon into Schumer's chest. With expert precision, Skorzeny twisted the blade just as it entered the heart.

"I regret to tell you that your loyal service to the Reich has come to an end."

One of Skorzeny's men dragged Schumer's body into a corner, while the SS colonel ensured the blade gleamed like new before sliding it back into its sheath.

***

With his team now alone inside the tunnels, Skorzeny walked back to the map he kept spread over one of the lab tables and leaned into the light cast by the single overhead fixture. From their current position in Upper Austria, their destination on the west coast of Italy lay beyond the towering Alps mountain range and over 400 miles of enemy-infested territory. But the rest of their escape route would be useless if they couldn't get across the nearby Danube River. The major's updated information about American troops capturing the last bridge over the river meant they would have to chance a risky night crossing in small boats. Their course would take them within a kilometer of the Abwinden Bridge. And with the enemy spreading like cockroaches across Austria and Italy, avoiding capture would take a miracle.

Skorzeny looked at his watch again. Sunset would arrive in twenty minutes, but it would take another hour for complete darkness to fall. When they entered the tunnels, low clouds filled the skies. But the weather made little difference. They would cross the Danube that night – or not at all.

To make matters worse, the SS colonel had no choice but to rely on unknown contacts, arranged by a man he had met only once, to meet them on the south bank.

Five months earlier, Skorzeny had received orders to report to a man calling himself the Deacon.

***

At 10:30 in the evening, an effeminate but efficient assistant showed Skorzeny into an empty conference room deep inside the Reich Chancellery to meet with a man identified only as 'the Deacon.' Skorzeny stood at attention, his black cap tucked under his arm. After a moment, he clicked his heels together.

"Colonel Skorzeny reporting as ordered," he announced in a clipped, military tone.

Across the room, the Deacon rose from a chair at the head of a long rectangular conference table. The man's eyes scanned the SS officer from head to toe, lingering uncomfortably on his tall, muscular physique.

"Thank you for coming, Colonel. I am not in the military, so please do make yourself comfortable," the Deacon said, motioning to a chair near his. He did not offer to shake hands. "May I say how honored I am to meet the Reich's most decorated commando? Your exploits in this conflict shall go down in history."

Skorzeny didn't care for the Deacon's smooth, fawning manner, and he carefully noted the other man's tailored silk suit, highly-polished black leather shoes, soft hands, and long blond hair. The Deacon bore no resemblance to the men of strength, action, and bravery Skorzeny admired. To the contrary, he looked like a wealthy degenerate.

"Thank you, Herr Deacon," Skorzeny managed to say without revealing his true thoughts.

The Deacon sat on the edge of his chair with his elbows resting on the table and his fingertips touching one another, forming a delicate triangle.

"Colonel, I'll get right to the point. The war does not go well for the Fatherland. Plans must be made."

The Deacon spoke the truth, but Skorzeny would not dare voice his agreement.

"I understand your silence, but facts are facts," the Deacon continued. "There is little I or anyone can do to change the inevitable. But the end of the war does not necessitate the end of our glorious cause. I have offered my assistance to preserve much of what the National Socialist movement has achieved. Such things that will create a strong foundation for rebuilding the Reich. I understand I can trust you with any vital information I deem necessary to share. Is that true?" the Deacon asked, seeing no reaction from the SS officer.

Skorzeny simply nodded, still wary but intrigued.

The Deacon continued. "Good. I, and others, have already arranged transportation for certain technologies to points outside the reach of our enemies. This has been accomplished by utilizing commercial transport through neutral and friendly countries. Those efforts do not concern you. But the following does. The rise of a Fourth Reich will require leadership. As I'm sure you agree, Germany's leaders cannot and must not fall into enemy hands. Their unique personalities are crucial to the rebuilding process for many reasons. Trials and other humiliations could irrevocably poison public sentiment against us. You will be instrumental in protecting and transporting certain, shall we say, important persons to safety."

Skorzeny nodded again and said, "I serve the Führer and the Reich. I will do whatever is required of me."

As a response, the Deacon reached into a slim folder, withdrew a single sheet of paper, and pushed it across the table. Skorzeny read through it twice. He had received ultra-secret orders directly from the top of the Nazi party before, but never like this. The handwritten order read:

To: Colonel Otto Skorzeny, SS

I place you under the permanent command of Herr Deacon. His orders are my orders.

Adolf Hitler

Skorzeny's brows knitted together for a brief moment before he carefully folded the paper and tucked it into his tunic pocket.

"I am at your service, sir."

"Excellent. When the time comes, I will call upon you to transport the Reich's most vital human asset to safety. He shall be referred to by his codename – Subject A. I have arranged several routes, utilizing capable contacts and assistance from various organizations. You will study those routes, make any recommendations and alterations you deem necessary, and stand ready to implement the operation. Do you understand?"

"I do," Skorzeny replied, his sense of duty, loyalty, and the orders in his pocket failing to dispel his suspicions.

He had often met such men as the Deacon, and they rarely acted out of pure loyalty or untainted motives. But his orders left no room for his personal opinions, and he would, as always, carry them out without hesitation and to the best of his ability.

*****

So far, The Deacon had managed to piece together a lifeline out of Europe, even after they barely survived a harrowing escape from Berlin. But Skorzeny knew his mission now stood on a precariously thin tightrope. One more misstep or another instance of bad luck could cost all their lives – including the one man who could ignite a Fourth Reich.

As the minutes ticked away in the tunnel, any lingering qualms Skorzeny still possessed about the Deacon's plans became academic. He had no choice but to trust the promised contacts and transportation would be waiting on the far side of the river.

Looking back at his watch, Skorzeny saw that sunset had arrived.

CHAPTER SIX

Before leaving the tunnel complex, Skorzeny explained their route to his team using a set of detailed maps. Subject A remained on the couch.

"There is a little-known exit to this facility, an underground passageway that runs from this laboratory to the outside. American forces hold the last bridge over the Danube at Abwinden. So, we will cross the river here, to the southwest, in small boats. Contacts will meet us on the other side with replacement vehicles. Any questions?"

With obvious reluctance, the doctor asked, "Colonel, I appreciate the necessity of your plan for tonight. But is there a chance air transportation can be arranged once we are clear of this area? I only ask because our subject's health is, well, less than perfect. As you have seen, traveling over land is quite difficult for him."

Skorzeny had to control his reaction to the doctor's question. He had explained time and time again that Allied aircraft dominated the skies all over Europe and would shoot down any unauthorized flights without warning.

"It is your job to guard our subject's health. Not mine. Do I need to remind you that if he dies during our little journey, you will be of no more use to me?"

The doctor physically cowered under Skorzeny's rebuke.

"My apologies for the interruption, Colonel," he managed to say.

"Let us move on. If we get separated during the crossing, move inland to this road and stay where you are," Skorzeny ordered, pointing to a small dirt track that paralleled the south bank. "Our contacts will find you."

***

After almost an hour in the claustrophobic escape tunnel, Skorzeny pushed through a massive metal door embedded in a hillside. Outside, the group stepped into near-complete darkness. Using only two small lanterns, Skorzeny led them through dense undergrowth to the bank of the Gusen River. After the journey through the long, dank tunnel and short hike through the woods, Subject A's doctor insisted on a short rest to administer an injection and medication for stomach ulcers.

While the doctor tended to his patient, Skorzeny's men located a small dock where two rowboats waited to take them on the next leg of their journey. Although far from new, a quick examination showed them to be sturdy little boats well suited for work along the river. Ten minutes later, Skorzeny personally took the oars of Subject A's craft and guided them the short distance along the Gusen River to the point where it emptied into the Danube. Looking across the quarter-mile expanse of water, he could barely see the opposite side. But just to the north, lights blazed on the bridge at Abwinden. The SS officer scoffed at the folly of the Americans. Instead of watching the river, they focused on people trying to cross the bridge. With the lingering overcast blotting out any moonlight, his team would be invisible to anyone looking down into the darkness.

They would pass right under the noses of the Americans.

The river remained calm, and with no water traffic in the area, the crossing proceeded smoothly. Having made several dangerous assaults across rivers during combat operations, Skorzeny and his men had no trouble navigating in the darkness. The SS guards' muscular arms expertly dipped oars into the water and powered the rowboats into the heart of the river. With no cover other than the night itself, reaching the relative safety of the far bank became their sole objective.

Subject A, wrapped in blankets, gazed blankly into the night. He didn't speak, a consequence, the doctor explained, of his hallucinogenic state. Skorzeny couldn't imagine being unconscious yet fully susceptible to others' commands. Knowing Subject A well, the SS colonel doubted he had voluntarily agreed to the doctor's treatment.

"Keep watch on the far bank," Skorzeny ordered quietly as outlines of trees became visible across the river. "Our contact will flash a light twice to guide us in. But remember, three flashes in a row are a warning the Americans have started patrolling the area, and we will have to divert further downriver."

A moment later, two flashes appeared from the riverbank.

The Deacon had kept his word.

CHAPTER SEVEN

"Where is Subject A now?" the Deacon asked without emotion.

"They left Gusen late last night. Our operators made contact after they crossed the Danube near the town of Abwinden. Colonel Skorzeny will have Subject A at the next safe house shortly, Herr Deacon," his secretary, Hans, reported, setting a cup of tea on the Deacon's gleaming black desk.

The Deacon rose from his high-backed leather office chair and picked up the cup with carefully manicured fingers. A mane of blonde hair, much longer than the current fashion, flowed over his ears and framed a high brow, blue eyes, and square jawline. He stood ramrod straight, his movements precise and measured. His tailored gray suit tapered from broad shoulders to a narrow waist. After a moment, he turned and peered down at a small part of his empire through a bank of floor-to-ceiling windows. Below, hundreds of construction workers swarmed over two immense factory buildings. Like ants feverishly repairing their mound, the men below worked twenty-four hours a day to rebuild the massive heavy manufacturing plant that Allied bombers had done their best to destroy. Months earlier, even as the Americans and Russians were still racing toward Berlin, the Deacon began marshalling resources, both human and material, to restore his immense manufacturing empire.

To his credit, the Deacon had anticipated that the end of the war would bring a great increase in demand for consumer and commercial products. The country would also be in desperate need of jobs. And the Deacon would be prepared to offer both.

Yet, even with the bright business prospects peace would bring, the Nazis had been the best possible customers.

The Deacon sipped his tea and marveled for the hundredth time at how simple it had been to prop up Hitler with money and influence. Once placed into power, the strange but charismatic man who had once been an Austrian corporal did just as the Deacon wished, feverishly rearming the German military. Under his leadership, Germany spent billions buying every conceivable weapon to rebuild its military after the Great War. The country had regained its strength, and the dictator's firebrand rhetoric and effective propaganda had inflamed the population into supporting a war that had been disastrous for Germany but colossally lucrative for the Deacon's companies.

As the war progressed, the Nazis hemorrhaged money replacing tanks, guns, aircraft, and ships lost in battle – most manufactured by one of the Deacon's companies.

Yes, Hitler and his Nazis had been a godsend. The perfect government at the perfect time. At least for him.

"And the others?" the Deacon asked.

"On schedule. Subjects C and F are in Denmark, awaiting transport to our U-boat facility in Norway. The others are currently in Spain, traveling under humanitarian papers issued by the Vatican. Per your instructions, we allowed SS Reichsführer Himmler to take his own life by cyanide rather than being turned over to the Russians. Reichsmarschall Goering has been handed over to the Americans for trial and execution. Neither knew of your plans."

"Good. Himmler's ambition and Goering's stupidity and corruption made them unnecessary liabilities," the Deacon commented. "I am pleased to say the Russians accepted our offer of technical and manufacturing assistance in exchange for a swift announcement in the newspapers of Hitler's death by suicide."

The secretary waited a moment before asking the Deacon a question that had been swirling around in his mind.

"Herr Deacon, may I inquire about something for my own education?"

The Deacon turned around and lifted his cup. "You may."

"Sir, has the Führer's and the Nazis' usefulness to you not come to an end? You are the leader of a great economic empire with manufacturing and construction companies in Europe, South America, and even the United States. Yet, you have gone to great lengths to protect the losers of this war. This seems to be a risk you do not need to shoulder."

The Deacon took a sip of tea and set the cup and saucer back on the desk.

"You make an excellent point, Hans. But you still possess the impetuousness of youth. Never simply react to the present. That is allowing circumstances to control *you*. Instead, always take action that allows *you* to control the future. The small risk and expense to ensure the survival of the Nazi cause will pay huge dividends. You will see."

CHAPTER EIGHT

Gusen, Austria
Two days later

Early in the morning, Jacobson found Tucker supervising the platoon while they set up camp in a park near the center of Gusen. A few curious locals watched with blank expressions from a distance as the American army took control of their town.

"We have our living quarters almost completed, sir," Tucker reported. "I don't think the folks around here understand why we're pitching tents in their little park, but they haven't caused any trouble. Why *are* we here anyway, sir? The captain fill you in?"

"Yeah, some," Jacobson said as he looked around the quaint Austrian village. "First, there's that underground aircraft factory or something near here. I'm supposed to get in there as soon as possible and report on anything the Germans left behind. He also said something about the work camp. We're supposed to do what we can for the prisoners. Have you had a chance to see either of those yet?"

Tucker's mood suddenly turned black.

"Haven't seen any factory. But we went over to the work camp as soon as we got here. It's a goddamn nightmare, sir. Just a goddamn nightmare," Tucker replied, his voice thick with emotion he couldn't hide.

"Explain," Jacobson ordered, not understanding Tucker's answer.

"I guess it hasn't got out in all the papers yet. The goddamned Nazis rounded up anyone they didn't like and stuck them in these camps. I don't know the whole story, but the Germans forced them to dig tunnels near here. Mostly by hand. Worked the poor devils to death. And I mean exactly that – to death. I've never seen anything like it. No one has."

"How many, uh, workers are at the camp here?" Jacobson asked, still not fully following Tucker's explanation but trying to tease out more information.

Tucker's voice dropped to just above a whisper. "Alive? Two hundred and sixty-two, at least as of this morning. There will be less than that this afternoon."

Jacobson stopped and saw the deep anguish written all over the man's face.

"Sergeant, what the hell happened here?" Jacobson demanded, needing to know what could so badly shake a man who had just endured a full year of heavy, close combat.

"I can't explain it. Not really. You'll just have to see for yourself."

***

Tucker drove Jacobson out of town, crossed the only bridge over the Gusen River, and along a narrow dirt road that ended at a high barbed-wire fence. Tucker drove through two open gates flanked by now-empty guard towers and into a compound filled with hastily constructed wooden barracks. Jacobson counted ten long windowless buildings lining a long dirt courtyard. To one side, a smaller office building sat empty and abandoned.

"What the hell is that smell?" Jacobson exclaimed suddenly, burying his nose in the crook of his arm.

"Death itself, sir," Tucker replied without a hint of sarcasm.

"Explain what that means, Sergeant," Jacobson ordered as nausea overwhelmed him.

Tucker stopped the Jeep in time for Jacobson to lose his breakfast.

"Sorry," Jacobson muttered, embarrassed.

"Don't worry about it," Tucker replied without judgment.

Recovering quickly, Jacobson looked around. At first, the camp appeared totally deserted. Then, slowly, gaunt, pale faces started to appear in several dark doorways.

"These are the workers?" Jacobson asked, watching a few strange figures emerge tentatively from the shadows.

Jacobson could hardly believe they were human. He noticed their eyes first. Sunk into deep dark sockets, they looked back at him with a mixture of fear and distrust. Cheekbones protruded from under their eyes, producing the terrible illusion of living skulls. Several skeletal apparitions leaned against doorways while others sat on the ground, too weak to walk more than a few steps. A few wore ill-fitting civilian clothes, while others remained draped in the striped rags of their prison uniforms.

"My God," Jacobson said under his breath. "Who? How?"

Tucker understood Jacobson's confusion. Very few people had seen the Nazis' evil handiwork. And nobody could be expected to comprehend this level of inhumanity until they had time to process what lay before their eyes.

After a moment, Tucker spoke, breaking the spell. "We've had a hard time convincing them the war is over. We brought over some clothes we confiscated from the people in town and started supplying the camp with food and water. Apparently, as the war got worse for the Germans, they stopped feeding these poor Jews altogether. The medics are trying their best, but some of them are just too far gone to save," Tucker explained.

"Are you saying all these people are Jews?" Jacobson asked.

"Yeah. Mostly. At least that's what the locals told us. We haven't gotten these folks to talk much yet."

Jacobson tried to coax some of the prisoners forward. One or two stepped timidly further outside, but none would approach the Jeep.

Jacobson's mind tried to make sense of the reality hitting him squarely in the face. He had no way of knowing that this small camp was just one of the many satellite installations of the much larger Mauthausen concentration camp, only a few miles away. The world would later learn of the true scope of the attempted genocide hidden behind the gates of hundreds of such concentration camps spread all over Europe.

"You may as well see the rest," Tucker said, getting back in the vehicle.

Still battling shock at his first impression of a Nazi slave labor camp, Jacobson climbed into the passenger seat.

The Jeep sped by the row of barracks and out a second set of gates. The stench that made Jacobson sick at the camp's gate grew even heavier, concentrating into an invisible soup of pure wickedness.

Tucker stopped at the edge of a trench one hundred feet long and twenty-five feet wide. Nausea nearly incapacitated Jacobson once again. He didn't want to get out of his seat. He didn't want to see whatever lay at the bottom of that hole. He wanted to turn and run. He wanted to go home.

A full minute passed before Jacobson forced himself to walk to the lip of the trench and look inside.

When he did, he found row upon row of corpses lying naked in the dirt. Mostly just skeletons with skin, arms, and legs tangled together in a grotesque puzzle. Men, women, and children had been tossed inside like so much garbage. Jacobson could see bodies on top of bodies, death on top of death, stretching far into the distance. The magnitude of the Nazis' crimes crashed into the twenty-three-year-old like a tidal wave. Nothing could have prepared him for the overwhelming sense of horror that shook his entire being to the core.

How can this be? Oh, God! How can this be?

His family lived in a quiet suburb of Chicago. His father, a lawyer, worked long hours but came home to his family every night. As a child, Cy Jacobson rode a bicycle on concrete sidewalks. Neat two-story houses with manicured green lawns lined smooth paved roads. In the safety and security of middle-class America, cold-blooded cruelty and violence such as this would be unthinkable.

Yet, it existed here. Depravity and inhumanity on a massive scale – perpetrated only a mile from a beautiful Austrian town where people, just like his neighbors back home, went to work, raised children, and worshipped together in church.

The young lieutenant stepped back from the edge and looked up. The striking contrast of fluffy white clouds floating in a pure blue sky above a vile mass grave brought heaven and hell into unambiguous reality. He tried to think of a prayer from his days as a boy at St. Catherine's Catholic Church, but none came.

Gathering himself, Jacobson looked back across the mass grave, finally noticing a dozen civilians with handkerchiefs covering their noses and mouths, reluctantly shoveling dirt into the trench. As he watched, the lieutenant caught several glancing in his direction with hate-filled eyes.

"Who are those people?" he asked Tucker.

"Civilians from the town. We've had groups of those sons-of-bitches out here since yesterday working to bury these poor bastards," Tucker explained, spitting into the dirt.

"They knew about this?" Jacobson asked incredulously.

"They claim they didn't, but that's just so much bullshit," Tucker said loudly enough for the people shoveling dirt to hear.

The civilians, men in sweat-stained suits and women in wrinkled dresses, stopped work and looked in their direction.

The young officer suddenly snatched his pistol from its holster and pointed it at the civilians.

"Get back to work, you filthy bastards!" Jacobson screamed.

The townspeople looked away and hurried back to shoveling, making at least a temporary show of working a bit faster.

"Uh, Lieutenant?" Tucker said quietly.

"What!" Jacobson demanded, the gun still aimed across the trench.

"You can't shoot them, sir."

"Why the hell not?" Jacobson shouted, his eyes locked on the townspeople.

"We have other jobs to do here, sir. Now, I'd like to pop a few of those assholes myself. But I'm hungry, and it's time for chow. We just ain't got the time right now," Tucker said, hoping to distract the incensed young man.

The veteran sergeant had seen this kind of thing many times before – men pushed to the edge of humanity by the inhumanity of war. Yet, Tucker realized the evil before his eyes had little to do with war. These people were not soldiers fighting for their lives, their families, their buddies, or their country. From the safety of their own homes, they witnessed the depravity and cruelty taking place before their eyes – and chose to applaud.

"What? What are you saying?" Jacobson asked, looking at Tucker for the first time.

"It's time for chow, sir. Maybe we can come back and shoot one or two after lunch," Tucker said, smiling.

"Oh. Yeah. Okay," Jacobson replied, lowering his gun and looking a little sheepish at losing his temper. "Sorry."

"Don't worry about it, sir. Everyone who comes here suffers in one way or another."

CHAPTER NINE

The green canvas army tent usually housed four enlisted men in cramped quarters. But Sergeant Tucker made sure only two others shared his.

"Hey, Sarge!" Pernell called out from his cot. "When are they going to move us into one of those fancy hotels in town?"

"You ain't got the social couth to be allowed in no fancy hotel, Pernell. You got a nice warm cot and three squares every single day, which is better than we've had in a long time. Try to be less of a pain in the ass, son," Sergeant Tucker shot back.

"I bet our shiny new lieutenant has a nice setup in a hotel. Maybe a pretty maid and everything," Downtown chimed in.

"So, why are you complaining, Downtown? You've been sniffing around that little blond fraulein in town ever since we got here," Pernell chided.

Downtown shot Pernell a withering look.

Tucker looked back and pointed a long, bony finger at Downtown's face. "I told y'all not to get cozy with the locals. You know the rules. These people are Nazi lovers."

"Aw, Sarge, what's the harm? She's nice and likes to play a little pinch and tickle every now and again. It's against the Geneva

Convention to deprive a man of female companionship," Downtown pleaded.

"Can it," Tucker replied. "You ain't no worse off than anyone else. Rules is rules. So don't let me catch you with her, or I'll have to write you up."

Downtown flopped back into his bunk. He didn't like the rules, but he figured Tucker had left him a loophole. As long as he didn't get caught...

With Downtown brooding over Tucker's admonishment, Pernell pressed on about their living conditions.

"I still don't get why we can't get decent quarters. Hell, I got a hole in my leg during D-Day. The lieutenant just got here. What's he got that I don't, may I ask?"

"He's an officer. And he's got brains enough to go to college," Tucker replied. "And that's something you ain't never going to have."

"College? Big waste of time. When I get home, I'm going to work at my Uncle Vincenzo's pawn shop in Brooklyn, marry a fat Italian girl, and have lots of little Pernells," Pernell declared, lying back and putting both hands behind his head.

"Sarge, what's the skinny on when we get to go home anyway?" Downtown asked.

"Same as two hours ago. I got no idea. So maybe do me a favor and hold off askin' again until sometime tomorrow. Indiana or Illinois or wherever you're from ain't going anywhere," Tucker replied, back to his usual easy-going way.

"It's Iowa. I told you that a million times. Iowa. Anyway, what's with the new lieutenant? He's as green as they come. Nearly got his ass shot off the other day a couple of times," Downtown asked.

"I don't know. He's fresh from the farm, alright, but I think he'll do okay. I took him out to the trench today. He nearly shot the locals we had out there shoveling," Tucker replied.

"Sounds like he got a little upset. He a Jew or something?" Pernell asked.

"I don't know. What do you care anyway?" Tucker responded.

"I don't! Hey, some of my family's best customers is Jews. I just like to know who I'm dealing with. That's all," Pernell answered defensively.

"I don't think I've ever met a Jew," Downtown added. "We don't have any in Ames."

"Yes, you do, you idiot. Plus, that Franklin guy, the replacement, he was a Jew," Pernell scoffed.

"The kid that got blown up in the foxhole at the Bulge?"

"No, you moron. Franklin was the guy that caught the sniper bullet a couple months ago," Pernell responded, irritated.

Downtown just shrugged. "Didn't know him."

"You guys pipe down for a change," Tucker said, stretching his lanky frame over his cot and pulling his cap down over his eyes. "And tomorrow, I want you two to start rounding up supplies from town for the survivors in the work camp. I gotta take the lieutenant over to some underground tunnels or something and have a look around."

"Tunnels?" Downtown asked. "What kind of tunnels?"

"Hell, I don't know, boy" Tucker muttered. "The Nazi kind, I suppose."

CHAPTER TEN

The following morning, Jacobson and Tucker drove back to the labor camp. The liberated prisoners, having eaten well and seeing that the American troops meant them no harm, now sat or stood outside in small groups, enjoying the warm morning sun.

"They look better already, Lieutenant," Tucker observed.

"Absolutely. Are they getting regular supplies?" Jacobson asked.

"Yes, sir. All they can eat. But we haven't convinced them they can leave if they want to. Maybe they don't understand my accent or somethin'," Tucker drawled.

As they climbed out of the Jeep, several laborers shuffled forward, smiling and offering their bony, callused hands. Jacobson couldn't help but notice every forearm bore a number tattooed in blue ink.

The two Americans smiled while they handed out packs of cigarettes and bars of chocolate. Jacobson certainly wasn't an expert on languages, but he thought he detected some of the laborers speaking Polish and Czech, along with German. He needed a translator.

"I don't suppose you or any of the men speak German?" Jacobson asked Tucker.

"Wasn't any use learnin' any, I suppose," Tucker answered, scratching at his head. "Our only job was to kill them. And very few of them Krauts did much talkin' afterward."

Jacobson just shook his head. He couldn't argue with Tucker's logic.

"Well, I guess there's no harm asking if any of these people happen to speak English."

Jacobson climbed onto the hood of the Jeep, motioned for the ex-prisoners to approach, and self-consciously tried out a few words of German.

"Komm, bitte," he shouted. "Come here, please."

The words weren't perfect, but his intended audience seemed to get the message. Some stood and walked forward immediately as if ordered. Others approached warily, not sure what Jacobson had in store. He understood their reluctance.

When a small crowd had gathered, he asked if anyone spoke English. In return, he got a sea of blank faces. Disappointed, Jacobson searched his memory, trying to recall the question in German. But before he attempted to communicate again, a thin arm rose tentatively from the back of the assembled workers.

A young female voice said, "I speak English."

"Sergeant Tucker, would you please ask that young lady if she would mind talking with us for a moment?" Jacobson asked, pointing to the back of the small crowd. "And Tucker, be gentle."

"I'll use my best manners, sir," Tucker replied, making his way past the other workers.

A moment later, the sergeant arrived back at the Jeep, trailed by an exceedingly thin young woman. She walked with her head down, hands picking at the sides of a dress at least four sizes too large. Jet black hair just covered her ears, and bangs hung over downturned eyes.

Jacobson smiled. "Good morning, Miss. I'm Lieutenant Cy Jacobson. Thank you for talking with us. May I ask your name?"

Hearing the kindness in Jacobson's voice, the girl visibly relaxed. She looked up, revealing wide-set black eyes under full eyebrows of the same color. She looked inquisitive rather than scared. But her body language gave away an underlying distrust. She stood awkwardly, bent slightly forward, with her arms folded tightly across her chest.

"I am Rachel Cohen. I speak English," the girl replied, looking from Jacobson to Tucker.

"It's a pleasure to meet you, Miss Cohen. This is Sergeant Fred Tucker. Thank you again for coming forward," Jacobson said. "Sergeant, would you get some chairs for us from the office? I don't suppose this young lady would care to talk inside."

Rachel shook her head. "No. My people are still deciding whether to trust Americans, and they would be frightened for me if they saw us go into the Commandant's office."

"No problem. We can talk out here," Jacobson responded quickly.

After finding a comfortable spot in the shade of one of the buildings, Jacobson opened the conversation by asking Rachel how she had come to be in the camp.

Rachel hesitated at first, unsure whether she should help the Americans. But something in Jacobson's eyes and the way he spoke put her at ease. When she finally started talking, the words seemed to tumble out of her, as if she had needed to tell someone her story for a very long time.

She explained that she and her family had lived in Munich. Her father, a professor of history at the local university, taught his two children English and several other languages. They led a relatively quiet life, went to synagogue regularly, and had many friends, both Jewish and Christian.

Then Hitler came to power.

When the Nazis began persecuting the Jews, her father had considered fleeing Germany. Still, he couldn't bring himself to believe his lifelong friends and neighbors would succumb to the racist Nazi propaganda.

As time passed, their non-Jewish friends grew distant and eventually stopped interacting with her family altogether. The Nazis passed laws forcing all the Jews to sew Star of David patches on their clothes. Soon thereafter, the university fired her father.

Finally, one dreadful night, a gang of thugs broke into their house. Neighbors they had known for years helped the Nazi goons throw their belongings out onto the street. As her family watched, huddled together in the gutter, the mob burned whatever they didn't steal. Her father had remained strong, reassuring them they would be alright. But when the crowd tossed his treasured books into the bonfire, he couldn't bear it any longer. As he tried to rescue some of his favorite volumes from the flames, the mob threw him to the ground, beating him with fists and clubs in a demented orgy of violence.

Minutes later, the police arrived. For an instant, Rachel believed they had come to help. But to her horror, they arrested her father and brother and dragged them into a nearby park. As Rachel and her mother huddled in the gutter, several shots rang out. Her mother became hysterical and tried to run toward the park, but the mob turned on her as well, bludgeoning her into unconsciousness.

An hour later, the police rounded up all the Jewish families in her neighborhood and marched them to the train station. Rachel and hundreds of other Jews left Munich packed like cattle inside freight cars.

That was over five years ago, when she was only 13. What followed had been an unending fight for survival in camp after camp.

Jacobson listened to her story, shocked that this timid girl had been fortunate enough to survive. But he quickly changed his mind. Rachel wasn't just lucky. She had to have remarkable courage, resourcefulness, and strength of character to stay alive. While obviously malnourished and exceedingly thin, she exhibited a sharp mind and keen intellect.

"Did you ever see any of your family again?" Jacobson asked, fearing he already knew the answer.

"No," Rachel answered quietly. "And I never shall."

"I'm sorry," was all Jacobson could think to say.

But what could be said? What would have helped?

Jacobson caught the Jewish girl looking at him with caring eyes. *Was she actually worried her story had caused him pain?*

"Thank you for listening. You are very kind," Rachel said after several seconds. "You are the first person I have told what happened to me. Now you are wondering how I stayed alive. The answer is simple. The guards found out I speak English and other languages. They always seemed to need a translator for one reason or another. I was useful. The only way anyone survived in the camps was to be useful."

"How did you end up here in Gusen?" Jacobson asked.

"They transferred me from camp to camp. I came here around a year ago when the tunnels were nearing completion. I helped translate technical documents from English and other languages into German. Most of my people here are manual laborers. They dug the tunnels. Others moved and assembled equipment. They suffered far more than I did. About six months ago, the Germans became worried about the progress of the war. Raw materials for building aircraft became hard to find, which caused research and production to fall behind schedule," Rachel explained, her voice now angry. "As a result, they doubled our work even as food supplies became more and more scarce. The Nazis murdered anyone too weak or ill to work in the tunnels. Many starved to death. Have you ever seen a person die of hunger, Lieutenant?"

Jacobson flinched at the question. Of course, he had never seen anyone starve. And, for some reason, he was ashamed of his answer.

"No. I haven't. I'm sorry."

Jacobson's face must have betrayed his discomfort because Rachel quickly added, "No. No. I am sorry. You have been good to us."

With a good deal of effort, Jacobson set aside his feelings and got back to doing his job.

"Miss Cohen, I need your help," Jacobson began.

Rachel interrupted. "Please call me Rachel, Lieutenant. Miss Cohen sounds too formal."

"I'll do that if you call me Cy. Lieutenant sounds too formal," Jacobson replied with a grin.

Rachel smiled for the first time. "Alright, Cy."

"Rachel, I have to find out what the Germans were doing in those tunnels. I need to speak with some of your fellow, uh, prisoners about what they saw and did in there. Would you be willing to help me? It's important."

Rachel didn't hesitate. "Yes. Have you been inside yet? The facility is complex with many rooms and levels."

"No. In fact, the first thing I need is a guide. Who would you recommend?" Jacobson asked, relieved to be making some progress on his mission.

"Me," Rachel suggested confidently. "I can guide you and explain at least some of what they were doing. I read many technical documents, and I learned the basics of their work. Most of my people here were laborers. They did not see or hear as much as me. And I am not afraid to go there. Not anymore."

Jacobson could see her determination and couldn't help but be impressed. Rachel had a quick mind and valuable knowledge. The young lieutenant had gotten lucky to find her, and he knew it.

"Excellent. That would be great. Thank you. I'll have Sergeant Tucker come get you after the noon meal. Perhaps we'll discover something important."

CHAPTER ELEVEN

Later that afternoon, Jacobson stood outside the tunnel complex, marveling at the two massive steel blast doors protecting its entrance. One of the doors leaned precariously to one side, its immense hinges bent and twisted by dynamite charges set by a detachment of engineers that passed through earlier that morning. Despite the damage, Jacobson couldn't help but be impressed with the expert engineering needed to build just the entrance into the facility. Wild rumors of advanced Nazi aircraft had circulated for years, including everything from advanced jet-powered bombers to gravity-defying flying discs. He didn't have any idea if those stories would prove true, but whatever the Nazis hid behind doors like that must have been vital to their war effort and highly secret.

Inside, a string of light bulbs powered by a portable generator disappeared into the inky black interior. Jacobson recalled a picture he once saw of Auguste Rodin's massive sculpture, The Gates of Hell. Like Rachel had pictured many times before, he too imagined that stepping through the doors would lead him deep into the evil, fiery underground world of the damned. He involuntarily shivered at the thought of what he might find inside.

A few minutes later, Tucker arrived with Rachel riding in his Jeep's passenger seat. For some reason, the appearance of the Jewish girl dispelled the unnerving feeling that had overcome him just moments before. She still wore the same ill-fitting dress, but now she also wore a light Army jacket and a pair of sturdy leather shoes.

"She said the tunnels are damp and much cooler than out here. So, I rounded up the smallest jacket I could find and a pair of shoes from the local shoe store," Tucker explained. "That's why we're a little late, sir."

"Did you pay for the shoes?" Jacobson asked.

"Nope. I mean, no, sir, I didn't. I'd say the owner of the store didn't much appreciate me insisting he make a charitable donation, either," Tucker said, smirking around the cigar jutting from his teeth.

"Excellent," Jacobson replied.

"Yes. Thank you, Sergeant Tucker. And thank you as well, Cy," Rachel said sincerely. "It has been a long time since I had a new pair of shoes. Or any real shoes at all."

"My pleasure, ma'am," Tucker responded.

"Uh, yes. Of course, no problem at all," Jacobson replied, a bit awkwardly.

Rachel didn't notice Jacobson's nerves as she got right to work.

"Supplies arrived by railcar and truck. These tracks run from this entrance to a loading platform and then to an exit on the other side of this hill," Rachel explained, pointing to the double set of railroad tracks. "Overhead cranes unloaded heavy equipment directly from the flatbed train cars. Further inside, you will find multiple loading docks for cargo arriving by truck."

"How often did they close these doors?" Jacobson asked, pulling a notebook from his tunic pocket to take notes.

"At first, they stayed open all the time. As the Americans got closer and bombers appeared overhead, they kept the doors closed unless they received supplies or shipped material away. I did not like being inside when I knew the doors were closed. I had nightmares about being buried alive," Rachel answered, her hands reflexively rubbing together at the memory.

"Yeah, I can see that. Are you ready to go?" Jacobson asked, walking toward the entrance.

"Cy, could we take one of your vehicles?" Rachel asked hesitantly. "Walking through all the tunnels would take days. Driving would be faster."

Taking Rachel's advice, Tucker drove them through the blast doors and into the main tunnel. The impressively wide passage could easily accommodate two trains side by side. Overhead, the arched roof showed signs of where the laborers had carved the tunnel through solid rock. Except for the tracks, smooth concrete covered the floor.

After driving several hundred yards, the tunnel split in two, each side disappearing deeper into the earth.

"Which way?" Tucker asked from the driver's seat.

"Engineering, laboratories, and technical development are to the left. The rails to the right lead to the manufacturing spaces. The manufacturing side is much larger, but the engineering areas may be more interesting," Rachel answered, warming to her role as the tour guide.

"Left it is then, Sergeant," Jacobson decided.

The Jeep followed the left spur of the tunnel. As Tucker increased his speed, bare lightbulbs flashed overhead at an ever-quickening pace, reminding Jacobson of a nighttime roller coaster ride.

Suddenly, Rachel shouted, "Stop!"

Startled, Tucker hit the brakes, propelling Jacobson from the small rear seat into the front of the vehicle. Only grabbing Rachel's seatback kept him from smashing his head into the windshield.

"Sorry, sir," Tucker said.

"What the hell?" Jacobson demanded, a bit more harshly than intended.

Rachel looked at him with a frightened look in her eyes.

Jacobson immediately regretted his outburst. Any reprimand by the Nazis probably brought instantaneous punishment.

"It's fine," he said, trying not to sound irritated and retaking his seat.

"We passed by the entrance to the laboratory and offices where I worked. I have never come here in an automobile, and I became confused," Rachel explained apologetically.

"Forget it. No harm done," Jacobson said with a smile. "Now, where's this laboratory?"

"Inside there," Rachel answered, pointing back over Jacobson's shoulder.

Tucker reversed the Jeep, stopping in front of the long, single-story structure Rachel pointed out. The two men jumped out of the vehicle and walked to the entrance without noticing their guide had remained behind.

Rachel looked up, her eyes shaded and darting from side to side. "I...I thought I could come back here without being frightened. But I'm not sure I can go inside now."

Tucker walked back to the Jeep and casually leaned against the windshield.

"Hey now, I won't let anything happen to you. I promise. All them Nazis ran away days ago when they seen old Tucker comin' up the road."

Tucker's sense of humor worked. Rachel smiled and said, "Yes. Of course. Perhaps I am being silly."

Tucker stuck out his hand, offering to help Rachel from the vehicle as if she were a princess arriving at a ball.

The girl blushed, took his hand, and led the two military men through the door.

The trio had to use flashlights and a lantern Tucker retrieved from the back of the Jeep to see inside the darkened space. A few scattered papers still littered the six desks once used by German clerks. In the corner, two blackened fifty-gallon drums underneath a smoke-stained ceiling evidenced a hurried attempt to burn documents.

"I sat over there," Rachel said, pointing to a single small table set back in a corner. "They would bring documents, and I would translate them into German. Male clerks worked at the big desks, answering telephones and handling paperwork. I kept to myself, and they mostly ignored me. That's where I was sitting when I saw him."

"Him?" Jacobson asked.

Rachel paused, and her eyes grew wide.

"Yes. He passed this way and went into the laboratory," Rachel answered, pointing at the swinging doors on the other side of the office space.

"Who are you talking about?" Jacobson asked, still confused.

"Him. Hitler," Rachel replied, her voice low and ominous. "He walked right by where you are standing now."

CHAPTER TWELVE

"Damn, now this place *really* gives me the creeps," Tucker exclaimed.

"Rachel, are you sure?" Jacobson asked, reluctant to believe that this young girl, a Jew and a prisoner, had been allowed in the same room as the Führer himself.

Rachel turned and looked Jacobson directly in the eye.

"Yes. And that was only two days ago. Just before you arrived. I remember clearly. It was Saturday. Shabbat."

Rachel's insistence on the timing of her close encounter with the Nazi leader made Jacobson even more skeptical. Hitler committed suicide almost a week before the platoon arrived in Gusen. There had even been pictures of Hitler's burned body in all the papers.

Seeing the cynical expression on Jacobson's face, Rachel added, "I was sorting documents. The Nazis were crazy to get out. The clerks worked like madmen to remove all the equipment and burn documents. Everything was so loud and confused that the clerks barely noticed when several SS soldiers came through the door. They had tasked me with identifying papers they wanted to keep written in English, French, and other languages. I stayed out of sight because when the SS comes, people die."

"And that's when you believe Hitler came in?" Jacobson asked.

"I do not believe. I know," Rachel stated firmly. "But yes. They rushed him past everyone. He wore a long tan overcoat and a black hat, regular clothes, not a uniform. The SS men led him into the laboratories. That happened on the last day I came to work here. Soon after that, all the Germans suddenly just left. I did not know what to do, so I walked back to the camp."

"And you didn't see Hitler come out again?" Tucker asked.

"No. I could hardly breathe the whole time, just knowing of his presence. The laboratories are large, but he could have walked around them in just a few minutes. And that door is the only way in or out," Rachel answered, confidently sticking to her story.

"So, a dead Hitler walked through here and disappeared into the laboratories?" Tucker asked. "Sounds like you seen a ghost."

Rachel turned to face the lanky American combat veteran and pointed a single thin finger at his face. "No, Sergeant, I did not see a ghost. I saw the devil. And he was very much alive. You may believe me or not as you please. But I was not the only one to see him. Ask Lou. He is a mechanic. He said he also saw Hitler while he worked on the engine of a transport truck. Hitler drove by him in a black Mercedes automobile. He will tell you!"

"Okay. Okay. We'll talk to this Lou fellow later," Jacobson said, trying to calm Rachel and get back on track. "Right now, we should see what's in the laboratory. I still have a report to write."

He didn't know what to make of Rachel's account, so he decided to move on. For now.

Rachel reluctantly put aside her story and led the way through the swinging double doors. The lantern cast a circle of yellow light that dispelled some of the darkness but couldn't illuminate the entire space. They found themselves in what had clearly served as a massive laboratory of some kind. Like the office, it appeared the Nazis had left in a hurry. Only a few test tubes, beakers, and small, unidentifiable electronic instruments remained, strewn across the tables or broken on the floor.

As Jacobson ventured deeper into the lab, a sense of foreboding made his stomach turn to ice. He couldn't shake the feeling that something truly evil lurked just outside the light of his lantern.

Suddenly, he felt a tug on his jacket sleeve.

Startled, he jerked his arm away, only to find Rachel standing beside him, pointing at three round pressure chambers. Jacobson had seen something similar used to treat polio patients. But these were much larger. They looked like giant white barrels lying on their sides. Each 10-foot-long welded steel chamber was tall enough for a man to stand inside.

Neither he nor Rachel said anything as they examined the pressure vessels. A simple gurney sat inside each chamber, leather restraint straps hanging ominously from their sides. A thick, round window in each door allowed those outside to observe the interior.

"Do you know what the Nazis used these for?" Jacobson asked, fearing he already knew the answer.

"I heard rumors. But it is horrible," Rachel answered quietly. "They wanted to see what would happen to a person's body if they flew at very high altitudes. Much higher than a regular airplane can go. Even as high as space. Many of our people went in. None came out alive."

Jacobson involuntarily shivered at the thought of being strapped onto a gurney and wheeled inside one of the pressure chambers. He recalled from biology courses how extremely low air pressure found high in the atmosphere would cause blood inside a human body to actually boil – even at normal body temperature. Why the Nazis wanted to confirm an already well-established fact eluded him.

Perhaps to confront his own fear, Jacobson stepped inside the last chamber and looked around. He found an empty steel tank with pressure fittings penetrating the walls to allow air to flow in or to be vacuumed out.

Then he noticed a second, smaller pressure hatch on the back wall with another locking wheel. Stepping out again, he checked the other two chambers. Neither had a second door. Even more confusing, all three pressure chambers appeared to be installed flush against the laboratory wall.

Stepping back into the third tank, Jacobson impulsively spun the locking wheel and pulled open the rear pressure door. He didn't know what he would find, but a short passage ending in steps leading deep into the earth hadn't occurred to him as a possibility.

What the hell did the Nazis use this for?

"You see! You see! That must be where Hitler went!" Rachel cried unexpectedly from right behind him.

***

Despite his intense curiosity, Jacobson decided to leave the investigation of the hidden stairway behind the pressure chamber for another day. Captain Feilding wanted a preliminary report on the entire tunnel complex as quickly as possible, and he had barely begun his inspection. Jacobson assured Rachel they would return, but he had to see the full extent of the facility's research and manufacturing areas first.

Jacobson and Tucker, expertly guided by Rachel, spent the rest of the afternoon exploring the vast underground facility. Jacobson took detailed notes while they examined several other research laboratories and drove through enormous now-abandoned manufacturing plants. Jacobson could only guess at the extent of aircraft production the Germans managed to hide deep underground. But there wasn't much to see.

The Nazis had efficiently and thoroughly cleaned out the entire complex. Jacobson could only make notes about the tunnel system's impressive size and ingenious layout. They found a few parts from airplane engines, some cockpit components, and stacks of what appeared to be aluminum sheet metal – most likely for use in forming the skin of various aircraft. Everything else, from overhead cranes to manufacturing jigs, had been destroyed with explosives. If the brass hoped to find futuristic prototype jet fighters or space rockets left behind by the Germans, they would be sorely disappointed. Besides his description of the pressure chambers, Jacobson's report to Captain Feilding wouldn't prove very interesting.

But that wouldn't be the case if he included Rachel's claim that Adolf Hitler made an appearance in the tunnels several days after his reported suicide in Berlin. Jacobson wrestled with whether or not he should even include that information. Without corroborating evidence, he would have dismissed Rachel's story as a case of mistaken identity. After all, she had been in the camps a long time.

God only knows what that does to a person's mind.

Yet, the secret tunnel he discovered in the lab did seem to support Rachel's story. Jacobson could only think of one reason to hide a tunnel behind the pressure chamber – somebody wanted a way out of the facility without being seen.

On top of that, after they returned to the camp, they tracked down Lou, the mechanic. With Rachel interpreting, Lou adamantly confirmed Rachel's story. He had indeed seen the Führer drive past him in a Mercedes automobile. Although Lou admitted he had only been able to see the evil dictator for a second or two, nothing would dissuade him. Jacobson could sense that the memory shook the older man to the core.

"I will tell you the truth, sir," Lou had said, looking Jacobson straight in the eye. "If I knew that bastard was coming one minute earlier, I would have tried to kill him with my own hands!"

Rachel and Lou's story left Jacobson with a difficult decision – whether to pass on what they told him about seeing Hitler to his company commander – or forget it altogether. Such an inflammatory report might not be well received. He could even be putting his short career in jeopardy. *Who would believe it anyway?* The Army and the government had already assured the world that Hitler had killed himself. *Who was he to rock the boat?*

Jacobson spent hours that night writing drafts of his report to Feilding and throwing each, in turn, into his wastepaper basket. His criminal investigation training told him he couldn't conclusively prove Hitler's presence in the tunnels. But while the evidence wasn't perfect, he also couldn't simply ignore the statements of two eyewitnesses and the existence of the second pressure hatch and stairway.

Realizing he needed more information before submitting his report, Jacobson resolved to thoroughly investigate the tunnel behind the pressure chamber and see where it led. Even if Hitler hadn't used what he already thought of as a secret escape route, maybe other high-level Nazis did.

If he could confirm that the tunnel was, indeed, part of an escape route, he would make a full report to Captain Feilding and let the chips fall where they may.

CHAPTER THIRTEEN

The following day, Jacobson rose early to deal with his backlog of tedious administrative duties. Afterward, he collected Tucker and Rachel and drove back into the tunnels. This time, they came prepared with several lanterns and a bag of tools to investigate the mysterious passageway they discovered the day before. For extra security, Tucker carried his trusty Thompson.

"Uh, Lieutenant, sir, are we really goin' to go sneaking around in that Nazi hole? Maybe there's still a bunch of them down there, you know, hiding out until they can slink off someplace," Tucker asked, not at all confident about his lieutenant's plan.

"Yeah, Tucker, we are. But if there's any Nazis still around, I'll tell you what – you can have the first crack at them. That work for you?" Jacobson answered.

"Now I'd sure like to bag me one or two more, and that's a fact. It's just that tight spaces give me the heebie-jeebies. I'm more partial to the outdoors, if you know what I mean," Tucker explained, his bravado masking a touch of claustrophobia.

From the passenger seat, Rachel reached over and touched Tucker on the shoulder. "You offered to ensure my safety when we arrived yesterday. I shall protect you today."

Tucker laughed. "Well, alright, then. I guess if Miss Cohen is going to watch my back, I'll be okay."

The entrance to the passageway from the pressure tank looked just as sinister as it had the day before. Light from Jacobson's lantern penetrated only a few feet inside. Stepping through the door at the back of the chamber, Jacobson wrinkled his nose at the cold, wet, slightly musty odor coming from below. The lieutenant hesitated a second, nearly overcome by an acute sense of dread at the prospect of descending into the darkness.

"Tucker, find something we can use to block both of the doors to the chamber open. I don't want to risk getting trapped down there," Jacobson ordered.

"He *had* to go through here. There's no other way out," Rachel proclaimed to bolster her own courage. "I just know he did."

Taking the lead, Jacobson drew his pistol, held up his lamp, and started down the steps. Rachel followed close behind.

Tucker paused, glancing into the stairwell. Except for the dim but fading light from Jacobson's lamp, all the massive sergeant could see were impenetrable walls and a low ceiling that led in only one direction – down.

"I guess I've walked into hell plenty of times already. I guess one more ain't going to matter," he finally said under his breath before ducking through the door carrying the heavy tool bag.

Jacobson led the way deeper and deeper into the earth. They turned left and right, seemingly at random, until they lost all sense of direction. Finally, the stairway ended at a steel gate, secured by a chain and padlock, blocking the way ahead.

A moment later, Tucker joined Rachel and Jacobson at the door.

"Someone sure didn't want to be followed," Tucker observed.

"Give me that crowbar," Jacobson said. "Maybe I can break this lock."

Jacobson jammed the heavy steel bar into the locking ring of the padlock and pulled with all his might. Nothing.

"Let me give you a hand," Tucker offered.

With both men putting all their weight on the heavy-duty crowbar, the lock suddenly snapped, sending them tumbling to the ground.

"Dang, I didn't think that would work," Tucker said in amazement.

After untangling themselves, they opened the door and continued their journey through the tunnel on the other side. The trio trudged through the seemingly endless black void for the next half-hour. No rooms appeared on either side, and they found no intersections with other passageways. Jacobson had to conclude that the Nazis built this for only one purpose – to provide a hidden exit out of the laboratory complex. But to where?

"How far do you think we have gone?" Rachel asked after a long period of silence.

"Two or three kilometers, a mile or more at least," Jacobson answered. "But it's hard to tell."

"I hope we find the end soon. It just don't feel right down here," Tucker groused.

"Well, I think you're about to get your wish. There's a door ahead," Jacobson responded, light from his lantern falling on a solid metal door built into a steel wall.

"You think that leads outside?" Rachel asked, hopefully.

"Only one way to find out, I suppose," Jacobson said. "Tucker, bring that Thompson up here just in case."

Tucker moved past Rachel, put his back against the tunnel wall and raised his weapon. Jacobson grasped the metal locking bar.

"On my go," Jacobson said. "One. Two. Three. Go!"

Jacobson raised the bar and pulled the door open. Light flooded into the tunnel, causing all three to squint into the bright sunlight.

As soon as he could see, Tucker slid around the edge of the door.

"All clear, Lieutenant," he called after a few seconds. "Nothin' out here but trees."

Jacobson and Rachel stepped through the door, both as relieved as Tucker to be back outside.

"Rachel, do you know where we are?" Jacobson asked.

Rachel looked around for a minute before replying.

"Yes, I think we are close to the Gusen River, near where it meets the Danube."

"Hey, Lieutenant! Rachel!" Tucker called from near the door they had just used.

"What have you got?" Jacobson asked, joining the Sergeant.

"Take a look at these," Tucker said, holding up several vines. "These have been cut. And not long ago. I think they completely covered the door until just recently."

"So, someone did come through the tunnel," Jacobson concluded. "Let's take a look around. Maybe we can find tire tracks or something."

The three spread out along the bank of the river. But they soon concluded that no vehicles could have passed through the dense vegetation.

"Cy! I found a dock!" Rachel called excitedly a few minutes later. "And some people have been here as well."

After Jacobson and Tucker joined Rachel, Tucker examined the ground nearby. He pointed out where five or more people had walked along a faint path toward the water, trampling the sparse grass and undergrowth. Jacobson leaned over to take a look.

"You sure, Tucker? I don't see anything."

"Yes, sir. I don't claim to be part Mohawk or nothing, but I've spent my life in the woods. Somebody wearing combat-style boots came this way from the direction of the tunnel. It's not easy to make out, but I'd stake my life on it. Plus, this is no game trail. Deer travel in single file. Men made this path walking side by side," Tucker explained. "And I can prove it."

Intrigued, Jacobson followed him to the riverbank.

"The last few days have been dry. But just before that, it rained," Tucker began.

"Yes," Rachel agreed. "The day I saw, uh, him, it had rained heavily the night before. I shall never forget that day."

"These footprints were made when all this was wet and muddy. Combat boots of various sizes made these prints. And see here? There's two sets of civilian shoes," Tucker said proudly.

Jacobson joined Tucker and examined the prints for himself. He couldn't discern all the details the sergeant pointed out, but he didn't have to be a woodsman to see that several people had trod through the mud to reach the dock.

"I wish we had a camera with us. Or plaster to make a cast of this. These prints might be important to somebody," Jacobson said, thinking out loud.

Tucker gave Jacobson a toothy grin. "Well, sir, you're in luck. I've been carrying this little thing around for a couple of months. I took it off a dead Nazi officer a while back. I thought it might come in handy today."

"I'll be damned," Jacobson exclaimed, examining a small Leica camera Tucker pulled from his pants pocket. "You know how to use it?"

"Kinda. You use this lever to roll the film. Look through this window at what you want to take a picture of, focus with this little ring on the lens, and then push this button."

Jacobson took a pen from his pocket and set it on the ground next to the footprints while Tucker snapped photos from several angles.

"Why did you put a pen in the pictures?" Rachel asked, intrigued.

"I trained in police work at the academy, uh, college. We can use the size of the pen to tell us how big the footprints are from the photos later on," Jacobson explained.

As they were preparing to make their way back to town, Jacobson found Rachel sitting on a fallen tree almost entirely covered with moss. Her arms were crossed across her chest, and she was staring pensively toward the river.

"We're ready to leave. Is everything alright?" Jacobson asked, a little hesitant to intrude.

"This has been quite an adventure. But suddenly, I felt like I had walked in that horrible monster's footsteps. For a second, his evil nature lingered in the air like a demon that wants me dead."

Jacobson sat down next to the girl. He wanted to put an arm around her and tell her she was safe. But that would be an empty gesture. Rachel had endured unimaginable horrors. What could he or anyone say or do to make someone like her ever feel safe again?

"I'm sorry if bringing you along wasn't the right thing to do," he said after a long moment.

"Oh, no. It is not that at all. I wanted to come. And I am glad I did. There is no doubt in my mind that he stood in this very place. Do you believe me now?" Rachel asked, her deep black eyes searching Jacobson's for acceptance of her story.

Jacobson found himself suddenly captivated by the young Jewish girl and he found it hard to pull his eyes away from Rachel's. They were like deep, dark pools that seemed to draw him closer and closer. After a moment, he tore his gaze away, stood, and walked a few feet toward the river, ashamed at his attraction to a girl that only days before had suffered and nearly died at the hands of the Nazis.

Rubbing at the stubble on his chin, Jacobson looked thoughtfully into the sky and answered Rachel's question.

"Yes. I think I do."

CHAPTER FOURTEEN

Jacobson's report described the empty tunnels and manufacturing plant in as much detail as possible, including the disturbing evidence of high-altitude pressure testing on living prisoners. But, the Germans' thoroughness in cleaning out the underground facility before their evacuation prevented Captain Feilding's newest lieutenant from reaching any conclusions about the extent of the Nazi's advanced technical ability. Feilding found Lieutenant Jacobson's report thorough and well-written, but the addendum to the report raised problems he didn't need.

Feilding feared the brass would not appreciate the part of Jacobson's report citing evidence of post-war sightings of Adolf Hitler. Since the fighting stopped, rumors that Hitler had not died in the Berlin bunker ran rampant. So far, the Army had suppressed most news stories alleging the dictator was still alive – and for good reason. The war in Europe had been long and costly. The Allies would have difficulty controlling the German population and dealing with

Russia's demands to occupy the country without the threat of Hitler re-invigorating the Nazi cause. Plus, the Allies were still involved in a bloody war in the Pacific. Japanese leaders needed to see Hitler's death as cowardly and without honor – a fate that awaited them as well.

"Damnit, Cy, you sure have put me in an awkward position. Sending a report like this up the chain of command is risky as hell," Feilding growled at the youthful lieutenant who had just hand-delivered his report to his company commander.

"I know, sir. But I've been trained to follow the evidence. Two eye-witnesses place Hitler in those tunnels five days after he was supposed to be dead. Plus, the passageway from the laboratory down to the river, the dock, and the footprints all support the fact that a group of soldiers and civilians recently used what can only be described as a secret escape route to the outside. Other Nazis escaped. Why not Hitler?" Jacobson responded.

"Yes, yes. I know. And, if we don't follow up on this lead, that son-of-a-bitch could well and truly get away scot-free," Feilding replied, turning the problem over and over in his mind.

Jacobson knew that the captain would be taking a chance submitting the report and that he had put his commanding officer in a difficult position.

After a few seconds, Feilding asked, "Cy, no bullshit. Do you believe your witnesses? Are they sure of who they saw?"

Jacobson had turned this very question over in his mind many times. And he had always come up with the same answer. "Yes, sir. I believe both are credible, particularly Miss Cohen. I had no choice but to put my findings in writing," Jacobson responded confidently.

"All right, all right. I'm going to submit your report as written. I don't know what it will do to our careers, but God help me, it's the right thing to do."

The fallout from the incendiary report arrived almost immediately. Within 48 hours of his return to Gusen, Jacobson's life changed completely.

CHAPTER FIFTEEN

Gusen, Austria

The brilliant spring sunshine of the last few days gave way to chilly temperatures and soaking rain. Jacobson was sitting at his makeshift desk plowing through another pile of mind-numbing administrative paperwork when his clerk stuck his head inside and announced a visitor.

"Fine. Fine. Send him in," Jacobson grunted, barely looking up from his desk.

A moment later, a short, thin man stepped through the door and removed his hat and lightweight overcoat, revealing a balding head and neatly-pressed civilian suit. The man's meticulous movements and round glasses gave Jacobson the impression of an overworked accountant.

He was anything but.

"Good afternoon, Lieutenant. Please allow me to introduce myself. I'm George Smith," the visitor said, closing the office door without consulting Jacobson. "I need to speak with you privately."

Jacobson didn't know what to make of the stranger. He hadn't expected an American civilian to suddenly appear in his backwater Austrian town.

The lieutenant leaned back in his chair, folded his arms across his chest and scowled at the pushy intruder. "May I first ask what this is about?"

"Ah, well, uh, no. But I'm sure you'd like to see my credentials. Please don't ask any questions until you have looked those over. It's really quite important. I'm sure you understand," Smith answered, reaching into his jacket pocket and handing over several sheets of paper and an identification card in a leather case.

Jacobson certainly did not understand. And if this stranger's arrival hadn't been the most intriguing thing to happen in the last 24 hours, he might have objected further. Instead, he remained silent while he studied the odd man's papers and identification. As he read, his eyes grew wide and his eyebrows rose higher and higher into his forehead.

"Okay, Mr. Smith, you have my attention. What can I do for you?" Jacobson asked, now more than curious.

Smith took a moment to look around the hotel room that acted as Jacobson's office as if inspecting it for hidden listening devices but said nothing.

"Mr. Smith, I have never heard of the OSS, but orders signed by General Eisenhower carry quite a bit of weight," Jacobson added, trying to move the conversation forward.

After another moment of awkward silence, Smith finally replied. "Yes. Yes. Quite so. The OSS, or Office of Strategic Services, is somewhat new. During the war, we inserted people behind enemy lines, gathered intelligence, intercepted radio and telegraph communications, coordinated with various resistant groups, that sort of thing."

"Ah. Spies," Jacobson stated.

"Yes," Smith agreed. "But I am here on another matter. One I believe you can help us with. You see, the OSS has been assigned the task of pursuing and apprehending missing high-ranking Nazis. As you know, The Nazi party's hierarchy has much to answer for. There is a small work camp here in Gusen, so you have seen some of their despicable deeds. I can assure you that this is only a very small example of the Nazis' handiwork. We now fear they murdered hundreds of thousands of Jews, political opponents, and others. Perhaps millions. As the war drew to a close, many of the most powerful party faithful, fearing capture and facing justice, arranged to escape using pre-established ratlines."

Jacobson had a hard time coming to grips with murder on the scale Smith described. If he hadn't seen the horrors of the Gusen concentration camp for himself, he might have dismissed Smith's revelation as exaggeration.

"Good God! I had no idea. But, ratlines, sir?" Jacobson asked, having never heard the term before.

"Yes. Ratlines are nothing but pre-planned escape routes. Soon after D-day, we started hearing rumors that top German officials were establishing these ratlines in case the war went badly for Germany. They set up pre-arranged contacts, safe houses, modes of transportation, and the like to get themselves out of Europe," Smith explained. "Remember, the Nazis had a broad base of support and could rely on many friends, some in high places, to aid with their escape."

"I can see that. But where would they go?" Jacobson asked, leaning forward in his chair.

"Almost certainly South America. The governments of Argentina and Uruguay, in particular, remain strong Nazi sympathizers. You might recall that the German battleship Graf Spee had mechanical difficulties in the South Atlantic and sought refuge in Uruguay. That was no fluke," Smith replied.

"I remember. So, sir, this is all interesting and, I have to say, somewhat frightening, but what can I do for you?" Jacobson asked, still confused but now extremely curious about the OSS agent's purpose in Gusen.

"Please allow me to explain. I decided to come here after reading your report indicating Hitler's presence here in Gusen as late as May 5. Do you still find that evidence credible?" Smith asked, looking Jacobson directly in the eyes.

The connection between his report and Smith's revelations suddenly became clear and Jacobson chastised himself for missing it.

"Yes, sir, I do," Jacobson responded confidently. "The witnesses are still here, and I'd be happy to let you speak with them and show you the escape route we found in the Messerschmitt tunnel facility."

Smith waved his hand, dismissing the idea.

"Thank you, Lieutenant. But that won't be necessary."

"Then I'm confused. If you don't want to see or hear the evidence for yourself, what more can I do for you?" Jacobson asked.

Smith didn't reply. Instead, he held up one finger, opened a thin briefcase and removed two pieces of paper.

"Since the end of hostilities, we have received hundreds of accounts from people all around Europe claiming they saw Hitler after the war ended. We found the great majority of those were nothing more than hoaxes, fantasies, or cases of mistaken identity. Yet several, like yours, merit further investigation. I wanted to meet you in person before giving you these orders," Smith replied, handing Jacobson the paperwork.

Jacobson quickly scanned through the orders. Astonished, he reread the two-page document, making sure he grasped its meaning.

"Are you serious? You want *me* to investigate whether Hitler was here in Gusen?"

Smith leaned forward in his chair.

"No, Lieutenant. The scope of your investigation is not limited to Gusen. You are hereby ordered to follow the evidence you have gathered and will gather wherever it leads you within Allied-controlled Europe. You will immediately choose a team of three or four members to provide aid and security for your assignment. You will, for lack of a better term, hunt down Hitler or any other Nazis who might have escaped through this sector. You will report to me and me alone. Do you understand?" Smith asked.

"Well, yes, sir," Jacobson replied, not at all sure he fully understood.

"Some think what we are doing is a fool's errand. But others, including President Truman and General Eisenhower, believe that if there is even a tiny chance Hitler survived the war, we must find him. Think of the ramifications for a moment. We know the Nazis plundered billions of dollars in gold from the countries they conquered, not to mention billions more in valuables of all kinds. With nearly unlimited resources, Hitler and his followers could find a way to reignite the Nazi nightmare. Maybe not in Europe. But there are dictators, tyrants, and opportunists all over the world that would welcome Hitler, the Nazis, and their treasure trove with open arms. The allies barely won this war. Next time, the outcome could be much different."

Smith watched Jacobson digest his orders, knowing the young Lieutenant would recognize the importance of the job he had just been handed.

Smith continued. "The OSS has been charged with either confirming Hitler's death or finding him before he and his true believers can regain power and influence. Despite what you see in the press, we have not been able to verify that the Führer died in Berlin. The Russians insist they found the burned bodies of Hitler and Eva Braun, but they have not been willing to share the remains with us so we can authenticate the bodies for ourselves. In addition, we have reliable sources and significant evidence suggesting Hitler escaped the city just days, maybe even hours, before the end of the war. So, we have no choice but to pursue credible leads," Smith explained.

"And you don't have enough personnel to follow up on every such report?" Jacobson asked, suddenly realizing why Smith would entrust the mission to a new second lieutenant.

"Precisely," Smith responded, impressed with Jacobson's perception. "Your team is just one of several others we have assembled for the same purpose. So, per the orders I just handed you, you and whoever you pick for your team are now attached to the OSS. Your team's code name is *Orion 6*. Use it only when you make contact in the future. I brought along a special long-range radio and instructions for contacting us as needs be."

"Sir, what resources will I have available other than a small team?" Jacobson asked, warming to his new, exciting assignment.

"Excellent question, Lieutenant Jacobson," Smith replied, handing his briefcase across the table. "That is now yours. In it, you will find authorizations and orders granting you unlimited access to all Allied resources in Europe. You will also find currency in various denominations as well as gold coins you can use for bribes, payoffs, and expenses as you deem necessary. You will contact me if you need more. If you reach a dead-end, so be it. We may be grasping at straws anyway."

"Yes, sir. Does Captain Feilding know about all this?"

"He only knows you have been reassigned and that a replacement will take over to administer Gusen. That's all. Otherwise, your mission is classified, and you will divulge your activities only to your chosen team members. Any other questions?"

"Yes, sir. Why me?"

"Simply put, you used your training to fully investigate the eye witness testimony presented to you when you could have more easily walked away. You sought corroborating evidence to back up the witnesses. By the way, one of the footprints you photographed turned out to be from the same size shoe worn by Hitler. Most importantly, your actions showed initiative. But don't get cocky. Teams like yours are a long shot at best. Also, be careful. The Allies defeated the Nazis militarily, but their cause survives. They still control a large base of support. Allied troops have begun occupying Austria and Italy, but we are still spread exceedingly thin and will not be able to offer you much in the way of assistance. Make no mistake. Your mission is not without risk."

As Smith stood to leave, Jacobson asked, "Sir, do *you* believe Hitler killed himself in that bunker?"

Smith turned toward the door but stopped and looked over his shoulder.

"Would a megalomaniac who damn near took over the world simply admit defeat and shoot himself in the head? I think not. So, the answer to your question is no. Not for an instant."

CHAPTER SIXTEEN

Still reeling from Smith's surprise appearance and new orders, Jacobson didn't hear his clerk's knock. After a moment, the private tentatively stuck his head inside and announced that the mayor of Gusen was in the office requesting a meeting.

Jacobson stifled a groan when the portly Burgermeister, or mayor, of Gusen, strutted through the door. Without asking, the man removed his hat, tossed it on the table Jacobson used as a desk, and planted himself on a rickety chair from the hotel's tiny dining room.

Without so much as a pleasant greeting, the mayor launched into his current set of complaints.

"Lieutenant, I must demand you stop commandeering supplies from the townspeople for the work camp laborers and forcing my people to bury the dead. I have a petition signed by the majority of our citizens to support that demand," the mayor announced.

"I see," Jacobson replied, trying not to sound annoyed. "And what does your latest petition say?"

"It attests to the fact that we had nothing to do with the, uh, activities undertaken by the Germans at the labor camp outside of town," the mayor announced, pulling several sheets of paper from the inside pocket of his black suitcoat and placing the document formally in front of Jacobson.

Without even looking at the damp papers, Jacobson looked the mayor in the eyes and said, "Atrocities."

"Excuse me?" the mayor responded, confused.

"You said 'activities.' I'm sure you meant 'atrocities,'" Jacobson said, trying to remain calm.

"As I told you when we first met, we had no idea what was happening inside that camp. You cannot hold this town responsible for the Germans' actions after they forcibly occupied our country!" the mayor shouted.

Jacobson's patience shattered.

Standing for the first time, he leaned over the table and put his face directly in front of the mayor's nose.

"Here's what I think," Jacobson snarled. "I think that when Austria *voluntarily* joined the German Reich, you couldn't wait to raise a Nazi flag right in the middle of Gusen. And when the SS goose-stepped into town to build those tunnels and that despicable work camp, you handed out little Nazi flags for all the children to wave. I bet you even had a little swastika pin stuck onto the lapel of that very coat!"

Jacobson punctuated his words by poking his finger into the mayor's suit jacket.

"I never..." the mayor stammered.

"Yes, you damn well did!" Jacobson shouted into the mayor's face. "And I have records from your office and the newspapers that prove you were the biggest goddamned Nazi-lover in this sector!"

The mayor's body visibly tensed and a line of sweat formed across his upper lip.

"They brought those Jews here! Not us! Not me! Before the Germans came, we were lucky. No Jews lived here. They brought trainloads of those dirty creatures to that camp. What were we supposed to do? *Help the Jews?*"

Jacobson walked stiffly around the table, lifted the mayor off the chair by his lapels, and propelled him violently backward into the wall.

With his nose only an inch from the other man's fat, sweating face, Jacobson hissed, "Yes. I do."

The mayor's eyes grew wide and his lower lip trembled. His back was against a wall – in more ways than one.

Jacobson wanted to beat the pompous ass to a pulp with his bare hands. The sniveling, whining, cowardly Nazi had earned that and much more. But he couldn't. He had orders to maintain peace in the town. *What a shame.*

Instead, Jacobson gave him another little shove to focus his attention.

"Mr. Mayor, your request to end the work parties is *denied*. You will now *personally* lead those work parties each morning until those poor souls are properly buried. If you fail, if you complain, or if I see you or any of your people even look at the laborers sideways, I shall see to it that the Provost Marshal receives a full accounting of your actions as a Hitler-lover. If that happens, I wouldn't be at all surprised if you stood trial as a war criminal. Do you understand, *Burgermeister?*"

Sweat poured from the mayor's head, soaking his starched white collar.

"Do you understand?" Jacobson shouted again.

The mayor managed to nod once.

Jacobson dropped his hands, and the mayor shot out of the office without another word, his face twisted into a mask of panic and rage.

CHAPTER SEVENTEEN

Jacobson couldn't have been happier to get away from Gusen and let the next guy juggle mountains of paperwork and listen to unending complaints. Logically, he could understand why the Austrians resented the Americans taking over their town. And the lieutenant could even see why they hated burying the dead from the labor camp. However, he found their utter disregard, if not outright support, for the human suffering just a mile away, to be offensive and unforgivable. While the people in Gusen remained stoically silent when the Americans were around, their looks of contempt told Jacobson everything he needed to know. They had learned nothing and still considered themselves part of Hitler's 'Master Race'.

But as Jacobson left his office, he had a spring in his step and new-found energy. His little encounter with the mayor had been therapeutic. Better yet, he now had a new, challenging, and critically important mission.

Jacobson found Tucker, Pernell, and Downtown loading a flatbed truck with food and water for the labor camp. The rain had stopped, leaving behind muddy roads and stifling humidity hanging in the air. Tucker and his men sweated through their undershirts as they manhandled crates of fresh vegetables onto the flatbed.

"Sergeant Tucker!" Jacobson called out as he approached the men. "May I see you for a second?"

Standing on top of the truck, Pernell leaned over to Downtown. "Well, if it isn't our clean and shiny lieutenant. I sure hope he doesn't get his shoes muddy again."

"Yeah, he's pretty brave coming out in this weather. The creases in his pants might fall out," Downtown added.

"Stow it," Tucker barked. "The guy is okay."

"Yeah?" Pernell asked. "He'll never be as good as Lieutenant Stephens. Never."

"Neither will you," Tucker replied, pulling on his shirt as he walked away. "Get back to work."

Tucker left Pernell and Downtown still complaining and joined Jacobson on a low rock wall along one side of the dirt road.

"What's going on, Lieutenant? You look like a kid on Christmas morning," Tucker began.

"Yeah? Well, I got some good news," Jacobson said, smiling.

Tucker's eyes widened. *Were they finally going home?*

Jacobson continued, "You and I have a new assignment."

That wasn't what Tucker wanted to hear.

"I was hoping you were going to tell us we were shipping out," Tucker said, trying not to sound disappointed.

"Oh. Well, no. Sorry," Jacobson responded, angry with himself for not realizing how much his men looked forward to going home.

Tucker stifled an urge to do a little bellyaching of his own.

"Okay, sir. Maybe I should hear about this 'new assignment.'"

Jacobson described his meeting with the OSS agent and the incredible orders requiring him to form a team and follow up on their recent investigation.

"That's got to be the craziest idea I ever heard of in my life!" Tucker blurted after Jacobson explained they would be pursuing Adolf Hitler. "Uh, sorry, sir. I don't doubt Miss Cohen thinks she saw that lunatic son-of-a-bitch. I really don't. But…"

"Your concern is noted, Sergeant. I sure didn't expect anything like this either," Jacobson responded, cutting off Tucker's objections. "But our orders come straight from the top. And by 'the top,' I'm not kidding."

"Captain Feilding?" Tucker asked, unimpressed.

"No, Sergeant," Jacobson replied, pausing a moment before continuing. "Eisenhower."

Tucker let out a long low whistle. "You're joshing me, sir."

Jacobson opened the briefcase Smith gave him, pulled out the orders, and pointed to Eisenhower's signature.

"Well, I'll be damned. And you said you could pick your own team?" Tucker asked, finally understanding Jacobson's enthusiasm.

"That's right. And I want you on that team. But I don't know the other men yet, and you do. I need a small team. Maybe two others. Who do you recommend?" Jacobson asked.

"Well, that's pretty simple," Tucker answered. "Those two knuckleheads over there – Pernell and Downton. They can be goofballs, but I've fought with them since Normandy, and there's nobody I'd rather have at my side. The skinny guy, Pernell, is from Brooklyn. He's tough and street-smart. The big one, Downton, we call him Downtown, is from Iowa. He's a farm boy. Strong as an ox and can fix anything."

"Excellent. They'll provide security. We'll pick up the last member of our team on the way out tomorrow morning."

"Who else is going along?" Tucker asked.

"Rachel."

"A *girl!?*" Tuck exclaimed, shocked. "I changed my mind. *That's* the craziest thing I've ever heard. You think that's really such a good idea, sir?"

"We'll need an interpreter. Plus, she knows the culture over here. I think she'll be a lot of help," Jacobson explained. "If she agrees to go, the matter is closed."

"So, let me get this straight. A young Jewish girl, a brand-new second lieutenant, and three dirty combat grunts are going Nazi hunting?" Tucker asked, a note of resignation in his voice.

Jacobson put one hand on Tucker's slumping shoulder.

"Yes."

CHAPTER EIGHTEEN

Near Traunsee Lake, Austria
The same day

SS Colonel Otto Skorzeny found himself irritated and tense as he walked the long halls of Schloss Weyer. The seventeenth-century castle had been a godsend since his team arrived with Hitler seven days earlier. Consumed by the precarious status of his current mission, he didn't even notice the bright sunlight streaming into the manicured open courtyard or the expansive views of Traunsee Lake. The harrowing escape from Berlin to the Gusen tunnels, crossing the Danube River in the dead of night, and subsequent ride along rural farm roads had taken a heavy toll on Hitler's health. The aging dictator had laid in bed for days afterward, fighting pneumonia and often unconscious. At times, Skorzeny feared death would overtake him. But, during the last forty-eight hours, Hitler made a remarkable recovery, reigniting Skorzeny's duty to get him safely out of Europe.

But they were over a week behind schedule. And with every passing hour, more Americans arrived in Austria and Italy.

"Colonel Skorzeny!"

The SS Colonel turned to find the overweight owner of the castle huffing and puffing up the hall, trying to attract his attention.

An ugly toad of a man, Skorzeny detested Herr Lowenstau's constant fawning and continuous demands.

Skorzeny reluctantly stopped walking and turned a smiling face toward Lowenstau. *What could he want now?*

"I hear the Führer is much better!" Lowenstau panted.

"Yes," Skorzeny responded.

"Wonderful! I suspect that he will continue on his journey shortly. Also, I have quite urgent news to pass on," Lowenstau said, still breathing hard.

"Then please, continue," Skorzeny replied calmly.

"We received a call less than an hour ago from the mayor of Gusen. I found you as quickly as I could..."

"Yes. Yes. Report what you know," Skorzeny responded, not entirely masking his impatience.

"Yes. Well. The mayor reported that the Americans were sending out teams to try and locate important Nazi leaders. And, he said one of these teams would leave Gusen tomorrow morning," Lowenstau reported excitedly.

"I see," Skorzeny replied without any visible reaction to the surprising news. "What else did he say?"

"Apparently, the team is being led by a certain Lieutenant Jacobson. He is young. And he has at least three other men with him. They will cross the Danube at Abwinden."

Skorzeny never believed that the Americans would accept the subterfuge that Hitler died in his bunker at face value. But he was genuinely surprised to learn about a team of investigators as close as Gusen. He had to assume that someone discovered their presence at the Messerschmitt facility.

"Did the mayor say how he came by this information?" Skorzeny asked, covering his concern with his usual set-jaw scowl.

"The Mayor of Gusen's daughter received the information from an American enlisted man who bragged about getting chosen for a special mission. With a bit of gentle persuasion, the mayor's daughter learned that he had been assigned to pursue the Führer. I did not ask what she had to do to get the information," Lowenstau replied with a lascivious grin.

"Yes. Thank you, Mayor Lowenstau," Skorzeny said, his mind already working on his next move.

As Skorzeny walked away, he sensed Lowenstau following close behind.

"Colonel, may I beg just another moment of your time?"

Lowenstau's voice irritated every nerve in Skorzeny's spine.

"Yes? What else?" Skorzeny growled, turning around.

The fat mayor stood greedily rubbing his two soft white hands together. He failed to notice Skorzeny's mounting temper.

"I was hoping the Führer might do me a great honor before he must leave?" Lowenstau asked.

Skorzeny knew he should have expected a final demand, even though Lowenstau had already been paid a king's ransom for their use of the castle and grounds.

"Your loyalty and hospitality have been most gracious. I expect we shall not intrude on you much longer. It is my understanding that Herr Deacon has already provided generous compensation for your inconvenience," Skorzeny responded stiffly. "What *else* may we do for you?"

Skorzeny's tone of voice should have been enough to deter Lowenstau from pressing his luck. But the obnoxious man's ambition blinded him to the SS officer's dangerously dark mood.

"A trifle really. A trifle. Would the Führer consider granting me an Iron Cross for my loyal service these last several days? It would be of great value when I enter the election for mayor of my little town," Lowenstau asked with a phony toothy smile.

Skorzeny had to restrain himself. The Reich reserved the Iron Cross for those displaying valor in the face of the enemy, not sniveling bureaucrats. Lowenstau had already appropriated this entire castle after forcibly evicting the Jewish owners and sending them off to die in the camps. A castle and the Deacon's payments should be reward enough. The very idea of this pathetic excuse of a man wearing the same Iron Cross he and several members of his outfit had won killing the enemy in the dead of the Russian winter sickened him.

Skorzeny approached Lowenstau and put a hand on the shorter man's shoulder.

"Herr Lowenstau, I think that could be easily arranged," Skorzeny replied smoothly. "I'm sure it would make your family proud."

"Ah, Colonel. Regrettably, I have no family. But it will certainly boost my reputation with my neighbors and friends," Lowenstau replied, excitement growing in his voice.

Lowenstau didn't notice Skorzeny quietly draw his Luger pistol from its holster. "Well, then. Let me be the first to offer my congratulations."

Without hesitation, Skorzeny suddenly pulled Lowenstau closer, jammed the pistol against the other man's sternum, and pulled the trigger. The castle owner died with a look of surprise plastered on his face when the 9-millimeter bullet tore through his heart.

They always look surprised.

After dragging the body into a nearby storage closet and washing the dead Austrian's blood from his hands, Skorzeny reported to Hitler's room. He found the Führer dressed and drinking tea next to an open window, the afternoon sun glinting off carefully-set porcelain cups and saucers.

"So, we continue our journey tomorrow, Colonel?" Hitler asked, dabbing at his lips with a white linen napkin.

"I had hoped to provide another night of rest, my Führer. But I must report the Americans have started sending investigative units into the field searching for high-ranking leaders of the Third Reich. We should leave immediately."

Hitler considered Skorzeny's words for a moment.

"I see. We shall do as you suggest. Do you believe these so-called investigative units pose a threat?" Hitler asked.

"I do not believe so, my Führer. Reports indicate they are using young officers and small, untrained teams. I suspect they do not have adequate personnel or resources for a serious manhunt. Yet, you are too important to accept even small risks," Skorzeny replied.

"I agree. Has my presence at this place been successfully kept unknown?"

"Yes, my Führer. I have silenced our host. My men are now doing the same to the cook and housekeeper. Nobody shall ever know you were here," Skorzeny reported, not mentioning Lowenstau's ridiculous request for an Iron Cross.

"Excellent. And the families of these people?" Hitler asked, as casually as if inquiring about the weather.

"None," Skorzeny said formally.

He was wrong.

CHAPTER NINETEEN

"Look around. See if you can find where small boats landed along the bank," Jacobson ordered.

A bright sun shining in a clear sky warmed the early morning air as Jacobson's team arrived at the south bank of the Danube River. They had assembled early and crossed the famous river on the same bridge their platoon had captured only days earlier. Jacobson had used a detailed map of the area to find where the Gusen joined with the Danube and estimated where small boats might have landed.

Tucker, Pernell, and Downtown left the dirt road alongside the river and made their way through the tall grass, trees, and shrubs to the shoreline.

Jacobson and Rachel followed a parallel path along the road, looking for telltale signs of cars or trucks that might have picked up Nazi fugitives.

"I haven't had a chance to properly thank you for agreeing to join us on this mission," Jacobson said as they walked along the dirt road.

Rachel stopped and looked into Jacobson's eyes. "I should be thanking you for requesting my help. I wanted to leave the camp but had no place to go. I have no family, and everyone I knew as a little girl is either dead or scattered to the four winds. And I wish to help. This is important work."

Jacobson could hear Rachel's sincerity and marveled again at her strength of character.

"Still. This mission could prove dangerous, and I have no idea if we will accomplish anything or not," Jacobson responded almost apologetically.

"We will. I know we will," Rachel replied, her eyes flashing with determination.

"How do you know?" Jacobson asked, taken aback by the certainty in Rachel's response.

"You believed in me when you had every reason to think I was crazy. Now, I believe in you," Rachel answered with a little shrug.

Jacobson blushed a bit at Rachel's answer. *She believes in me?*

Rachel turned and started walking again. "Now, back to business. Why do you think Hitler would have crossed the river in a small boat?"

Forcing himself to stop musing about what Rachel might have meant, Jacobson explained his thinking. "Well, we followed the escape tunnel out to the Gusen river. We found a place to launch small boats and footprints proving someone had been there. The evidence suggests that someone left the Gusen area just before we arrived in this sector. If I were in their shoes, I wouldn't be concerned with patrols on the river itself, but the bridges would have been closed to them as an escape route. They almost certainly crossed at night to avoid being seen. As best I can tell they probably came ashore somewhere around here."

"We will have a difficult time finding any evidence in this area," Rachel responded skeptically. "The trees and brush are quite thick near the river."

"I know. But I think we're on the right track. I want to see if we can find anything at all that might help confirm our theory."

After searching for nearly an hour without finding anything, Jacobson worried that his new assignment would be very short indeed.

"Hey, Lieutenant! Over here!" Tucker called from the direction of the river.

Jacobson and Rachel had to force their way through a mass of dense brush before finding Tucker. Nearby, an old man sat on a log with a fishing pole and empty bucket at his feet.

"I found this old boy doin' a little fishing. I know fishermen. He probably comes down here all the time. He seems okay. Wasn't even frightened when I came through the woods. I thought Rachel could talk to him some. Maybe he saw something," Tucker suggested.

Rachel sat on the log next to the fisherman. She decided he must be over eighty years old. His hands were bony and lined with protruding blue veins. His hair had thinned to a wisp of white threads. But she also saw that his blue eyes sparkled with curiosity at the appearance of American soldiers.

After a short conversation, Rachel learned his name was Rolf, and he did, indeed, come to the river every day to fish. And, because he had a hard time sleeping, he usually arrived extremely early every morning.

"Ask him if he has seen any small boats crossing the river late at night," Jacobson suggested.

"I am going to," Rachel replied. "I just want to make sure he is friendly first."

Rachel turned back to Rolf and asked a couple more questions, which seemed to upset the old man. Their conversation became animated, and Jacobson worried for a minute Rachel might have gone too far.

Suddenly, Rolf pushed himself off the log and stood as straight as his arthritic bones would allow and said, "Hitler!" before spitting on the ground at his feet.

"I ain't sure," Tucker said, standing to one side. "But I don't think good old Rolf here approves of Herr Hitler much."

Hearing Hitler's name, Rolf spit on the ground a second time.

"Did you ask him about the boats?" Jacobson asked.

"Yes, I did. Rolf saw two rowboats, loaded with soldiers and other men, cross the river. But that happened a week or more ago. He does not remember exactly when. They came from upriver, near the mouth of the Gusen, and landed only fifty meters downriver from here. He remembers because crossing the river at night in rowboats was, as he put it, stupid. He did see that several of the soldiers wore SS uniforms."

Hearing Rachel mention the SS, Rolf said, "SS! Schiest!" before spitting on the ground again.

No one missed Rolf's meaning.

"What else did he see?"

Jacobson wanted to get every possible morsel of information.

"The boats came out of the dark, and the men rowing them knew what they were doing. He couldn't see much through the trees, but he did hear several cars leave and head toward the town of Steyr."

Rolf volunteered to show Jacobson's team exactly where the Germans landed. When they arrived, they found nothing to indicate boats or humans had ever touched the spot.

Nevertheless, Rolf's information gave Jacobson some hope, and the lieutenant led everyone back to the road to look for additional clues. Rolf tagged along, his curiosity piqued by the appearance of American soldiers searching for escaping Nazis.

Tucker started poking around in the grass at the bottom of a shallow ditch that separated the road from disused fields on the far side. After a few minutes, he found a small glass vial of some kind.

"What have you got there?" Jacobson asked, seeing Tucker holding the glass container up to the light.

"Medicine ampoule of some kind. Strange to find it in a place like this, though," Tucker replied.

"Sure is," Jacobson said, taking the glass container. "But it could be important."

"How so?" Tucker asked.

"OSS intelligence reports indicate that Hitler suffered from several illnesses. Mostly stomach problems. This little piece of trash isn't much, but it at least fits our theory that Hitler crossed the river."

Rachel and Rolf joined Jacobson as he unfolded a detailed map.

"Rolf, if I wanted to get to Steyr without being noticed, which way would I go?" Jacobson asked, with Rachel interpreting.

Rolf studied the map for a moment before using Jacobson's pencil to trace a route along backroads to the nearby town.

"One last question," Jacobson said. "The people of Steyr, did they support the Nazis?"

Rolf's eyes grew cold and he spit on the ground again. "Steyr! Nazi!"

"I guess that answers that," Tucker commented.

After being thanked by Jacobson, Rolf made his way back to the river to continue fishing while Jacobson met with his team to discuss their next move.

"We're definitely onto something. I bet Hitler or some other high-ranking Nazi crossed that river and is now headed south. Steyr seems a likely place to go since old Rolf believes it's still crawling with Nazis. But what other options do you see?" Jacobson asked.

Tucker answered first. "Well, I sure wouldn't stop so close to the river. Steyr is only ten kilometers from here. I bet they went further than that."

Jacobson studied the map thoughtfully for a minute.

"I agree. The Army will be in these towns close to the river by now. He can't go north. That would just take him back to Germany. East is also out. He can't show his face in Vienna, and the Russians have Hungary locked down," Jacobson said, running his finger across the map one way and then the other.

"Italy. He must be going to Italy. Once he's there, he can escape by sea or maybe fly to North Africa," Rachel suggested.

"That makes sense," Jacobson replied. "But Italy, like Austria, is going to become more and more dangerous for him as the Allies move in."

Jacobson's team faced an obvious problem. Even if Hitler had no choice but to head toward Italy, they didn't know where to go next. Hitler could be anywhere between the Danube River and the Italian border – over a hundred miles from where they stood. He needed more information.

"Other than multiple escape routes, why would Hitler want to go to Italy?" Jacobson asked, almost to himself.

Rachel had the answer. "There is a formidable network in Italy that supports the Nazis and has tremendous assets all over the world. He could find help there."

"What sort of outfit has that kind of pull?" Tucker asked. "The mafia?"

Pernell spoke up from his perch on the back of the team's Jeep. "The mafia is big, but they don't have that kind of juice. Plus, the mob hates Nazis. Bad for business."

"Pernell, shut your trap and keep your eyes open!" Tucker snapped. "You're supposed to be on security. Move out to the right flank."

Pernell muttered something about the war being over, but jumped off the Jeep, stuck a cigarette in his mouth, and took up a sentry position as ordered.

"So, what's this network you were talking about?" Jacobson asked.

"The Catholic Church," Rachel said without emotion.

The answer shocked Jacobson to his core. *The church? Impossible!*

He was about to challenge Rachel's wild accusation when three shots rang out.

CHAPTER TWENTY

"Are there no airfields? Why must we crawl along these back roads when there must be loyal Luftwaffe pilots brave enough to fly their Führer to safety?" Hitler demanded from the back seat of a dirty 1938 Mercedes 170v sedan.

Having grown accustomed to the trappings and luxury of unlimited power, the Führer complained constantly as they bounced along the rutted, dusty farm roads. He had completely forgotten his upbringing in a poor Austrian village and his time cowering in the muddy trenches of Belgium during the First World War. Now, he failed to see the reality of his precarious situation or the immense effort necessary to protect him.

"We must ensure your safety, my Führer. Our enemies operate many airfields in northern Italy and constantly patrol the skies. Flying is too risky," Skorzeny explained for the fourth time in so many hours.

"Yes. Yes. So, you keep saying. Have arrangements been made to get us over the mountains?" Hitler demanded, referring to the Alps that stood between Austria and northeastern Italy.

"Of course, my Führer. I shall show you on the maps as soon as we reach our overnight destination," Skorzeny replied.

"Very well. I shall try to be patient," Hitler responded, still sulking.

The pothole-covered back roads rattled and shook the old Mercedes. Hitler grunted and cursed at the constant abuse as the three-car convoy traveled toward the mountains. They made agonizingly slow progress, sometimes moving at no more than a walking pace, but they had no choice. Hitler had to remain unseen by anyone other than the few trusted and meticulously chosen contacts that would provide shelter and assistance along their pre-planned escape route. But the honor of serving the Führer's needs as he fled came with a price – the same price paid by Herr Lowenstau and his staff at Schloss Weyer.

"How much longer?" Hitler wanted to know after another thirty minutes of bone-jarring travel.

"Another hour, my Führer," Skorzeny replied.

The driver shot Skorzeny a look. It would be at least twice that long before their next stop.

Hitler didn't react to the news, apparently satisfied. But suddenly, he asked, "Otto, do you believe the Americans are pursuing me? The lieutenant you described?"

Skorzeny turned around in his seat. Hitler could be fired by supreme confidence one moment and plunge into a morass of paranoia the next. He had to be careful with his answer.

"My Führer, if such a team exists, they will be dealt with. I sent two of my best men back along our route to find out if anyone is following us. They are ordered to eliminate any such threat, no matter the cost."

"No matter the cost. Excellent," Hitler cooed, pleased by the thought of men laying down their lives to protect his own.

***

Thirty miles back, Skorzeny's two SS men watched Jacobson and his team through binoculars as the Americans huddled around a map spread across the hood of a Jeep. Tucked into thick bushes across a field a hundred yards from their targets, the SS soldiers planned their attack.

"I see an officer, three enlisted men, and a girl," the older of the two said, peering at the group.

"A *girl?*" the other soldier said, surprised. "Why would they have a woman with them?"

"Who knows? The officer, Jacobson, is young and doesn't appear to have much experience. His sergeant and the other two look like they have seen combat. See how they have found proper sentry positions?"

"If I had my 98k sniper rifle, I could take out the officer and at least one of the others before they knew they were under attack," the younger man said wistfully.

"I have no doubt, Karl. You killed many communists with that fine weapon back in Stalingrad. But we must make do with what we have," the older man, Franz, said, carefully stroking his well-used submachine gun like a favorite pet.

"How do we take them? We are outnumbered two to one," Karl asked.

Karl wasn't frightened. He had already seen more than his share of brutal combat during the war. If anything, he was over-confident. Two seasoned SS commandos with the tactical advantage of surprise should quite easily eliminate the small contingent of Americans.

"We'll get on their flanks. You move right and take the guard on that side. I'll take the left. After they are dead, we will have the others trapped in a crossfire with the river at their backs."

The two men inched slowly backward into the dense trees, their camouflage combat fatigues helping them blend into the foliage as they maneuvered into position.

***

Pernell had just flicked the butt of his cigarette into the road when he caught a slight movement in the tree line. With instincts honed by near-constant combat, his rifle flew up to his eye.

"Contact left!"

Tucker grabbed Jacobson and Rachel and pulled them to the ground behind the Jeep just as he heard Pernell's M1 fire three quick shots. From the opposite direction, he recognized the staccato of a German submachine gun firing toward Downtown's position.

The firefight intensified quickly. Single shots from the Americans were answered by long bursts from the Germans' submachine guns. The SS men fired on full automatic to keep the Americans' heads down while they moved from position to position. But their weapons lacked accuracy. They would have to get much closer to ensure a kill shot.

Pernell and Downtown conserved their ammunition, taking opportunistic shots at the Germans. Meanwhile, Tucker supported his men from behind the Jeep, swinging his rifle from one side to the other, snapping off rounds whenever he caught a glimpse of the enemy.

Despite his assistance, Tucker watched the overwhelming firepower of the Germans' machine guns force Pernell and Downtown to retreat back toward the Jeep. The sergeant could see that they would soon be trapped against the river if they couldn't take out at least one of the Germans. He had to do something.

"Sir," Tucker shouted, ducking down to where Jacobson knelt with Rachel, "I have to support Pernell. You and her stay here."

Jacobson wasn't about to overrule his sergeant.

"Go."

Tucker used Pernell's next shots to cover his sprint to the side of the road. Finding cover in the ditch, he poured a hail of bullets from his Thompson in the general direction of the advancing German.

Jacobson knelt behind the Jeep with Rachel. Quick glances around the rear wheels allowed him to take stock of the situation. With Tucker's help, Pernell had stopped one German's advance, but now Downtown was in trouble. The private had taken shelter in the shallow ditch thirty yards down the road from Tucker. Small explosions of dirt over Downtown's head made it obvious the big Iowan didn't have a chance to return fire. With increasing confidence, the German ran toward him, firing from the hip.

Pausing only to wipe his sweaty palms on his uniform, Jacobson snatched his M1 from the back of the Jeep and chambered a round. He had only seconds to act.

Ignoring the gunfire to his left, Jacobson steadied the barrel of his weapon on the edge of the Jeep. He had been a good shot back at West Point, but not great. He would have to be better than that now if he wanted to save Downtown's life.

Jacobson aimed at the German, trying to keep the fast-moving target in his sights. His first shot missed badly. But suddenly, he got the lucky break he needed. Instead of charging forward, the German paused to pull a hand grenade from his belt.

Jacobson held his breath, centered the iron sights on the German's chest, and pulled the trigger a second time.

The round slammed into the German's shoulder, spinning him counterclockwise. The hand grenade pirouetted around his helmet in a wide arc – still clutched in his outstretched hand. In the next second, the grenade exploded, and the SS soldier seemed to just vanish.

Hearing the unexpected explosion, Downtown peeked over the edge of the ditch and gave Jacobson a wave of thanks.

"Come on!" Jacobson shouted, motioning Downtown back to the Jeep.

Suddenly, the firing from Tucker and Pernell stopped. As an eerie silence returned, Jacobson saw the two men dragging a second dead German out of the field.

Dumping the body on the dirt road, Tucker said, "Goddamned SS. These guys don't die easy, that's for sure."

"Nearly got us all," Pernell added, wiping sweat from his face with a dirty handkerchief.

"The dead one over there would have gotten me for sure if the lieutenant hadn't helped out," Downtown added, taking off his helmet and rubbing his head. "Nice shot, sir."

Tucker gave Jacobson a nod of approval, leaned over, and ripped the "SS" badge from the dead man's collar.

Handing the trophy to Jacobson, Tucker said, "Here, sir. You kill one of these SOBs, you get to keep this as a souvenir."

"But you guys killed this one," Jacobson objected.

"Aw, that's okay, sir. The one you shot blew up. We all have a pocketful of those. You keep that one. You earned it," Pernell responded.

The men didn't notice Rachel walk tentatively up behind them and peer down at the body.

"SS? Yes?" the girl asked.

"Yes," Jacobson replied, not seeing the fury burning in Rachel's eyes. "Are you alright?"

Rachel didn't answer.

"Zevel! Ben Zona!" Rachel screamed in Hebrew. "Bastards! Bastards!"

Rachel punctuated her curses by slamming her foot again and again into the dead man. Her near-unhinged rage and the ferocity of her attack surprised even the battle-hardened soldiers.

Tucker reached out to stop the assault, but Jacobson pulled his hand away.

"She needs this."

When the storm of anger finally cooled, Rachel stepped back, sat on the ground, and began sobbing.

"I...I am sorry," she managed to say.

"It's okay," Jacobson said softly.

"When we find Hitler, I am going to kill him with my own two hands," she said, her eyes steely, even as tears flowed down her cheeks.

Jacobson knelt next to her.

"Given the war is over, and we just got attacked by the SS out here in the middle of nowhere, I'd say someone doesn't want us following them. So, who knows? Maybe you'll get your chance," Jacobson said, lifting the Jewish girl out of the dirt and setting her soundly on her feet.

CHAPTER TWENTY-ONE

After sending Pernell and Downtown out to be sure there were no more threats, Jacobson spread the map over the hood again.

"Hell of a job, sir," Tucker said, noticing Jacobson's hand shaking.

"I don't know. I was scared shitless, and now I've got the shakes. I got lucky."

"Yeah? But you stepped into the fight anyway, and that's as good as it gets, sir," Tucker replied. "I've seen other officers freeze up when the real shooting starts. You didn't."

"Well, at least not this time. But thanks, Sergeant. You guys sure know your stuff," Jacobson commented, smiling to himself at what he considered high praise from a combat veteran.

"You think these two guys knew we are out here chasing Hitler or whoever?" Tucker asked, standing next to Jacobson.

"Yes, I do," Jacobson replied thoughtfully. "First, they were SS. Hitler would have a contingent of SS guards at his side. Second, two highly-trained troops wouldn't be operating rogue out here in the Austrian countryside. If we were in Germany, that might be different. Finally, they knew precisely where to find us."

Rachel, sitting in the Jeep, added, "That's frightening. If they knew where to find us, they must also have known who we are and what we are doing. How is that possible?"

Rachel was right. Their mission was supposed to be a secret. Even Captain Feilding didn't know why Jacobson had been reassigned or what the OSS had asked him to do. All three suddenly realized that someone had betrayed their mission.

"I informed Pernell and Downtown about our mission the night before we left," Tucker offered. "I told them to get their gear together and that we had been reassigned to look for Nazi fugitives. I also told them to stay in camp until we left."

Rachel looked at both men. "I did not know anything until you asked me to come with you just before we left. Some of my people wanted to know where I was going, but I only told them the Americans needed me as a translator."

Tucker stuck a cigar in his mouth and looked in the direction he sent Pernell and Downtown. "I got a bad feeling maybe one of my boys blabbed to somebody."

***

"It ain't like that, Sarge!" Downtown pleaded a few minutes later. "I didn't tell her nothing important!"

Tucker released Downtown's uniform shirt from an iron grip and shoved him bodily into the spare tire mounted on the back of the Jeep.

"No? Bullshit! What *did* you tell the little tramp?" Tucker demanded, the burning end of his cigar just an inch from Downtown's face.

"Honest! Nothing important!"

Tucker slapped Downtown's helmet off his head.

"You snuck out of the tent and thought you might have a good shot at getting the pants off the mayor's daughter one more time. And, to make yourself look like a big man, you shot your mouth off about hunting Nazis. I'm right, aren't I?" Tucker shouted, shoving

Downtown again. "Spill everything, or, I swear on my mama's grave, I'll shoot you right here and now!"

Tucker made a show of putting his hand on the holster of his sidearm.

He had trusted the younger man with his life many times. But he had to know the truth.

Downtown turned his head and looked to Jacobson for help.

Jacobson didn't bat an eyelid. "I think you should tell Sergeant Tucker everything. And you better be damn convincing about it."

Before Pernell and Downtown returned from their scouting mission, Jacobson had agreed to allow Tucker to handle the situation. His sergeant knew the men. He had fought shoulder-to-shoulder with them for over a year. Jacobson decided he would back up whatever action Tucker took to find the truth.

"Okay, okay," Downtown said, holding up his hands. "Yeah, it's just like you said, Sarge. I wanted to see Helga one more time. She acted like she hated to see me go and made me promise I would come back. All I said was I had to go and look for some missing Nazis with the lieutenant, and that I thought I would be back in a few days. That's all – I swear!"

Tucker stepped back and considered Downtown's story. After a few seconds, he decided the private had told the truth. Turning to Jacobson, he nodded and asked, "What do you want me to do with this stupid son-of-a-bitch, sir?"

Jacobson let Downtown stew for a few seconds before responding.

"Let him go. Downtown, this Helga, do you know for sure she's the mayor's daughter?"

Relieved, despite the fact Tucker still held him in a fiery glare, Downtown answered, "Oh, yeah. I mean, yes, sir. She introduced me to him once. Kind of a fat, sweaty guy? He acted like he was pleased to meet me, but I don't think he was. He seemed more like a slippery politician. You know, talking out of the side of his mouth and lying and all. Just like the mayor of my hometown, come to think of it."

"Yeah, I had some dealings with the man. I think I know what happened. Helga ran back to Daddy and reported what you said. The mayor somehow knew Hitler, or maybe someone else important, had been in town, and he called ahead to warn them we were on their tail. Goddamnit! I have to report this to Smith," Jacobson said, thinking out loud.

"Pernell, unpack the radio and get the aerial up."

CHAPTER TWENTY-TWO

Gusen, Austria

The OSS agent who called himself 'Mr. Smith' stood behind the mayor of Gusen with the barrel of his pistol inserted into the squirming Austrian mayor's right ear.

"You should stop fidgeting, Mr. Mayor," Smith said calmly into his other ear. "My finger is on the trigger, and I wouldn't want any accidents before we've had a chance to have a nice long conversation."

Smith had interrogated loyal Nazis many times and had learned they didn't respond well to a gentle touch.

Stripped to his underwear and socks, the mayor had little room to struggle. The ropes on his wrists and ankles bound him tightly to the same chair he had used while arguing with Jacobson about burial work parties. Removing the man's clothes not only served to humiliate him and make him vulnerable but also took away his trappings of power.

"I am the mayor of this town! You have no right to hold me here!" the pudgy man responded, trying desperately, but pitifully, to hold on to his dignity.

Smith wanted to laugh out loud at the mayor's empty bravado. Sweat stained the Nazi's undershirt and dripped off his nose. The mayor's belly folded over the waistband of his thin white shorts, and his sagging socks only stayed up due to a well-worn pair of garter belts that cut off the circulation below his calves. Smith half-expected the mayor to have a heart attack or urinate on himself. He had seen both before.

Smith pushed the barrel of his gun a little further into the man's ear canal.

"You are a loyal Nazi who has committed acts of inhumanity and depravity, and I have the authority to summarily execute you here and now. But, as a lesson to other Nazi lovers, maybe I should take you outside and shoot you in your underwear in the middle of the street."

The prideful man visibly shook at the prospect of a humiliating public execution. Smith could sense he was close to breaking through the mayor's thin crust of bravery.

"All you have to do to stay alive and go home to your family is cooperate with me," Smith coaxed. "But I have to tell you, my patience is wearing thin. I'm a busy man. And I have other disgusting Nazis to visit today. So, this is your last chance to answer my questions."

The terrified mayor sagged in his chair, and tears flowed from his eyes.

"Yes. Yes. Alright, yes. Please. I received a call. I can't remember when precisely. They informed me that a high-ranking party official would secretly pass through the Messerschmitt facility to access the Danube. They did not tell me when he would arrive, but they ordered me to call a certain number if the Americans became suspicious or asked questions. That's all. I swear. *I swear*!"

Smith enjoyed watching cowardly Nazis betray other Nazis to save their own skins. These people upheld their sacred vows only as long as it benefited them personally. The followers of oppressive, authoritarian regimes were almost exclusively motivated by the chance to grab power and accumulate wealth. And they espoused a deep commitment to ideological purity only as an excuse for their repugnant behavior.

"And the identity of this party official?" Smith demanded, suddenly moving the pistol barrel from the man's ear to the back of his skull.

The abrupt change in the placement of the weapon shocked the mayor.

"I swear I don't know! They had no reason to tell me. My only job was to report any investigation!" the mayor blubbered pitifully.

Smith removed the gun and walked around the chair so he could look directly into the mayor's face. He leaned over, coming nose-to-nose with the terrified politician. Tears streamed down his captive's now colorless cheeks. Smith wrinkled his nose at the smell of cheap cologne and pungent body odor.

"I don't believe you, you fat Nazi pig! You know more!" Smith screamed in the other man's face. "I don't have time for this. Goodbye, Mr. Mayor."

Smith made a show of cocking his pistol, standing back, and aiming at the man's face.

"No! No!" the mayor cried, his chest heaving and his hands and feet straining at their bindings. "I know only that the number I called was for Schloss Weyer. Schloss Weyer! It is near Traunsee Lake. Please, sir. I have a wife and daughter."

"Who did you speak to there?" Smith asked, holding the gun steady.

"Someone, I don't know who, answered the phone. I said Lieutenant Jacobson and his men left that morning in the direction of the Danube and that they had been assigned to search for party members escaping from Germany. Nobody on the other end ever said a word. I reported, and they hung up. That's all!"

Smith lowered the gun.

"If you have lied or withheld a single thing, I will return. There will be no second chances. Do you understand?"

The mayor looked at Smith with hope in his eyes. His breathing slowed a little, and his body visibly relaxed. "I...I understand. I have told you everything."

Smith left the mayor tied to the chair. Finding a phone on the clerk's desk outside, Smith dialed and waited.

"Message to Orion 6 from Smith. Schloss Weyer. Lake Traunsee. End message."

CHAPTER TWENTY-THREE

Schloss Weyer
Near Lake Traunsee
Austria

After receiving Smith's new information, Jacobson's team sped 30 miles across the Austrian countryside to the town of Gmunden. Schloss Weyer sat just outside town on the shore of Traunsee Lake. As soon as they arrived, Tucker dispatched Downtown and Pernell to scout around the castle and report any activity. Each man carried his M-1 rifle and a BC-611 walkie-talkie. Waiting for Downtown and Pernell to report back, the others stayed hidden in a shady, secluded stand of trees not far from the lake's glittering water.

"You think there's any chance Hitler is still here?" Tucker asked from the driver's seat.

"Not really," Jacobson replied, looking away from the map he had been studying. "I bet they kept moving. Staying in one place too long would be dangerous. Anyway, Rachel saw Hitler eleven days ago in the Messerschmitt tunnels. So, no. I'm almost certain he's not here now."

"Not to throw cold water on all this, but if he has that much of a lead on us, is there any real chance of us catching him?" Tucker asked, throwing one leg onto the fender and stretching his lanky frame out as far as possible.

"There has to be!" Rachel responded. "Why would they try to kill us if they didn't consider us a threat?"

"Exactly," Jacobson agreed. "For some reason, they must have gotten delayed. If I had to guess, I'd say there was some failure in their pre-positioned support. Or maybe Hitler got sick, and they had to stop. Either way, I'm certain we're not two weeks behind. A few days, maybe. But not more than a week."

Just as Jacobson finished, a scratchy voice came from Tucker's walkie-talkie.

"Pernell to Tucker. How do you read? Over."

"Go ahead. We read you loud and clear. Over," Tucker replied, hefting the heavy device in one hand.

"No vehicles on the grounds and no movement at the castle except for one female civilian, maybe thirteen years old, hanging laundry from the exterior gates. Otherwise, the place looks deserted. Over."

From the other side of the castle, Downtown reported seeing nothing but a pair of goats lazily munching on trash outside the kitchen door.

Jacobson listened to the reports, folded his map, and put on his helmet. "Okay, have them stay in position. We'll drive over and have a look around."

A few minutes later, Tucker parked the vehicle twenty yards or so from the entrance to the castle's courtyard. The young girl, who had been using the tall iron gates as a clothesline, stopped working and stared wide-eyed at the Americans and Rachel as they approached.

Barefoot and wearing an oversized maid's uniform, the girl looked like she was about to run.

Rachel, seeing the fear on the girl's face, called out in German, "We're friends! You have nothing to fear."

Unconvinced, the girl backed away, but she didn't run.

"Stay here," Rachel said to the men. "I think she is frightened of you."

Rachel walked ahead smiling, and the girl seemed to relax a little.

Turning back to Jacobson and Tucker, Rachel added, "Let me talk to her before you come over. And try to look less, uh, threatening. Put your guns away."

Jacobson slung his rifle onto his back and casually lit a cigarette. Tucker followed suit, leaned against a tree, and stuck a cigar in his mouth.

Rachel picked up a wet apron from the basket of laundry sitting on the ground close to the girl and hung it on the iron gates using two clothespins. After a moment, the girl stepped closer and began working alongside Rachel.

After hanging a child's blanket, Rachel asked the girl's name.

"Mila," she answered, not looking at Rachel.

"Do you live near here, Mila?" Rachel asked.

"Yes," Mila responded warily. "In the servants' quarters."

"Do you work in the castle?" Rachel inquired, hanging another item.

"My mother worked here. Now she is dead, and nobody works here," Mila answered, tears filling her eyes. "I only come here to use the well and do the wash."

Rachel sat on a shaded cast-iron bench and pulled a candy bar from her pocket. Patting the seat next to her and holding out the chocolate bar, Mila joined her. They sat for a minute while Mila slowly opened the candy and took a small bite. The sweet chocolate brought a little smile to her face, and she stopped crying.

"Can you tell me what happened? Why does nobody work here now?" Rachel asked.

Between bites of chocolate, Mila explained how her mother worked as the cook for Herr Lowenstau, the owner of the castle, and how she would sometimes help her mother in the kitchen and with the laundry. But, about two weeks ago, Herr Lowenstau became more demanding than usual and said Mila could not work there anymore. Her mother made her stay home, and she wasn't allowed to come back to the castle. But Mila became worried and found a hiding place where she could see the kitchen door.

A day or so later, soldiers came in two cars. Mila snuck behind the castle every day and watched. Her mother cooked all day and into the night. Lowenstau often went to the kitchen and shouted at her mother, ordering her to prepare certain unusual foods. Once, she believed her mother had seen her hiding outside.

Mila suddenly burst into tears. The candy forgotten, she buried her face in her hands and sobbed uncontrollably.

Rachel let her cry, stroking Mila's stringy blonde hair. When the girl's sobs subsided, Rachel asked gently, "What happened next, Mila?"

"One day, a huge soldier came into the kitchen and pushed Mama outside. I saw everything. Mama must have known about my hiding place because she looked at me and shook her head. Then..."

Mila's tears returned.

"The soldier killed her," Rachel said.

Mila nodded.

"A German soldier?" Rachel asked.

Mila nodded again and knelt in the dirt. After a moment, she drew 'SS' into the dust with her finger.

Rachel took the girl in her arms and held her tightly. "I know," she said over and over. "I know."

With a bit of coaxing, Mila revealed the soldiers had left the castle just a few days before. Soon after, she and other locals discovered the bodies of Herr Lowenstau and Emma, the maid, in the courtyard. Nobody had dared venture back inside since.

***

After hearing Rachel retell Mila's story, Jacobson and Tucker pushed through the iron gates and into the castle, leaving Pernell and Downtown on guard outside. They moved slowly through the massive structure, finding it deserted and quiet, just as Mila described.

"I thought castles had drawbridges and moats and towers and such. This place is more like a big white school," Tucker complained.

"I know that 'Schloss' means castle, but I'd call this more of a palace or a mansion. Maybe whoever built it way back when added fortifications, but it sure doesn't have any now," Jacobson offered.

The three-story structure was impressive, to be sure, but it looked nothing like King Author's Camelot. Constructed in the 1600s, Schloss Weyer consisted of four wings arranged in a square, surrounding a large open courtyard. Walkways lined with arches ran the length of each wing. Below, neatly trimmed shrubbery and now-empty flower beds filled the interior courtyard gardens. Inside, massive rooms overflowed with expensive-looking furniture and artwork. The castle's bedrooms and living quarters overlooked the lake from its west wing.

Jacobson found the interior oppressively Germanic, with heavy dark furnishings and paintings of past battles, boar hunts, and the like adorning every wall. He wasn't surprised to find medieval armor and weapons lining the interior hallways.

Tucker couldn't believe anyone could actually live in a place that fancy.

The pair moved quickly from room to room, scanning for evidence of Hitler's presence. After searching for over an hour, they finally came to a large suite with tall windows framing the lake and surrounding countryside. A four-poster bed dominated the space. Across the room, a fireplace with two wing chairs facing each other provided an intimate seating area. Jacobson and Tucker agreed that the accommodations would be suitable for the dictator of Germany.

"Now, this is interesting," Tucker commented, standing near a table and two chairs placed beside an open window. "Looks like someone didn't finish their breakfast."

On a table set for one, Jacobson found the remains of several uneaten boiled potatoes and now-unidentifiable green vegetables. A partially evaporated cup of tea sat to one side.

Jacobson scrutinized the table and said, "You're right, Sergeant. This is interesting."

Tucker didn't know what Jacobson meant.

"It's not definitive evidence by any means," Jacobson observed. "Mila said something about her mother cooking unusual dishes. And it's well known that Hitler was a vegetarian."

"What's that mean?" Tucker asked, having never heard the term before.

"It means he didn't eat meat. Only vegetables," Jacobson replied.

"Well, I'll be damned. Never heard of such a thing," Tucker scoffed, shaking his head.

Jacobson continued, "Remember that medicine vial we found at the river? Hitler believed eating vegetables helped his stomach condition."

"I'm no expert on rotten food or old tea. But this doesn't look like it's been sitting here a week," Tucker remarked.

"I agree. Let's keep looking."

They continued to search the room, looking for anything else that might suggest Hitler's presence. Jacobson finally arrived at a massive armoire set against one wall and decorated with a gold leaf inlay of some ancient coat-of-arms.

The doors were locked, but Jacobson immediately noticed a key lying on the floor at his feet. He picked up the key and inserted it into the keyhole in the right-hand door. Turning the key produced a satisfying click. As he opened the door, a string holding some sort of pin swung out of the opening.

"No!" Tucker shouted.

Standing a couple of yards away, the sergeant saw Jacobson turn the lock and open the door. When he heard a pin sliding between metal, he launched himself across the room, knocking Jacobson away from the front of the cabinet.

Exactly one second later, the armoire exploded, blowing out the windows and hurling lethal shards of wood and metal across the room. Almost immediately, drapes and bedding caught fire. The blaze quickly climbed the walls, threatening to engulf the bedroom – with Jacobson and Tucker still inside.

Stunned from the concussive blast and being knocked to the floor by Tucker, Jacobson found himself lying on his side with the lanky sergeant draped over him like a massive blanket.

Pushing the larger man off to the side, Jacobson leaned over the unconscious Tucker.

"Sergeant!" Jacobson yelled, shaking him by the shoulders.

Then he saw the fire. They had landed in the corner of the room, and he knew they only had seconds before the flames trapped them inside.

Though shaken, Jacobson grabbed Tucker's shoulders and managed to drag him to the door. Bits of flaming drapes and wallpaper rained into the bedroom, and long fingers of flame licked at the ceiling. As they left the room, dark gray smoke spilled out the door and into the long hallway.

With most of his strength gone and choking on the acrid smoke, Jacobson couldn't have been happier to see Pernell and Downtown burst into the hall, grab Tucker, and take them both outside.

Rachel had heard the explosion and saw the men carrying Tucker out of the castle with Jacobson limping along behind. She ran to the well, filled a bucket with cool water, and grabbed a piece of Mila's clean laundry off the gate.

Pernell laid Tucker next to the Jeep while Downtown helped Jacobson sit on the ground next to him.

"Is he alive?" Jacobson asked.

Rachel wet the cloth and wiped it across Tucker's forehead. The cool water revived the sergeant, who looked up at Rachel and said, "Well now, I always wondered what heaven would be like."

Rachel turned to Jacobson. "Yes. He is most definitely alive."

"What happened, Sarge?" Downtown asked.

Jacobson answered for him. "Booby trap. Hand grenade, I think. If the sergeant hadn't knocked my dumb ass away, I would be nothing but a splattered mess all over the walls in there."

Tucker was too busy enjoying Rachel's nursing to hear Jacobson's explanation.

"You thinking hand grenade, Fred?" Jacobson asked, using Tucker's first name.

"Yeah. No doubt about it. Rigged just right to take out anyone nosing around after they left," Tucker replied, sitting up. "But one thing's for sure."

"What's that?" Rachel asked.

"These guys are really starting to piss me off."

CHAPTER TWENTY-FOUR

Bad Ischl, Austria

Late in the evening, Hitler, Skorzeny, and the four remaining members of Hitler's escort drove through the quaint spa town of Bad Ischl. Sitting at the foot of the Alps, Bad Ischl was the gateway to the popular Alpine lake region. The town also guarded one of the few passes through the mountains separating Austria from Italy.

Bad Ischl had suffered dramatically during the war. People stopped coming to the town to enjoy the salt springs, ski in the winter, and explore the beautiful Alpine lakes in the summer. Now economically devastated, nobody strolled along the picturesque streets or sat in the numerous outdoor cafés.

To reach the mountain passes, Hitler's party had no choice but to cross the Traun River and drive through the middle of town. Skorzeny breathed a silent sigh of relief as the last of the town's buildings receded into the night.

Soon, the tiny convoy turned off the main road and onto a well-manicured gravel drive that twisted up into the mountains. After less than a mile, they stopped in front of a small but luxurious hotel overlooking Bad Ischl that would serve as their overnight refuge.

Normally, the hotel pampered wealthy Austrians and Germans with high-end services and private mineral springs. But Skorzeny cared about none of that. He had chosen this location after painstakingly researching the entire area almost a year earlier as the best location for an alternate safehouse. Tactically, the site overlooked both the town and the only road through the mountains – a critical chokepoint from which they could observe anyone approaching.

Skorzeny found the owner of the Sommer Hotel, Herr Gosser, waiting in the circular gravel drive to greet his guests. A man of extreme discretion, Gosser said little as he ushered Skorzeny, Hitler, and the others into the hotel. The hotel owner had not known before that moment that he would be hosting the Führer himself but managed to suppress his surprise at the appearance of a man universally reported to be dead. His long experience with famous and infamous guests in the past gave him impeccable insight into their preferred treatment. He would have to call on all that experience over the next 24 hours.

Thirty minutes later, Gosser had Hitler settled in the hotel's most luxurious suite. After he had guided everyone else to their rooms and provided a hot dinner, he met with Skorzeny, as instructed, in the gardens overlooking the town and valley.

The SS commando stood smoking one of his caustic Russian cigarettes, a taste he had developed while operating in and around Russia during Germany's invasion back in 1941.

"All is in order?" Skorzeny asked as the impeccably-dressed Gosser approached.

"Of course, Colonel Skorzeny," Gosser replied. "How may I be of service?"

Skorzeny examined the portly, five-foot-five-inch-tall hotel owner for a moment, sizing him up in more ways than one. While physically unimpressive, Skorzeny noted how the hotel owner's keen intellect and confident nature made him far more formidable than his diminutive stature would otherwise suggest.

"You know who I am, then?" Skorzeny asked.

"Of course, Colonel. I am deeply honored to meet the Reich's most decorated officer," Gosser replied with a slight bow.

Without acknowledging the compliment, Skorzeny said, "Tell me about your staff."

"As instructed, there is no staff. I prepared tonight's meal myself earlier this afternoon. The rest of my employees have been on holiday now for ten days. After I received word that my hotel might be utilized, I personally made all the preparations for your arrival."

Skorzeny considered Gosser and his answer carefully. At least according to the hotel owner, he had followed the Deacon's orders perfectly. But Gosser needed to answer the following question correctly to live another day.

"Who gave you the notification of our arrival?"

Gosser didn't hesitate. "Herr Deacon, of course."

"Yes, of course. Other than my identity, what do you know of your guests this evening?" Skorzeny asked, taking a long pull on his cigarette and looking out over the darkened valley below.

"It is my duty and honor to serve the Reich. I have been tasked with providing hospitality and comfort to those chosen by the Reich. I have no other desire or need to know anything more," Gosser replied.

"Hmmm. You choose your words carefully, Herr Gosser," Skorzeny replied.

Gosser did not say anything in return.

Once again impressed, Skorzeny asked, "Is the cable car in proper operation?"

"Of course. I ran a full test this morning. If necessary, it can carry your entire party to the summit of Salzkammergut mountain."

"And the access road in the other direction?" Skorzeny asked.

"Yes, the wooded track begins on the other side of the hotel and takes a circuitous route back down the mountain to Bad Ischl. The path is little used, but I examined it yesterday on my motorbike to be sure it is open and passable."

"Herr Gosser, your excellent service is much appreciated. I anticipate us being here only one night. Should that change, I shall let you know immediately," Skorzeny said, offering a rare compliment.

"My pleasure. I have taken the liberty of placing a beef steak and cabbage in your room along with an Asbach of good vintage," Gosser replied with another slight bow.

"My favorite food and drink. You have done your homework, Herr Gosser. I shall enjoy them shortly."

After dismissing the hotel owner, Skorzeny walked the grounds for another half-hour, contemplating how they had arrived at the foot of the Alps.

***

Once the Allies successfully landed in Normandy and the Russians fought their way into the Fatherland from the east, German military leaders, including Adolf Hitler himself, questioned the Reich's ability to survive the war. But moving people crucial to the Nazi agenda and enough plundered wealth to reconstitute the Reich would require colossal resources and steadfastly loyal relationships.

As the Allied forces tightened the noose around Germany's neck, the Deacon came forward offering the assistance of his worldwide contacts and massive wealth. After Skorzeny's meeting with the reclusive benefactor, the SS Colonel had a new mission. He would no longer face the enemy on the field of battle. He was tasked with nothing less than ensuring the survival of the Nazi leadership, who would be key to the creation of the Fourth Reich.

The Deacon had masterminded the creation of four routes out of Europe, utilizing loyal supporters and others who would protect Hitler and high-ranking Nazis as they escaped the Allies. Skorzeny spent months reviewing each route, painstakingly creating back-up means of travel and safehouses so that there would be no delay transporting the Nazis' leadership out of the country. But Hitler had stubbornly refused to leave his bunker even in the face of inevitable defeat. When he finally agreed to abandon Berlin just two days before his contrived suicide, it had been almost too late, and the Führer's escape nearly ended in the first few minutes.

Skorzeny took a long drag on his cigarette, removed his cap, and ran a gloved hand through his bristly salt-and-pepper hair, remembering the harrowing trip through a maze of Berlin subway tunnels that ended at the Tiergarten, the massive park in the heart of the city. German troops had collapsed around the park and the Reichstag, Germany's capital building, in a suicidal last line of defense against the barbarous Russian hordes.

At the Brandenburg Gate, they boarded a lone Junkers Ju-82 transport plane. Using the long, straight avenue through the middle of the park as a makeshift runway, they climbed into the air just before the first barrage of Soviet artillery shells landed. Looking down from a thousand feet, the explosions reminded Skorzeny of great ugly flowers blooming into the sky.

Skorzeny originally planned to fly Hitler north to the still-occupied coast of Denmark. They would then refuel and continue to the safety of a secret U-boat base near Narvik, Norway.

But none of that happened.

Minutes after taking off, a Russian fighter pilot spotted the slow and cumbersome three-engine Junkers passenger plane. The Yakolev Yak-3 fighter made one pass, destroying the port engine and peppering the fuselage with short bursts from its machine guns. Skorzeny had watched in horror as the Russian banked hard to get behind them again for a second and, undoubtedly, lethal attack.

If not for the immense skill of their pilot, Hanna Reitsch, Germany's top test pilot, they would all be dead.

Reitsch dove hard into low-hanging clouds, risking a collision with the treetops. After the harrowing descent, Skorzeny caught only one more glimpse of the other plane, a thousand feet above, and turning away. Incredibly, the Russian pilot failed to spot them again, never knowing how close he had come to killing history's most notorious dictator.

With the northern route now out of the question, Skorzeny ordered Reitsch to turn south and land at an abandoned airfield near Berchtesgaden on the Austrian border. The female test pilot masterfully wrestled with the ungainly and damaged plane for several hours, struggling to keep it in the air. The flight had been a nightmare for everyone on board, particularly the Führer. They shivered in the freezing wind that whistled through bullet holes in the plane's thin aluminum skin while choking on fumes and smoke from the smoldering engine. After what seemed like an eternity, they finally bounced onto a deserted grass airfield. From there, they struck out in hastily arranged cars for the safety of the Messerschmitt tunnels near Gusen.

***

Skorzeny shook his head and forced himself to focus on their current situation. High mountains and treacherous roads separated them from their next rendezvous point in northern Italy. Despite near-crippling delays, the SS colonel swore to himself they would succeed. They had to. The survival of the Reich depended on it.

Skorzeny paused another moment to look out over the Austrian countryside, now lit by a bright half-moon. The darkened village of Bad Ischl lay far below, its inhabitants unaware that Adolf Hitler himself rested just above them in the beautiful hills. He enjoyed the cool breeze at his back and thought about Franz and Karl, whom he had deployed as a rear guard against the Americans' pursuit. They were two of this best men, and should be back by the next morning. If they didn't reappear, he would know with certainty that he faced an unexpectedly dangerous adversary in this Lieutenant Jacobson.

CHAPTER TWENTY-FIVE

The appearance of American soldiers and the fire at Schloss Weyer created an unwanted stir in the town of Gmunden. Jacobson and his men were the first American troops to appear in this part of Austria since the end of the war, and the lieutenant worried that Nazi sympathizers might have some way to warn Hitler's guards of their arrival, just like the mayor of Gusen managed to do. Somehow, they needed to blend into the population – or at least become less conspicuous.

The problem turned out to be obtaining local clothes, and even more difficult, how to get their hands on a different vehicle. Even if they wanted to, they couldn't simply drive into Gmunden and buy new clothes at a local store, then pick out a car or truck at a used car lot. The war had brought shortages of every kind to Austria, including consumer goods like clothing. And, with the German war effort monopolizing every scrap of steel, rubber, and machine goods, no new vehicles had been manufactured for the civilian market in almost six years. The locals didn't own many cars and trucks before the war. The ones that still survived sat unused due to a complete lack of gasoline.

Yet, after Rachel explained the problem to her new young friend, Mila offered to find appropriate clothes for the men.

Herr Lowenstau had fired most of the servants, cooks, and gardeners at Schloss Weyer after he appropriated the castle from its rightful owners. So, when Jacobson, with Mila acting as a middle-man of sorts, offered to buy several sets of workmen's clothes for the Americans at a premium price, the unemployed locals gladly accepted the money.

"I look like a farm boy in this getup," Pernell griped, pulling on an old gray cap that smelled like sweat and cow manure.

"Well, so do I," Downtown replied after donning a torn pair of overalls and a thick plaid work shirt.

"You *are* a farm boy," Pernell chided. "I wouldn't be caught dead in this getup back in Brooklyn."

"We don't live on a farm," Downtown objected. "My father owns a tractor repair shop in Ames."

"Everyone in Iowa is a farm boy," Pernell replied.

"Pipe down," Tucker barked. "We ain't doing this for fun. Get your gear together. We're going to move out as soon as we can find us a vehicle."

Pernell and Downtown stopped picking at each other and entertained themselves for a few minutes watching Tucker try on civilian clothes. Almost nothing fit. The biggest problem turned out to be finding a shirt big enough for his immense frame and long arms. It wasn't easy, but he finally settled on a pair of hunting pants held up by long suspenders and, after ripping off the rank and unit patches, his uniform shirt.

Rachel couldn't help but giggle as the men struggled with their unfamiliar attire. She didn't think they could pass as Austrians, but, at least from a distance, they didn't look like American combat soldiers.

"Where's the lieutenant?" Downtown asked, noticing Jacobson had disappeared.

"In the castle, last time I saw him," Tucker replied as he tightened his bootlaces.

Just then, Jacobson emerged from the courtyard gate, grinning sheepishly and wearing civilian clothes much different than those Mila had arranged for the other three men.

Unlike his men's work clothes, Jacobson sported a brown tweed coat with an attached belt over a clean white shirt and dark blue tie. Suede patches at the elbows and right shoulder gave the impression of a hunting jacket. Crisp khaki pants tucked into calf-high boots completed the gentleman-sportsman look.

"You look quite handsome!" Rachel exclaimed.

Jacobson couldn't help but blush at Rachel's comment. He had found a closet full of clothes in one of the castle's suites, which probably belonged to a previous owner. And while dated in style, they wouldn't be entirely out of place for a well-to-do Austrian landowner.

"How come he gets a fancy suit?" Pernell complained under his breath.

"He's the boss. He needs to look like one," Tucker explained.

"Sergeant, let's take a look at that map," Jacobson ordered, getting back to business. "Pernell and Downtown, you guys take the Jeep and go with Mila. She says she knows of a truck we might be able to buy. If it looks reliable, trade for the Jeep or buy it outright. Price is no object."

After they left, Tucker spread their map on the ground, and he, Jacobson, and Rachel gathered around.

"Okay, we're here in Gmunden. I'm convinced Hitler has been here. But the real question is his next destination. Any ideas?" Jacobson asked.

"I still believe he is traveling toward Italy," Rachel replied. "He doesn't have any other choice."

"Miss Rachel is right," Tucker agreed. "And I don't think we're too far behind."

"Agreed," Jacobson said, "But the question is, again, where did he go from here? If he wants to get into Italy, he has to pass through the Alps. Assuming he can't fly across the mountains, how does he do that?"

"I have not been to this part of Austria, but, as a young girl, my family took several trips to Italy. I remember my father saying that the Alps have protected Italy for millennia from invasion from the north and that only a very few safe passes cut through the mountains. The roads were always narrow, and the trips would take a long time."

Jacobson studied the maps carefully. From Gmunden, he found two major roads that headed through the mountains and into Italy. One ran to the west toward Salzburg. The other headed east toward the city of Liezen. Dismissing both routes as dangerously close to major cities, Jacobson looked to the south and found the town of Bad Ischl nestled at the foot of the Alps.

Pointing to the town, Jacobson asked, "Here. Bad Ischl. What do you think?"

"I have heard of this town. People go on holiday there to visit the mountain lakes," Rachel replied.

"It would be a long, hard ride on bad roads to get through the mountains from there," Tucker observed, pointing out the thin, winding line representing a narrow, dangerous road through the Alps. "But it's a good choice if they want to stay out of sight."

"Without definite intelligence, our only choice is to make the best guess we can. So, it looks like we're agreed. We'll head toward Bad Ischl as soon as Downtown and Pernell deliver our new truck."

***

"Uh, Lieutenant, that thing ain't exactly new," Tucker commented as a ragged old Opel farm truck approached the front of the castle.

The once red cargo truck now sported more surface rust than red paint. Chipped markings on the door advertised some previous owner's fresh produce business. As it bounced into the yard, the patched and faded-green canvas cover over the cargo area swayed and flapped in the wind until the truck came to a stop, throwing up a cloud of dust.

Pernell and Downtown hopped out of the cab, grinning like a couple of teenagers who snuck their daddy's car out for a joy ride.

"This is it?" Tucker asked, dismayed at the appearance of the ancient-looking vehicle.

"Yep!" Downtown replied, patting one dented fender. "Isn't she a beauty?"

Tucker walked around the truck, a look of dismay slowly changing to anger.

"Now, Sarge, let me explain before you blow your top," Downtown insisted, seeing Tucker's evident dissatisfaction.

"Okay, but it better be good," Tucker replied, annoyed.

"She may not look like much, but she's a German Opel Blitz or at least the civilian version. They used thousands of these things to carry troops and supplies during the war. Don't you remember us dynamiting a bunch of these after the Bulge?" Pernell explained. "This is the best truck they ever made."

"Yeah, Sarge. It's got a Kraut diesel engine, the brakes are one hundred percent, and we have enough diesel fuel to get us to the other side of Italy if we need to. I checked it out, and it's all there mechanically. I hate to say it, but the Germans make the toughest vehicles anywhere," Downtown added.

Tucker knew he was right. German tanks, aircraft, trucks, and weapons had drawn reluctant admiration from the Allies and had almost won the war for the Nazis.

Jacobson joined them a moment later and gave the vehicle a cursory inspection. He knew nothing about cars or trucks and had never been mechanically inclined.

"You men satisfied with this vehicle?" Jacobson asked.

"Yes, sir," Pernell and Downtown said almost in unison.

"Then let's go," Jacobson said, helping Rachel into the cab before swinging in himself.

Pernell and Downtown exchanged looks. Good officers relied on their men. In exchange for trusting Pernell and Downtown, Jacobson had just earned some of their respect.

***

Jacobson tried to remain optimistic as the Austrian countryside wandered past his open window. He realized the decision to drive toward Bad Ischl was a long shot. In reality, Hitler could have left Schloss Weyer and gone anywhere – even doubling back to the Danube River. Or, he might risk Allied air patrols and fly out of some secluded field to an unknown destination. One thing was certain, though, if they didn't reacquire Hitler's trail quickly, his mission would be over after only a few days.

Pushing aside his doubts, Jacobson focused on the information he had in hand. Hitler had not flown out of Gusen even though it had an intact airfield less than a mile from the Messerschmitt aircraft facility. Plus, Hitler and whoever guarded him had been extremely cautious, staying on backroads while moving from town to town. He had to believe they would maintain that pattern. As the most recognizable man on the planet, any sighting of Adolf Hitler, even passing in a car, would launch rumors that would spread like wildfire.

"You have been quiet," Rachel commented, interrupting Jacobson's mental analysis.

"You haven't been chatty either," Jacobson replied.

"Yes, I have many questions running through my head at the same time. May I ask you one of them?"

Jacobson shrugged. "Sure. Shoot."

Rachel didn't grasp the American slang but took it to mean she should ask her question.

"Do you believe we are now truly following Adolf Hitler?" Rachel asked.

Jacobson looked over at the determined Jewish girl who had survived years in Nazi concentration camps. His answer mattered to her, so he spoke carefully.

"Back in Gusen, you asked whether I believed you saw Hitler, and I answered that I did. Now, I believe Hitler is alive and that we are indeed chasing him. All the evidence points to it, even though we couldn't prove it in court if we had to. I don't have to tell you this is dangerous work, and if ever you want out, all you have to do is say so."

"Please don't take my question the wrong way, Cy. I am not asking because I am scared. I need to know where you stand because I want to find him and kill him worse than anything in the world."

"I hope we do just that," Jacobson answered. He had first met Rachel less than a week before. But in that time, she had been unwavering in her belief that Hitler had survived. And her determination to kill the monster responsible for her family's death didn't surprise him in the least.

"I have more than hope. I have faith. Faith we are getting close."

CHAPTER TWENTY-SIX

Sommer Hotel

Early in the morning, Skorzeny finished organizing the two-car convoy that would carry the Führer over the Alps and into Italy. After arranging everything with typical German efficiency, he turned his attention to the final matter he needed to address before they departed – Herr Gosser, the hotel's proprietor. Skorzeny had to admit he liked the odd little man. But, despite the hotel owner's discretion and exacting attention to detail, duty demanded he eliminate Gosser.

The Deacon and his web of collaborators could modify the route, arrange for alternate overnight stops, and assign additional personnel. But regardless of any change in the plan, the Deacon ordered Skorzeny to eliminate every witness to Hitler's presence. No exceptions. Even for loyal Nazis.

Skorzeny slammed the trunk of Hitler's vehicle and walked back inside the hotel. One of the remaining three SS guards snapped to attention with a crisp Nazi salute as the heels of Skorzeny's polished black boots tapped in precise rhythm across the marble-tiled lobby.

"Heil Hitler!"

"Where is Herr Gosser this morning, Sargent?" Skorzeny asked, looking across the open space and into the dining room.

"Herr Gosser appeared at 0530 this morning and said he would be in the kitchen preparing the morning meal, sir," the sergeant reported.

"Carry on," the SS Colonel replied, walking away.

Skorzeny's fingers wound around the hilt of his SS dagger as he marched quickly through the hotel's elegant dining room. He paused outside the double swinging doors to the kitchen and listened carefully for any activity. Met only by silence, the SS commando pushed quickly through the doors. Inside, he found the kitchen brightly lit, but the stove and oven sat cold and unused. And Gosser was nowhere in sight.

The hotel owner had disappeared.

Skorzeny slammed his fist on a long wooden table, rattling the pots and pans stacked on one side. He should have known. Gosser had fooled him with feigned loyalty and remarkable service. But unlike Herr Lowenstau back at Schloss Weyer, Gosser was no fool. He must have suspected he wouldn't be allowed to live after witnessing Hitler still alive. Even knowing he had little chance of finding the hotel owner, he had to try.

But where would Gosser go? And how?

Running out the back door, Skorzeny saw Gosser's convertible still parked under an open shed. Then he remembered how the hotel owner had assured him that he had personally inspected the secondary escape route through the woods *on his motorbike.*

Sure enough, the motorcycle had also disappeared. Skorzeny immediately realized that Gosser had used the escape route through the woods for himself.

Grabbing a set of keys from a hook by the back door, Skorzeny ran to Gosser's car, started the engine, and threw the transmission into reverse. Skidding in a tight turn, Skorzeny aimed at the entrance to the old track leading downhill toward Bad Ischl and gunned the engine.

Low branches whipped at the windshield as the car slid from side to side on the slick mud surface. Skorzeny sawed at the wheel, barely able to keep the car under control on the steep descent.

After less than a half-mile, the road curved sharply to the left. Skorzeny muscled the car around the curve, counter-steering to keep from plunging into a deep ravine. Suddenly, the massive trunk of a fallen tree filled his windshield. He slammed his foot onto the brake pedal – but it was too late. The grill smashed into the tree, throwing the SS officer into the steering wheel.

Shaken and bruised from the impact, Skorzeny climbed from the wreck and slammed the door behind him. He had lost. Gosser had lied about the road being open. He could see how a motorcycle could easily bypass the downed tree that now prevented anyone from following by car.

Out of options, Skorzeny set off at a trot back toward the hotel. Hitler would surely ask if the devious hotel owner still lived, and Skorzeny would have to lie to his Führer.

"Scheise!"

The SS colonel could only hope his failure to eliminate the single witness to Hitler's presence in Bad Ischl wouldn't come back to haunt him.

CHAPTER TWENTY-SEVEN

Bad Ischl, Austria

Gosser rode his motorcycle down the old logging road with practiced precision. As soon as the Deacon informed him that a high-ranking German might be using his hotel as an overnight stop while escaping from Allied-controlled territory, he made preparations to protect himself. Most notably, regular rides through the woods on his trusty BMW.

For over a decade, Nazi leaders frequented his hotel, often in the company of movie stars and famous sports figures. Gosser never accepted the Nazi's insane beliefs, but he had no problem taking their money. By providing top-flight hotel amenities, accompanied by brilliant lip service to the Nazis' odious philosophy, profits from his hotel rose year after year.

But his experience with the Nazis also taught him an important lesson. They would protect their power and demented agenda at all costs – and having seen Hitler with his own eyes put him in mortal danger.

Gosser burst out of the trees and onto the roads of Bad Ischl. He didn't expect any pursuit, but he couldn't help looking over his shoulder. To be doubly sure he wasn't being followed, the hotel owner stayed on side streets and sped through several narrow alleys before heading toward his secret hideaway.

On the north end of town, Gosser pulled the motorcycle into a tiny garage behind a building where he rented a little two-room apartment under an assumed name. He maintained the one-bedroom flat for clandestine trysts with lovers of both sexes – a fact he kept well hidden from the homophobic Nazis. Today it sat empty.

Once safely inside, he dropped into his favorite leather club chair and poured the last of his finest cognac into a crystal snifter. Somewhat to his surprise, his hand shook as he brought the glass to his lips. The liquor helped. In a moment, the fiery liquid settled in his stomach, lighting a warm glow that helped calm his tattered nerves.

He needed another bottle.

***

"Hey, Sarge! When is chow time?" Downtown called from the back of the old farm truck.

"Stifle it, Downtown. You ate last night," Tucker replied from the driver's seat.

"We're just outside Bad Ischl. We'll get some provisions there," Jacobson added.

The overnight trip from Schloss Weyer had taken its toll on Jacobson and his team. The truck had performed well, but it wasn't the most comfortable form of transportation. Bouncing along neglected roads for hours kept everyone awake, and Jacobson couldn't fault the men for becoming grouchy.

"There is a market," Rachel said, pointing to a row of storefronts near the edge of town. "I would be happy to go in if you would like."

"Good idea. Pull over, Sergeant. We have some shopping to do," Jacobson ordered.

Jacobson gave Rachel a stack of money and told her to buy whatever she thought they needed. He also told her to get a few bottles of beer for later.

Dressed as a servant girl in clothes Mila provided from her mother's closet, the bored shopkeeper barely gave Rachel a second glance as she grabbed a shopping basket and made her way through the store. She selected several jars of pickled vegetables, cans of potted meats, coffee, slabs of ham, eggs, and five loaves of dark bread. She hadn't been inside a store in years and marveled at the sparsely-stocked shelves. While nearly empty compared to before the war, to her, they held a wealth of food beyond her wildest dreams.

At the counter, she asked for several bottles of beer and two bottles of local wine. She didn't notice the man standing behind her holding a bottle of cognac.

"That's quite a lot of groceries for a young lady," the man said, leaning in closely to Rachel's ear. "Perhaps I could be of service by helping carry your purchases?"

Rachel recoiled. The man's voice reminded her of lascivious German guards in the camps. "Thank you. But I'm sure I can manage, sir. My employer is waiting outside."

"Oh, I'm sure that's correct. You look like a strong girl," the man said, putting his hand on Rachel's shoulder. "A little on the thin side, but quite sturdy. My name is Herr Gosser. Is there no way I could help? I would be quite pleased to do so."

Gosser stroked the back of Rachel's head and ran his hand down her back, stopping just above her waist.

Rachel took a step away and clutched the heavy basket in front of her.

"Thank you again, Herr Gosser. But I must go," Rachel said, turning her back and walking toward the door.

Gosser paid for his bottle and quickly followed her outside. He quickened his pace and caught up with Rachel as she stepped into the road across from where Tucker had parked the truck. He didn't see Jacobson and Tucker watching from inside the cab.

Gosser grabbed Rachel by the elbow, stopping her in the middle of the street.

"Now, that was not polite, young lady!" the hotel owner said. "I was only trying to be…"

Gosser's sentence ended when he found himself flat on his back.

Seeing Rachel being accosted, Jacobson jumped out of the truck and shoved Gosser bodily into the dirt. Tucker grabbed Rachel's basket and helped her into the truck's cab.

Shaking off the surprise assault, Gosser looked up to find Jacobson standing over him with fists clenched in rage.

"Who the hell are you?" Jacobson growled.

Gosser slowly sat up, brushing dirt off his pants and jacket before replying.

"Ah, an American," Gosser replied in English. "I suppose I owe you and the young lady an apology. I had a rather upsetting morning, and I'm not myself. May I stand?"

Jacobson, angry with himself for revealing his identity, motioned for the other man to get up.

"You didn't answer my question," Jacobson said, seeing Downtown and Pernell standing at the ready.

"Yes, of course. I am Herr Gosser. I own the Sommer Hotel. I offer my apologies to you and the young lady for my intolerable behavior," Gosser said, bowing.

Jacobson didn't know what to make of the man who, only a minute earlier, had been rudely hounding Rachel but now stood scraping and bowing like an English butler.

Jacobson looked briefly back at the truck where Rachel sat, glaring at Gosser. "Are you alright?"

Rachel nodded.

"Tucker, what do you think we should do with this guy?" Jacobson called back to where Tucker now leaned on the hood of the truck.

"Well, I'd say let the asshole go, except for now he knows we're in town," Tucker answered.

"He's what some guys in my neighborhood would call a loose end," Pernell offered, although nobody had asked.

While not thoroughly appreciating Pernell's meaning, Gosser got the gist and became agitated.

"Sir, all I know is that an American came into town. Your business is your own. Discretion is part of my nature, and I assure you, your presence here will be kept in utmost confidence by me. This is something I learned long ago while serving the wealthy and powerful at my hotel."

Gosser's comment caught Jacobson's attention, and he let the odd little hotel owner squirm another minute under the glare from four heavily armed Americans.

"So, Herr Gosser. You own a fancy hotel here? Ever have any Nazis as guests?" Jacobson asked.

"Oh. Uh, yes, of course. As you are probably aware, this area is favored by many Europeans as a place to holiday, or vacation, as you Americans say. I had little choice, but yes, Nazis of many ranks paid handsomely to stay at the Sommer," Gosser replied, hoping some amount of honesty would extricate him from what appeared to be an increasingly perilous situation.

The overly polished hotel owner disgusted Jacobson. He was an opportunist, willing to prey on vulnerable young women and cater to Nazis. But Gosser would also be in an optimal position to know if Hitler had indeed come through Bad Ischl. He decided to play the strange little man's game.

"Well, I'm not surprised. I'm going to tell you something I shouldn't. But you strike me as a man with some insight," Jacobson began. "I'm charged with looking for any high-ranking Nazis that might be trying to escape from justice. I can use whatever means I see necessary to achieve my objective. That includes everything from, shall we say, physical coercion to payment of large sums of money."

"Ah, the carrot and the stick," Gosser observed. "Of the two choices, I prefer the metaphorical carrot. What may I ask is the going rate for information on Nazi fugitives?"

"Simple. The bigger the Nazi, the bigger the rate," Jacobson said, pulling three gold coins from his pocket.

Looking at the gleaming gold, Gosser's dread of the Nazis battled with his greedy nature. If he blurted out Hitler's name, the Americans would probably not believe him. But if he chose the truth tempered by careful omissions, he might be able to extract a rather significant amount of gold from the young man's pocket.

"I do, in fact, have information you will wish to purchase," Gosser said smoothly. "It will cost you those three coins and two more like them."

"Talk first. I'll decide what your information is worth," Jacobson responded, dropping the coins back in his pocket.

The hotel owner looked at his watch before responding.

"Yes, of course. I can see you are not a man to be trifled with," Gosser said, looking Jacobson in the eye. "A very important person of the type you seek stayed at my hotel only last night."

"Uh-huh. And who might that be?" Jacobson answered skeptically.

"I never actually laid eyes on this person, and nobody revealed his identity to me. But I can tell you that he traveled with four SS guards and a doctor," Gosser replied. "They planned to leave this morning, but I left the hotel early to, well, avoid complications."

"Damnit!" Jacobson exclaimed. "How long ago?"

"I'm not sure," Gosser answered. "There is a small chance they may still be there. In that case, they would be exceedingly unhappy to see either of us."

"Get in!" Jacobson ordered, shoving Gosser toward the back of the truck. "We have to go there. Now."

"I don't… That is impossible…" Gosser stammered, refusing to move from the road.

Tucker grabbed Gosser by the collar and goose-walked him to the bed of the truck, where Pernell and Downtown hoisted him inside. With Pernell pointing a rifle at his chest, the hotel owner had no choice but to cooperate.

Gosser cursed his carnal appetites and uncontrollable greed. A dead man has no use for pretty girls or gold coins.

CHAPTER TWENTY-EIGHT

Following Gosser's reluctant directions, Tucker drove like a madman through Bad Ischl. After only fifteen minutes, the sergeant gunned the truck's engine for the final steep ascent to the Sommer Hotel.

"The hotel is just around the next corner!" Gosser shouted. "They will hear us coming!"

"Okay, pull over, Sergeant," Jacobson ordered. "We'll approach on foot."

As soon as the truck skidded to a stop, Downtown and Pernell jumped out and ran forward, one on each side of the narrow road. Tucker grabbed his weapon and followed close behind. Within seconds, Pernell and Downtown had placed themselves in defensive positions to cover Tucker as he scouted the hotel's entrance.

Jacobson watched the sergeant advance. Tucker held his Thompson low at his hip as he scanned for threats. A moment later, the sergeant signaled they could follow him up to the hotel.

Jacobson took the wheel and drove into the deserted parking area.

"They have already departed, Lieutenant," Gosser said, looking over Jacobson's shoulder. "They had two cars parked here earlier this morning."

"Damnit," Jacobson spat, not hiding his disappointment. "Sergeant, you and Pernell sweep the hotel and make sure nobody is home. Downtown, patrol around the perimeter outside. Rachel and I will see what Herr Gosser knows. And guys, be careful. Watch for booby traps like back at the castle."

Turning to the hotel owner, Jacobson demanded, "Alright, where did they go?"

"I have no idea, Lieutenant," Gosser replied with a shrug. "I truly do not."

Rachel climbed out of the truck to join the conversation. She studied Gosser carefully, especially his overly sincere manner and contrived willingness to accommodate the Americans. The Austrian's lack of morality sickened her. She had no doubt this little man would do anything necessary to enrich himself – or save his own skin.

"He is lying," Rachel snarled into Gosser's face. "He knows. He wants the gold, but will tell you as little as possible to earn it."

"I'm sure I don't know what you mean, young lady," Gosser huffed. "I've received no recompense as yet. Only promises."

"And you'll receive none if I think you're lying," Jacobson threatened. "You might remember our conversation about the carrot and the stick. The stick is still on the table."

"I swear, they did not share their plans with me, Lieutenant," Gosser answered smoothly.

Rachel had heard enough. This Austrian's calm assurances and slick politeness sounded like the lead scientist back in the underground lab. As victims of the low-pressure chambers shuffled through the doors to the laboratory, he would promise safety and comfort. Rachel only heard the dying screams of his victims twice. Those screams would have haunted her dreams, except that they amounted to only a tiny part of the suffering she witnessed at the hands of the Germans.

"This Nazi bastard is not telling us the truth!" Rachel shouted. "He knows Hitler was here and at least which direction he went. He must tell us!"

Rachel lunged at Gosser. Jacobson barely had time to grab the enraged girl around the waist before she physically assaulted the Austrian.

"Keep that dirty Jew away from me!" Gosser cried, backing away from the incensed young woman.

Jacobson released Rachel, turned, and smashed his fist into Gosser's face, causing blood to erupt from the other man's nose. Gosser dropped to his knees, whimpering and trying to staunch the flood of blood with both hands.

Jacobson put a foot on Gosser's shoulder and shoved him backward into the gravel.

"That's the second time you have disrespected my friend. Once more, and I'll kill you," Jacobson growled, drawing his sidearm and aiming it at Gosser's head.

Blood still streamed over Gosser's mouth and chin as he slowly climbed back to his feet.

"I know nothing of Hitler," the hotel manager croaked. "Nothing."

Jacobson couldn't tell what Gosser feared more – him or revealing that Hitler had stayed at his hotel. He decided to make the hotel owner an offer he couldn't resist.

"Too bad. Despite being a despicable pig, I would have given you the gold if you had helped us. But suit yourself. I'll be happy to tell any Nazis I come across about the excellent assistance Herr Gosser, owner of the Sommer Hotel in Bad Ischl, provided us," Jacobson promised.

Gosser's eyes burned with indecision. Naziism didn't disappear with the end of the war. If he aided the Americans, stubborn Nazi sympathizers might label him a traitor and target him for retribution.

On the other hand, if Jacobson made good on his threat, he would still be in mortal danger, only without the gold.

"You have me at a disadvantage," Gosser responded, pulling a white handkerchief from his pocket and dabbing it under his nose. "I see no choice but to cooperate."

"Alright. Talk."

"The girl is correct. Hitler slept here just last night."

"I knew it," Rachel said quietly. "I knew it."

"Which way did they go?" Jacobson demanded.

"I don't know exactly. I was instructed to prepare two emergency escape routes. One goes up the mountain on a cable lift. The other is a little-used track through the forest back to Bad Ischl. I blocked the forest path, so they could not have doubled back to town that way. I also prepared the cable lift to the top of the mountain. But that is a dead end to be used only as an extreme last resort. The main road below the hotel goes to the Lake District, and eventually winds through the mountains into Italy. They must have gone that way," Gosser responded, seemingly fully committed to earning his reward.

"Are there other roads from here into Italy?" Jacobson asked.

"No. That is the only one that cars can travel safely," Gosser replied. "I can show you on a map."

Jacobson turned to Rachel. "Would you ask Sergeant Tucker and his men to get back here as quickly as possible?"

Rachel nodded and ran off toward the hotel.

While Rachel collected Tucker, Downtown, and Pernell, Jacobson grabbed the radio from the truck, raised the aerial, and made contact with Agent Smith's office.

"This is Orion 6. I have a priority message for Smith," Jacobson said into the microphone.

A second later, a voice responded, "Proceed."

"Tell Smith we have credible information that Hitler, repeat, Adolf Hitler, was present in Bad Ischl at the Sommer Hotel on this date. He is accompanied by SS and traveling in two cars. Also, they are crossing the Alps into Italy. Recommend air patrols at grid J-57. Over."

"Message received. We will inform Smith," the voice said before the transmission ended.

Tucker and his men appeared in time for Gosser to trace the route on Jacobson's map with a pencil.

Jacobson looked at his watch. "If they left here two hours ago, they are at least thirty miles ahead of us. That would put them, uh, around here."

"Can we catch them?" Rachel asked, looking over Jacobson's shoulder at the map.

"I greatly doubt that will be possible," Gosser replied, looking at the old farm truck.

"Don't listen to him, Lieutenant," Tucker urged. "I thought the guys were crazy choosing it, but our truck has some grunt left in her. My daddy taught me how to drive while hauling moonshine all over Tennessee. We're just wastin' time sittin' here chewing on it."

"Yeah, let's get that son-of-a-bitch!" Pernell agreed.

Gosser shook his head. "The problem is not the truck. It's the road. More specifically, the roadway narrows considerably as it runs across the south face of the mountains near a tiny town called Muth. Explosive charges could send that part of the road into the valley. Colonel Skorzeny indicated they would do as much, and I have no doubt he is capable of that and more."

"Skorzeny?" Jacobson asked.

"The Führer's personal SS bodyguard. A commando. And the most decorated soldier of the Third Reich," Gosser explained. "Probably the most dangerous man in the world."

"Yeah? Well, good for him," Jacobson replied, trying to sound like he didn't care. "Mount up!"

CHAPTER TWENTY-NINE

Although Herr Gosser had escaped his grasp, the drive into the mountains proceeded more smoothly than Colonel Otto Skorzeny anticipated. Hitler seemed comfortable and remained quiet in the back seat. The late-spring snow that threatened early in the morning never materialized, easing the difficulty of navigating the tight mountain pass.

The Germans followed the dirt and gravel road higher and higher into the grandeur of the Austrian Alps. At first, the route wound through deeply forested hills. But as they climbed higher, the landscape became more and more desolate. Steep, barren slopes covered in rocks seemed to go on forever. Yet, every curve revealed a more stunning view than the one before. Massive granite peaks stood shoulder to shoulder, their summits gleaming with pure white snowcaps. Far below, Skorzeny could make out narrow valleys covered in lush green meadows.

The SS colonel shook off the distraction of the magnificent landscape. Two of his trusted soldiers never returned after he sent them back along the escape route to intercept the Americans. This could mean only one thing – Jacobson managed to kill both men. Otherwise, nothing would have prevented his loyal SS commandos from rejoining his team. He could leave nothing to chance. He had to assume Jacobson was still in pursuit.

"How far to the chokepoint?" Skorzeny asked his driver.

"Approximately ten kilometers, Colonel. At our speed, we will be at the place Herr Gosser identified in another thirty minutes," the muscular sergeant replied, not taking his eyes off the narrowing roadway.

Skorzeny looked back to be sure the other car remained close behind. Losing two of his best men left Skorzeny with only three other combat-ready SS soldiers. He would need them all for his escape plan to succeed.

"Colonel! I see an aircraft in the distance," the driver suddenly exclaimed.

Skorzeny grabbed binoculars from under his seat and aimed them in the direction his driver pointed. Sure enough, in the distance, a single strange-looking aircraft swung around a mountain peak. Skorzeny knew the deadly plane immediately. With its twin engines and double-boom tail, the P-38 Lighting had caused havoc and mass destruction as the war in Europe came to a close. The SS Colonel had personally witnessed its four fifty-caliber machine guns and single 20mm cannon decimate German troops and tanks. His men called it 'the fork-tailed devil.'

"I see it. Halt!" Skorzeny ordered.

Steep cliffs on both sides of the road and the complete lack of trees meant they had nowhere to hide. They could only stay still to avoid drawing attention to themselves.

For a moment, the Germans believed they had escaped detection when the airplane disappeared into the valley below. Skorzeny almost ordered the driver to proceed when the aircraft suddenly passed overhead, its powerful propeller wash buffeting the cars even as it disappeared into the distance.

"Reconnaissance," the driver said, relief evident in his voice.

"Yes. Otherwise, we would already be dead," Skorzeny agreed. "But we have been thoroughly photographed."

Skorzeny turned to see Hitler still bundled in blankets and all but invisible in the dark back seat. Even with the sophisticated cameras the Americans used, he doubted anyone would be able to identify the Führer. But that didn't change Skorzeny's analysis of what the aircraft's sudden appearance meant to his mission.

They were being hunted from above as well as from behind.

***

Tucker's aggressive driving threw Jacobson left and right across the truck's cab. He barely noticed Rachel's death grip on his left arm. He would have ordered Tucker to slow down, but he could sense they were closing in on their quarry.

As they rounded yet another harrowing curve with a steep drop-off just a few feet away, Pernell banged on the back of the cab.

"Lieutenant! Radio transmission from Smith!"

"What's the message?" Jacobson shouted over his shoulder.

"The guy says he has to talk to you personally, sir. You'll have to come back here."

"Damnit! Tucker, pull over for a second," Jacobson yelled over the screaming engine.

Intensely focused on driving, the lanky sergeant didn't hear Jacobson's order. But Rachel did. She spoke directly into Tucker's ear, "Cy needs you to pull over!"

His concentration broken, Tucker eased them to a halt.

Jacobson climbed quickly into the back of the truck, pulled on the radio's headphones, and spoke into the hand-held microphone. "Orion 6 here."

The mountains blocked most of the signal, badly garbling Smith's message "Orion 6. This is Smith -- last transmission -- recon pilot -- your grid coordinates. -- two cars traveling together at grid J-59 -- pictures -- for twenty-four hours."

Jacobson couldn't help pumping his fist in quiet celebration and relief. Gosser had not led them on a wild goose chase after all.

"Roger that. What assets are available that could cut them off around, uh, Obertauern?" Jacobson asked, looking at a map for the next town of any size along the mountain pass.

"Sorry, Orion -- your own -- none available. Good hunt --. -- out."

Jacobson tossed the headphones and mic back to Pernell and ran back to the cab.

"Go! Go! We're right on their butts!" Jacobson yelled, jumping back into his seat next to Rachel and pounding the outside of his door with his fist.

Tucker slammed the truck into gear and dropped the clutch. He didn't hear the cursing from the back as Pernell, Downtown, and Gosser all ended up in a heap against the tailgate.

"How far ahead are they, Cy?" Rachel asked, leaning over Jacobson to see the map that flapped wildly in his hands.

Jacobson struggled to smooth the paper enough to read the grid coordinates. With Rachel grabbing one side to hold it steady, Jacobson ran his finger along their route.

"Here! The transmission was garbled, but I'm positive Smith said a reconnaissance pilot spotted two cars right here!" the lieutenant exclaimed, holding the map so Tucker could see. "Only five or six kilometers. We can catch them!"

Rachel grabbed Jacobson's arm again and squeezed tightly. "Praise God!"

Tucker wasn't quite as excited. Without taking his eyes off the road, he asked, "Uh, Lieutenant? What's the plan? This road isn't exactly someplace I'd like to get into a fight."

"Can't say I have a plan right now, Sergeant. Let's see if we can catch up to the bastards first. If they blow up the road like Gosser said, we'll be out of luck. But I assure you, I'll be extremely open to suggestions once we have them in sight."

***

Skorzeny urged his small convoy forward as quickly as possible. The appearance of the P-38 could not have been a coincidence, and he had to assume its pilot would summon more lethal assistance. Even more ominous, its presence meant somebody knew their exact position.

Skorzeny couldn't escape the possibility that Herr Gosser betrayed Hitler's overnight stay in Bad Ischl to the Americans. He should have killed the hotel owner when he had the chance. While he never informed Gosser of their exact route, any competent pursuer would recognize that they intended to cross the mountains into Italy. The few roads through the Alps had limited his choice of routes, yet once they left the mountains and entered the Italian countryside, they could disappear in any number of directions.

But Italy's relative safety remained many miles in the distance.

"Colonel, the road narrows half a kilometer ahead. I could see the area as we rounded the last bend," the driver reported.

"Excellent. Drive to the other side and stop. We'll lay what charges we have behind us and be on our way," Skorzeny ordered.

"And the aircraft?" the driver asked, still shaken by their encounter with the American plane. Even seasoned SS commandos feared modern fighters.

"We can fight only one battle at a time. We cannot control whether another aircraft finds us, but we can prevent anyone from following us further," Skorzeny replied logically.

At that moment, Hitler's hand appeared on Skorzeny's shoulder.

"Are we being followed?" the Führer demanded. "And what is this of aircraft?"

Skorzeny couldn't afford one of Hitler's tantrums. They didn't have time.

"My Führer, we spotted an aircraft in the distance some time ago. It posed no threat. In a moment, we will stop and destroy the road to ensure nobody can follow us," Skorzeny explained quickly.

"No! No! You said to stop anyone from following us *further*. Explain yourself, Colonel," Hitler shouted.

"My Führer. As you know, I sent two men back along our route to act as a rear guard. They did not return. I must therefore *assume*, for your safety only, that we are being pursued," Skorzeny answered.

"Do not coddle me, Colonel. I may be old and sick, but I will not be manipulated!"

Skorzeny had to think quickly. Despite his illnesses and frailty, Hitler still led the Nazi cause and needed to be handled carefully.

"My Führer, nothing could be further from the truth. I didn't wish to bother you with the mundane tasks of the journey. Even now, we are approaching a narrow portion of the road that we can destroy, preventing any possibility of anyone following us. I would appreciate your opinion on that plan," Skorzeny said, pointing vaguely through the windshield.

To his amazement, Hitler laughed.

"Alright, Otto. Alright. I appreciate your attempt to offer me a diversion from my anxiety. But we both know I would be a fool to advise you in such a manner. Carry on, Colonel," Hitler chuckled, sitting back in his seat.

Skorzeny marveled at the Führer's manic behavior. One moment lashing out in paranoia and anger, and the next, laughing as if dining with old friends. In any event, Hitler appeared mollified – at least for the moment.

A few minutes later, Skorzeny ordered the convoy to stop twenty yards beyond what turned out to be a short stone bridge that spanned a deep gash in the mountainside. The colonel immediately decided the one-lane crossing, constructed of concrete and heavy stonework, would not be easy to destroy with the limited explosives available to the SS men.

A hurried inspection confirmed Skorzeny's first impression. Even all ten hand grenades he had on hand would not be enough to bring down the structure. He needed another option.

Skorzeny gathered his men and explained what he had in mind.

"Men, you remember our pesky Russian friends? How they tracked us through the frozen Russian woods tripping over the grenades we left behind? Let us do the same here."

Under Skorzeny's direction, two of his men ran back over the bridge and placed two grenades against the mountainside, attaching the detonator pins to a thin trip wire. When a vehicle hit the wire, the resulting explosion would blow it over the side of the cliff and into the ravine hundreds of feet below. They set a second set of grenades in the same manner on the opposite end of the narrow crossing in case their pursuers had two vehicles or an unsuspecting motorist happened by first.

Satisfied with their work, Skorzeny ordered the men back into the cars. As he approached Hitler's vehicle, the SS officer paused. He couldn't be sure, but he thought he heard the sound of a truck engine bouncing off the mountainsides.

CHAPTER THIRTY

Jacobson peered intently ahead as if he could will the sight of Hitler's cars into existence. He had to restrain himself from constantly urging Tucker to drive faster.

Beside him, Rachel sat stoically, still clutching Jacobson's arm. If anything, she wanted to catch Hitler more than the young lieutenant. Suddenly, she sat forward in her seat.

"I think I see the bridge!" she shouted, her thin arm outstretched and pointing ahead.

A moment later, Jacobson also saw the narrow stone bridge.

Turning backward in his seat, the lieutenant called for Gosser.

"Is that it?" Jacobson asked when the hotel owner's face appeared in the window.

"Yes, Lieutenant. The bridge traverses a deep cleft in the mountainside. But I'm confused because it is still intact. If Colonel Skorzeny passed this way, I am quite certain he would have destroyed it to prevent you from following."

Gosser had a point. The bridge would have been a perfect place to cut the road. But there it was, completely undamaged.

As they closed the distance to the bridge, Tucker stopped the truck.

"What's going on, Sergeant?" Jacobson demanded. "Why did you stop?"

Tucker carefully studied the bridge for a few seconds before replying.

"That right there is the perfect place for a trap, Lieutenant. We need to check it out before crossing," Tucker replied.

"Goddamnit, Sergeant, we're losing time! Get this vehicle moving!" Jacobson shouted.

"No can do, sir. If I was the guy in front of us, I'd plant me some kind of explosives right up there and blow us clean off this mountain," Tucker replied, a little surprised Jacobson, who had been cool-headed for days, had suddenly become reckless.

"Sergeant...!" Jacobson began before Rachel put a hand on his shoulder. "What?"

"Cy, he's right," Rachel said, ignoring Jacobson's outburst. "If we all die on the bridge, who will be left to continue our chase?"

It took Jacobson a few seconds to comprehend Rachel's point. Slowly, his blood cooled.

"Alright. Yes. Go take a look. But make it quick," Jacobson reluctantly agreed.

Tucker, Pernell, and Downtown jumped from the truck and ran forward, their eyes scanning the road and mountain for anything unusual. Slowing as they neared the entrance to the bridge, Tucker raised a fist in the air, ordering an immediate halt.

Leaving Pernell and Downtown behind, Tucker walked forward, looking at every crack and crevasse in the stonework. At first, he saw nothing, but then something caught his eye. Eighteen inches off the ground, a thin, almost invisible wire stretched across the roadway. Following the wire, Tucker found exactly what he feared would be there – two powerful German-made hand grenades rigged to explode against the rock wall. Just as he suspected, the booby trap would have sent their vehicle plunging off the side of the mountain. And whoever planned the ambush knew their business. Defusing the grenades or trying to cut the wire would be foolhardy. That left only one way to get across the bridge. He would have to set off the charges from a distance. If the detonations didn't damage the structure, and he figured they wouldn't, they would be back in the hunt with only a minimal delay.

"Downtown, go tell the lieutenant what we found and that we are going to blow the charges ourselves. Pernell, give me a grenade."

While Downtown ran back to the truck, Pernell and Tucker each took one grenade and pulled the pins. On the count of three, they tossed the grenades simultaneously, knowing the concussion would either trigger the hidden German explosives or cut the wire, causing the same result. As their grenades arched through the air, the two soldiers sprinted backward, hugging the mountainside for protection.

Seconds later, all four grenades, the Americans' and the Germans', detonated nearly simultaneously, propelling a massive cloud of broken rock and dust across the road and into the valley.

From the cab of the truck, Jacobson watched Tucker save their lives. If the sergeant hadn't refused to obey his hotheaded order, they would have all died five minutes ago.

While Tucker and Pernell detonated the hand grenades, Downtown stood by the cab of the truck, casually watching and smoking a cigarette.

"What's he doing now?" Jacobson asked as Tucker and Pernell disappeared into the dust cloud.

Downtown squinted forward and answered as casually as if Jacobson had asked the time of day, "He's going to blow the other booby trap."

"The *other* trap?" Jacobson inquired.

"Yeah, Lieutenant. There's always two," Downtown replied.

A few minutes later, another enormous blast reverberated off the mountainside and echoed off into the Alps.

CHAPTER THIRTY-ONE

A few miles ahead, Otto Skorzeny heard the distant boom of the first explosion. Another blast followed not long afterward. But the SS officer didn't congratulate himself. Hearing two detonations minutes apart most likely meant his ambush had failed.

The game was still very much afoot.

The road along the western side of the Alps became steep and ever more dangerous. It clung precariously to the mountainside with tight, blind corners that skirted around ancient rock outcroppings. Not much more than one-lane wide, the lack of guardrails on one side and jagged rocks on the other left no room for error. Skorzeny chose this route because of its remote location. But he also had to accept the inherent risk of the road itself and the loss of any way to evade someone chasing them from behind.

Skorzeny glanced into the back seat. Thankfully, Hitler had fallen asleep, saving him the task of dealing with the Führer's unending questions and ever-present paranoia. The SS colonel knew they would have to deal with this Lieutenant Jacobson, probably sooner than later. But his first priority was to get Hitler out of the mountains.

Mile by mile, the valleys below seemed to rise toward the cars. Indistinct shapes in the green meadows sharpened into pictur-esque farmhouses and lazy cows. The stark contrast between the inhospitable peaks of the Alps and the welcoming landscape several thousand feet below made Skorzeny daydream, for a moment, about a simple life on a secluded Alpine farm. But the enticing mental picture didn't last.

As they rounded a sharp right-hand curve, the driver suddenly stood on the brake pedal. The car swerved slightly as the already overworked brakes fought with momentum and gravity. Several huge boulders had torn away from the mountain and found a new resting place directly in the middle of the already-constricted roadway.

Skorzeny could do nothing as the driver balanced his use of the brakes and steering to maintain control. One misstep, and their car would smash into the field of boulders or plunge off the road entirely. Skorzeny braced for the inevitable impact.

But then, with an astonishing amount of finesse and timing, the driver swerved right, missing the first boulder, and then quickly nudged the wheel back to the left. A horrifying grating sound and vibration shook the car as they side-swiped a second massive stone. Within seconds, the vehicle came to a stop, one fender wedged against a huge boulder resting precariously close to the cliff face.

Skorzeny jumped from the car and pulled open the back door. He found the Führer lying in a heap on the floor, still wrapped in several blankets. Hitler's personal physician leaned forward and placed two fingers over the Nazi leader's carotid artery, checking for a pulse.

Skorzeny remained silent while the doctor finished his examination.

"Doctor?" Skorzeny asked, fearing the worst.

"Help me get him back on the seat," the doctor said, cradling Hitler's head in his hands.

Skorzeny scooped Hitler off the floor and placed him gently back in his usual position.

Almost too afraid to ask, Skorzeny said, "Is he…"

At that moment, Hitler's mouth opened, and he drew a deep, sonorous, snoring breath.

Skorzeny looked at the doctor, who gave a little shrug in return. "You said to give him whatever I thought necessary to keep him comfortable. Our Führer is uninjured."

With his invaluable charge safe, Skorzeny took stock of their situation. The second car had stopped in time to avoid the rockfall, and two of his SS men had already taken up positions to guard against anyone approaching from behind. The small avalanche that left the road completely blocked occurred behind a blind curve, and his driver could have done little to avoid the boulders. Skorzeny made a mental note to congratulate the sergeant for his quick reactions and skillful driving.

Beyond the point where his car now rested near the edge of the road, several more sizable boulders cut off any chance of continuing. Clearing the debris would take time – time they didn't have.

Skorzeny immediately set everyone to work. He didn't have to urge them to hurry. With Allied aircraft in the area and the Americans following close behind, they were dangerously exposed and vulnerable.

While his men worked feverishly to open the road ahead, Skorzeny prepared for Jacobson's arrival. He wouldn't have long to wait.

***

"How far ahead do you think they are?" Rachel asked. The irrepressible girl hadn't taken her eyes off the road for even a second after they crossed the booby-trapped bridge several miles back.

"No way to tell, little miss," Tucker replied. "Ain't nothing to do but charge ahead as fast as we can, I suppose."

Jacobson looked up from his map when Rachel didn't respond to Tucker. The determination in her eyes made them sparkle in the clear mountain sun. He had never found a pair of eyes so beautiful or so indomitable. He had to pull his gaze away. Now wasn't the time or place to become distracted.

Tucker caught Jacobson's admiring look and smiled just a bit. Over the past few days, he had noticed his lieutenant taking a shine to the Jewish girl.

Can't blame the boy.

Almost as if he intended to dispel the intense mood in the cab, Pernell stuck his head through the rear window.

"Hey, Lieutenant, Mr. Gosser back here says he wants to get out."

Jacobson turned around in his seat. "Tell Gosser we aren't stopping. If he wants to jump out without his gold, he's welcome to suit himself."

Pernell laughed. "I'll let him know his choices, sir."

A moment later, Gosser himself appeared at the window. "Lieutenant, I've kept my part of the bargain. I led you through the mountains and to the bridge as you requested. We must be close upon Skorzeny and the Führer. I would like to be paid and let out before you actually encounter them."

Jacobson barely turned in his seat before replying, "Like Pernell told you, we aren't stopping. So, sit down and shut up."

"Lieutenant, please," Gosser pleaded, genuine fear creeping into his voice. "They will kill me."

Tucker interjected. "Couldn't happen to a nicer guy."

Jacobson looked at the hotel owner over his shoulder. "Forget it, Gosser. You'll get paid when this is over. After that, you can go wherever you want. Until then, you stay with us."

"But..." Gosser began.

The argument ended when Tucker shouted, "Get down!

***

Suddenly, little craters seemed to appear as if by magic along the front fender, accompanied by what sounded like someone hitting the truck's steel body with a ball-peen hammer. Tucker instinctively swung the truck right and hit the brakes. The big vehicle skidded sideways in an ungraceful pirouette, its grill and front fender smashing into the mountainside before coming to rest against the sheer rock wall facing back in the opposite direction.

"Contact behind!" Tucker shouted as he tried to restart the stalled engine.

Jacobson grabbed Rachel and pulled her below the dashboard. Glancing into the big rearview mirror mounted outside his door, he could see two German soldiers advancing up the road with submachine guns held low at the hip. Turning around, he saw Pernell and Downtown trying to recover after being violently tossed around inside the bed. With Tucker's door jammed against the rock wall, Jacobson knew it was up to him to do something.

Taking one breath, Jacobson drew his .45 automatic, pulled the door handle, and jumped to the ground. Now crouching, he snapped off three rounds in the general direction of the advancing SS soldiers.

As he hoped, his wild shots made the Germans pause, but also drew their attention. Almost immediately, staccato blasts from the submachine guns ripped through the air.

With no other cover available, Jacobson rolled under the truck, finding as much protection as possible behind the double rear wheel, and fired three more shots. He couldn't hold them off for long.

Pernell and Downtown need to get into this fight, or we're all dead.

Seconds later, more gunfire destroyed both rear tires, causing the truck to settle close over his head. Jacobson only had a few shots left. They had to count.

"Aw, the hell with it!" Jacobson said to himself before rolling out from under the truck and squeezing the trigger over and over until the slide on his weapon snapped back. Empty.

He hit nothing.

Now emboldened by the feeble return fire, the Germans ran forward behind short bursts from their submachine guns.

As the two SS soldiers sprinted toward the damaged vehicle, one of the side flaps covering the truck's bed opened. Jacobson watched in disbelief as Gosser's legs appeared, quickly followed by the rest of his body.

With more agility than he would have thought possible, the short man landed on his feet and tried to escape with a suicidal run back up the road.

"Come back!" Jacobson shouted. But it was too late.

Several shots rang out. Gosser collapsed, arms and legs splayed out to both sides.

Gosser's attempt to get away ended poorly for him, but bought Jacobson and his men a few precious seconds.

The lieutenant had just enough time to roll back under the truck when the familiar sound of an M-1 Garand barked from somewhere above. One of the Germans fell, writhing on the ground. With no cover of their own, the second SS soldier retreated, dragging his comrade backward. A second rifle shot missed, ricocheting off the cliff face, just before both Germans disappeared behind the sharp curve in the mountainside.

Jacobson lowered his head into the crook of his arm for a moment. But he knew this wasn't over.

"Lieutenant, are you okay?" Jacobson heard from the back of the truck.

"Yeah, Downtown, I'm fine. What's your status?" Jacobson responded, still lying under the truck.

"We got the wind knocked out of us back here when we hit the wall. Pernell almost got his block knocked off, and he's still coming around. The Krauts scurried back where they came from. It looks like the road makes a sharp right fifty yards ahead. I've got that covered. Unless they got a tank, nobody's coming around that corner again."

"Good work, keep your eyes open. I'll check on Tucker and Rachel," Jacobson ordered as he crawled out from under the truck.

Inside the cab, he found Rachel tending to a nasty cut on Tucker's forehead. With practiced skill, she used tape from their first-aid kit to neatly close up the wound. The big sergeant sat motionless, stoically ignoring the pain.

Finishing her work, Rachel asked, "Are you injured, Cy?"

"I'm fine. You?"

"I am unhurt," Rachel replied. "You saved our lives."

"That's yet to be seen," Jacobson responded. "Sergeant, we have a problem."

Tucker sat up in his seat, pulled on his helmet, and stuck a cigar in his mouth.

"Yep, that's a fact, sir. I couldn't see around the corner, and those two Krauts just sprang out from nowhere and started shooting," Tucker answered. "They had to be waiting on us to show up."

Jacobson laid out their situation. "So, right now, they can't see us, and we can't see them. On one side, we have a sheer drop of hundreds of feet, and on the other, a practically sheer wall of rock. We can't get around that curve without getting our asses shot off, but neither can they. Goddamnit! For all we know, Hitler himself could be sitting in a car just around that bend, and we can't get to him."

"They teach you the name for this sort of thing back at West Point, Lieutenant?"

Jacobson had no idea what his sergeant was talking about.

"Well, what we got here, sir, is technically referred to as a Mex-i-can Standoff," Tucker drawled around his cigar.

CHAPTER THIRTY-TWO

On the other side of the curve, Skorzeny listened to the brief firefight. When sergeant Bentler appeared, pulling the body of his SS corporal back toward the cars, Skorzeny ran forward.

As soon as he arrived, the uninjured sergeant snapped to attention.

"Per your orders, we successfully disabled the Americans' vehicle. They will not be able to proceed. I saw three men wearing civilian clothing. One coward tried to run away. He is dead. The other two had combat experience. I cannot confirm whether or not that is the total number of enemies present. Corporal Wolfe did his duty before giving his life for the Führer."

"As I knew he would. The corporal's death will not be in vain. You mentioned a 'coward' running from the truck. Explain further."

"I believe the man that tried to escape was the proprietor of the hotel from last night," the sergeant reported.

Skorzeny's blood ran cold. His worst fear had come true. Gosser must have informed the Americans of his plan to get Hitler through the Alps and into Italy. The SS colonel silently vowed to seek revenge on the traitorous Austrian.

Skorzeny stiffened and addressed the sergeant directly. "You will now listen to me carefully. That was not the hotel owner. I repeat. That was *not* the hotel owner. Are we clear, Sergeant?"

The sergeant looked straight forward, formally clicked his heels together, and saluted.

"Yes, sir!"

"Now, what is our tactical situation?"

The sergeant explained how neither side could round the corner without being cut down by the other.

"How badly damaged is their vehicle?" Skorzeny asked.

"When we commenced our attack, the truck slid sideways and struck the side of the mountain, causing heavy damage. The tires on one side are destroyed. Also, I heard them trying to start the engine without success."

"Remain here as rear guard. We will have a path through the boulder field clear in five minutes. Gather the corporal's personal effects, drop his body over the cliff, and be ready to leave."

The sergeant hesitated a beat before responding. "Sir, I volunteer to remain behind to slow or stop any continued pursuit by the enemy."

Skorzeny considered the other man's request.

"Thank you, Sergeant. Request denied. I am already short on good men."

With their rear flank covered, Skorzeny returned to the boulders, adding his considerable physical strength to clearing the last of the immense rocks blocking their path. Sweat poured down the Germans' backs as they used anything they could find to lever away stones bigger than they could move by hand.

Finally, after one final great effort, the last massive boulder slipped over the side of the road and tumbled into the valley below. The Germans watched it gain speed, starting a new avalanche of its own.

Without wasting a moment, Skorzeny gathered his men back at the cars, explained the situation with the Americans waiting just around the corner, and laid out their next move.

"We must leave this place without giving our enemies an opportunity to interfere. So, we will use gravity to our advantage. Load your vehicles and let them roll silently through the remaining boulders. By the time the Americans discover we are gone, we will be well out of range of their guns. And, without a working vehicle, they will be unable to pursue us further."

Skorzeny pulled the sergeant back from his post and loaded the cars as quietly as possible. Both drivers placed their vehicles in neutral and steered through the minefield of rocks. They gained speed quickly on the steep downhill grade. In minutes, they covered almost a full kilometer.

A few moments later, Skorzeny heard the crack of several rifle shots echo off the mountains. Turning, he could make out a single soldier futilely aiming his weapon in their direction.

With characteristic bravado, Skorzeny stuck his arm out the window and waved goodbye.

Despite the show of defiance, the SS colonel knew they had managed to dodge a much bigger bullet than the ones the American had just fired. And he wouldn't let himself fully believe he had seen the last of Lieutenant Jacobson.

CHAPTER THIRTY-THREE

"What's going on, Pernell?" Tucker called from behind the wrecked truck.

Having seen and heard nothing from the Germans for several minutes, Pernell had volunteered to creep closer to the sharp bend in the road by hugging the side of the sheer rock wall while Tucker kept him covered from behind the truck.

With his back pressed against the mountainside, Pernell held up one finger.

Unable to see around the sharp curve, Pernell listened for anything that would provide a clue about what was happening on the other side. The Americans hadn't yet seen the rockfall that brought the Germans to a dead stop.

Pernell could make out the sound of combat boots running along the road. The next moment, someone quietly closed a car door, and he thought he could hear tires crunching across gravel.

Edging closer, he took a chance and glanced around the blind corner. He could see a field of huge boulders, but nothing else. No Germans. No cars.

A longer look, a few seconds later, presented him with the complete picture. Two cars emerged from another sharp bend farther down the road and were rolling quickly downhill.

Pernell stepped into the open, raised his rifle, and released three rounds at the German vehicles. Even as he did so, he knew he didn't have a chance of hitting anything. But he could have sworn someone waved at him from the window of the car in front.

***

As soon as the shooting stopped, Tucker and Jacobson dragged Gosser back to the truck. Unconscious but alive, Tucker checked for wounds and applied a field dressing over a bullet hole in Gosser's left side. With Rachel's help, the sergeant added a wide linen bandage around Gosser's waist.

"How is he?" Jacobson asked, his voice lacking much compassion.

"He'll be fine. Flesh wound," Tucker reported.

"Rachel? Would you mind looking after that sniveling weasel while we take a look at the truck?" Jacobson asked.

German bullets had shredded the double tires on the right rear side, and the impact with the mountain had smashed the front fender and punctured the radiator.

Just as Jacobson was about to ask if they could get the truck moving again, Pernell ran up with more bad news.

"They're gone, sir. They got stopped by a bunch of rocks in the road just around the curve. They bought themselves enough time to clear a path by attacking us. Then they snuck away without starting their engines. By the time I figured out what was happening, they were out of range. I popped a few rounds at them anyway. But you know what happened? I think one of them goddamned Nazis waved at me out of the car window!"

Jacobson took stock of their situation. A wrecked truck. An unconscious informant. And worst of all, with every passing second, a high-value target, probably Hitler himself, was disappearing into the distance.

"Sergeant, you guys see what you can do with this vehicle. Get it going if you can. If nothing else, see if the goddamned thing will roll. I'll try to figure out where they might go once they get out of these mountains," Jacobson ordered, trying his best to hide his deep disappointment.

They had been so close.

Grabbing his map from the truck, Jacobson planted himself on a low stone wall at the side of the road. He didn't know what to do next. If they couldn't get the truck moving, their hunt would end right there on the bleak mountain pass. Even if, by some miracle, Tucker, Downtown, and Pernell repaired their vehicle, they would be many miles behind. By then, they wouldn't have any hope of catching up to the Germans before they disappeared into northern Italy.

Lost in a black mood, Jacobson didn't see Rachel walking toward him.

"Are you alright, Cy?" Rachel asked, planting herself next to him.

"Yes. I mean, well, no. This could be the end of the line for our little adventure," Jacobson replied, clearly disappointed.

Rachel snaked her hand around Jacobson's arm and put her head on his shoulder.

"We are not finished," Rachel said soothingly.

But Jacobson didn't want to hear it. He stood and angrily threw his maps to the ground.

"No? I've gotten us stuck here in these goddamned mountains. Our vehicle is wrecked, and I've got not one damn clue where Hitler is headed next. How is this not over?" Jacobson shouted.

Rachel didn't even flinch at Jacobson's outburst. Her mother had always told her that women handled tense situations better than men.

Men often reacted with anger – mostly at themselves. The key, she had said, was to gently remind them of their positive accomplishments.

"Cy, I think you have forgotten that less than an hour ago, Adolf Hitler himself sat just around that curve. You got us this far. You will figure this out," Rachel declared without a hint of doubt.

Jacobson looked around to find Rachel's deep black eyes searching for his. His heart skipped a beat when he saw how much she cared – about him. It helped, but his self-esteem had taken a big hit. Did he ever have a chance to prove Hitler had escaped Berlin? More absurd yet, he had actually pictured himself capturing the most wanted man on earth. Less than two months ago, he was a college senior who had never left the United States. And now he had managed to strand his entire team in the middle of the Austrian Alps.

Jacobson turned back to Rachel.

"I'm sorry, there's no way..."

Jacobson stopped talking when he heard the truck's engine come to life.

"Hey, Lieutenant! You want to go catch this guy or what?" Pernell called out.

Jacobson sprinted back to the truck, where he found Downtown tightening the last lug nut on the rear wheel.

"Those tires were shredded to bits. How did you...?" Jacobson asked, astonished.

Downtown beamed as he tossed the tire iron into the truck's bed.

"Well, sir, we just took one wheel off the other side of the axle, walked it over here, and stuck it on this side. We only have one wheel per side now, but that's all we need," Downtown explained in overly simple terms.

"And the radiator?" Jacobson asked.

"I got an old family trick for that," Downtown responded, pulling some chewing gum out of his mouth.

Jacobson was too happy to notice the sarcasm.

"Where to, Lieutenant?" Tucker asked.

"Down, Sergeant. Get us out of these mountains. Then I need to use the radio."

CHAPTER THIRTY-FOUR

With the threat from Jacobson seeming to fade in the rearview mirror, Skorzeny turned his attention to their next destination. Thirty minutes earlier, they had turned off the treacherous mountain pass and now sped along a paved highway running east and west through the Puster Valley.

Skorzeny barely noticed when they crossed the Italian border. Unexpected delays had caused them to fall behind schedule, which would, in turn, force further alterations to their route and safe houses. More importantly, Skorzeny knew they had only days left to reach the Italian west coast, where Hitler was supposed to board a U-boat for the next part of his escape from Europe. But every day, even every hour, the Allies hunted down and destroyed the few remaining German submarines still operating in the Mediterranean Sea. Of the five men accompanying Hitler at that moment, only he knew how grave their situation had become.

He needed a telephone.

At the ski resort town of Innichen, Skorzeny changed into civilian clothes and walked the last half-mile into the center of town.

He had been to Innichen several times before the war. He remembered how the quaint town bustled with wealthy and famous vacationers from all over Europe enjoying the world-class ski slopes and magnificent Alpine vistas. Skorzeny could picture the brilliantly lit shops and cafés that lined the streets, welcoming cold skiers with warm fires and hot drinks.

But now, as night fell, the town seemed nearly abandoned. What little tourist business Innichen could attract during the war had disappeared altogether with the warmer weather.

Walking the darkened streets, Skorzeny searched for a telephone without success, finding the doors of every shop, café, and hotel locked tight.

Looking around, almost in desperation, the SS colonel finally spotted two young boys watching him from behind a stack of firewood.

"Hello!" Skorzeny called in what he hoped sounded like a friendly voice. "Can you help me find a telephone? I'll give you some lira for your trouble."

The two blonde heads didn't move, so Skorzeny reached into his pocket and withdrew several shiny coins. Holding them out toward the boys got their attention.

They emerged slowly, wary of the big man standing by himself in the middle of the road.

"Come. You have nothing to fear. I only need to use a telephone, and nothing is open tonight," Skorzeny explained, plastering a rare smile on his face.

Finally, the two boys came forward and stood before Skorzeny, their eyes fixed on the money in his gloved hand.

"My family owns that café," one of the boys said, pointing up the street. "We have a telephone."

"Excellent!" Skorzeny replied. "Here, each of you take one coin. You shall have another after I make my call. Yes?"

The two boys shuffled closer, and Skorzeny bent over a bit to offer payment.

Suddenly, one of the boys screamed and bolted in the opposite direction. Just in time, Skorzeny grabbed the other boy by the arm before he, too, could run away.

The boy's eyes grew in terror as he looked Skorzeny in the face.

"What is it, boy?" Skorzeny demanded as he held the squirming child in an iron grip.

The boy didn't answer, but his unblinking eyes betrayed his thoughts.

The scar. They are frightened of the scar.

"It is only a scar. I got it fighting a horrible pirate with swords," Skorzeny said, smiling. "You see? There is nothing to be frightened of."

At the mention of swords and pirates, the child stopped struggling, and his eyes widened with curiosity. Skorzeny often forgot how the prominent slash mark on the side of his face affected other people. He had never considered how it might frighten a child.

"Really? Pirates?" the boy asked.

"Oh, yes. Terrible pirates from the East!" Skorzeny exclaimed dramatically. "Now, will you take me to the telephone? You shall have four coins all to yourself for being brave."

Without hesitation, the boy led Skorzeny around to the back of the café and the door to the kitchen.

With the child waiting outside admiring the fortune in his mittens, Skorzeny called the number given to him by the Deacon himself.

*****

"You are behind schedule," the Deacon stated.

"Yes, our Subject A has been ill and required unexpected stops for rest and recovery," Skorzeny explained.

"You are in Innichen, yes?" the Deacon asked. "Can you drive on to Chiusa tonight?"

"I am afraid not," Skorzeny answered. "Subject A can go no further. Is there someplace nearby we can rest for the night? Tomorrow. Tomorrow we can get to the Brenner Pass and Chiusa."

"Stand by."

Almost five minutes passed as Skorzeny held the receiver to his ear, impatiently shifting his weight from foot to foot.

Finally, the Deacon's voice returned.

"Go to the abbey in the middle of town. The monk there will provide you with refuge for the night."

"Who do I ask for?" Skorzeny wanted to know.

"You'll be met at the gate. Call me again only after you successfully reach the monastery at Chiusa."

The phone went dead in Skorzeny's hand.

Skorzeny found the boy still patiently waiting when he emerged from the café.

"Where is the abbey?" Skorzeny asked.

The boy just shrugged, smiled, and held out his hand. The urchin had found a way to make some money and had a taste for more.

Skorzeny dug out another coin and flipped it through the air to the child. Motioning for the SS colonel to follow, the boy walked back to the front of the shop and pointed up the street before scampering away laughing.

There, standing only two blocks away, the SS Colonel saw a tall square bell tower built from crude stone blocks and capped by a triangular roof. Narrow mullioned windows pierced the sides of the tower.

Even his incredible stamina was fading. He should have seen it as soon as he entered the middle of town.

CHAPTER THIRTY-FIVE

The perilous path through the Alps ended at an intersection with a paved road. The drive out of the mountains had gone smoothly, but now Jacobson and his team faced a choice. Left. Or right.

As sunset approached, Tucker brought the truck to a halt and climbed out of the cab. Using the last of the fading light, he walked back and forth across the intersection, carefully studying the ground.

"See anything?" Jacobson asked, walking up behind Tucker.

"I'm hoping I can pick out which direction our friends went. I'm lookin' for tire tracks. But the dirt is packed into the gravel almost as hard as the asphalt road right there."

"Keep at it. I'm going to check on Gosser," Jacobson said.

Climbing through the canvas flaps at the back of the truck, Jacobson found Rachel expertly changing the field dressing covering the bullet wound in Gosser's side. The hotel owner calmly watched as Rachel removed the blood-soaked bandage and replaced it with another from Pernell's pack.

"How's he doing?" Jacobson asked.

"I'll live. Thank you, Lieutenant," Gosser replied, still groggy from the ampule of morphine Pernell had administered earlier. "And, thank you, young lady. Your hands are as skilled as any doctor's."

"Stop moving about," Rachel ordered, finishing her work.

"You still want to get paid and go home?" Jacobson asked Gosser. "You kept your end of the deal. Say the word, and we'll drop you at the next town."

"Lieutenant, as much as I'd like to get back to my hotel and re-cover in bed under the influence of a fine brandy, I can't. Not yet."

Puzzled, Jacobson asked, "Really? Why not?"

"When I jumped out of the truck, I wasn't running away from you. I was running from Colonel Skorzeny and the SS. I am ashamed to say my actions were those of a coward. I must somehow rectify that embarrassment, or I won't be able to live with myself. So, if you will have me, I'd like to continue. I think I can be of help."

Pernell scoffed at Gosser's admission.

"Right," Jacobson said sarcastically, agreeing with Pernell's assessment. "How do I know whose side you are really on?"

"First, you have offered to pay me in gold. Second, the Germans shot me. Whose side would you be on? Further, my motivation for catering to Nazis at my hotel arose from my own greed and not any love of their ridiculous agenda. I'll help you. You have my word."

"That sounds like more bullshit to me. But it also kinda makes sense," Downtown said.

Jacobson considered Gosser's offer. "Alright, you can stay with us a while longer. And I'm going to hold you to that word. Downtown, if Herr Gosser steps out of line, shoot him."

"My pleasure, sir," Downtown replied, flashing Gosser a wide smile.

A moment later, Tucker called from outside the truck. "Hey, Lieutenant!"

Jacobson found Tucker examining a patch of grass near the edge of the gravel with a lantern.

"We need to go right," Tucker said, pointing west.

"What did you find?" Jacobson asked, seeing nothing for himself.

Tucker placed his head near the ground and peered across the road.

"It's faint, and that's a fact. But right here, there's a narrow tire mark running through this grass and dirt. I believe one of the cars cut this corner, squashed down this grass and stuff, and headed off in that direction."

Jacobson leaned over and peered at the ground, but he couldn't make out what Tucker saw.

"I don't see anything," he said.

"That's okay, sir. I wouldn't be able to pick out the right fork to use in a fancy restaurant, either. You have to know what you're lookin' for before your eyes can see it," Tucker responded with homespun wisdom.

"Good point, Sergeant," Jacobson replied. "Since that's all we have to go on, I'm sold. Let's mount up and get moving."

Before Tucker turned west, Jacobson had Pernell charge the short-wave radio with its hand crank. "This is Orion 6, over. How do you read? Over," Jacobson said into the mic after donning headphones.

A moment later, a scratchy voice in Jacobson's ear responded, *"Orion 6. Read you loud and clear. Go ahead. Over."*

"Our position is map grid J62. We lost our target in the mountains but believed headed west through the Puster Valley. Is there any recon available?"

"Negative on recon. But Smith said to relay that intelligence reports indicate subjects relying on churches and church personnel for aid in escape. Repeat. Subjects using churches. Do you copy? Over."

Jacobson asked for confirmation of the church's involvement with Nazis.

"Affirmative. Base out."

After the radio had been packed away, Jacobson turned to Rachel and Tucker.

"You aren't going to believe this," Jacobson said. "They say that the church is actually helping Nazis escape."

"That don't sound right," Tucker said as the truck accelerated into the dark valley.

"I tried to tell you as much already," Rachel replied, her face betraying a wave of seething anger.

"Yes, you did. What else can you tell us about the Nazis and the church?" Jacobson asked.

Through near-clenched teeth, Rachel related how the Nazis lied to the German people, blaming the Jews for Germany's problems. Rachel's father steadfastly but wrongly believed the people would reject such patently false accusations. The heavily Catholic population of Munich and other German cities had, indeed, turned on their Jewish neighbors and friends. Most galling to Rachel and the utter astonishment of her father, the local priests and even the Bishop of Munich remained silent in the face of increasing persecution of the Jewish community. And in that silence, they had become complicit in the destruction of her family.

Jacobson couldn't imagine how such insanity could overtake an entire country or infect a religion that espoused "love thy neighbor as thyself" as a core belief.

"What happened then?" he asked gently.

Rachel's hands balled into fists.

"I'll tell you everything that happened in Munich later," Rachel said, her eyes burning with anger. "For now, you should know that many important people visited the laboratories during my time in the tunnels. On two occasions, priests came there. I know one was of particular importance because he came accompanied by many other priests and Nazi officers. Everyone kissed his ring and addressed him as 'Your Eminence.' Do you know what that means?"

"I don't really. Does it mean he was some kind of bishop?" Jacobson guessed, trying to recall his Catholic upbringing.

"That man was a Catholic cardinal. One step below the pope. And he seemed quite pleased with the sadistic murder of my people."

CHAPTER THIRTY-SIX

As the Germans drove through Innichen Abbey's heavy iron gates, moonlight illuminated the five-story-tall square bell tower that loomed high above their heads and stood in silence visage over the town. Skorzeny could see how the imposing medieval stronghold and thick stone wall that surrounded the abbey's perimeter had allowed the church to project its power over the entire valley for hundreds of years.

Pulling into the interior courtyard, Skorzeny and his men leaped from the cars with their weapons at the ready. With deep shadows concealing most of the open area, the SS colonel wasn't taking any chances.

After a moment, the gate they had passed through groaned loudly, and a metallic clang announced a security bar of some kind falling into place.

"Who is that?" Skorzeny demanded into the blackness now obscuring the entrance.

"You may put away your weapons, Colonel," a voice said from the dark. "You are safe here."

Peering across the courtyard, Skorzeny could make out the figure of an old monk dressed in long brown robes, limping toward him, holding a white cane.

"Who are you?" Skorzeny asked, cocking his head to one side and scrutinizing the figure before him.

The monk pulled back the hood of his robes, revealing a bald head covered in a constellation of age spots. Two thick patches of wiry gray eyebrows stood over two milk-colored eyeballs that saw nothing.

The monk sniffed the air and appeared to look straight at Skorzeny.

"Your two men can also put away their weapons."

Astonished, Skorzeny asked, "How did you know our number, and for that matter, that we hold weapons?"

The monk smiled, revealing a set of gleaming white teeth.

"I am not a magician, I assure you. I heard your heavy footsteps as soon as you emerged from your vehicles. And I can smell gun oil. I lost the use of my eyes a long time ago, but God has granted me other gifts to compensate."

"And, you know who I am?" Skorzeny asked.

"Of course not. I have merely been informed that an SS Colonel and others require sanctuary for the night. The bishop only informed me of your arrival a short time ago, so my preparations are incomplete. I was also instructed to use the phrase 'die Spinne' upon your arrival, for what reason, I do not know. I have several rooms in the abbey you are welcome to use if you can forgive the sparse accommodations."

"And who else is here with you? How many other monks?" Skorzeny asked, now peering over the monk's shoulder.

"You can look, Colonel. But you will find no one else here. During the winter, I watch over this abbey alone. My brothers will not return for another week. Now, shall I show you to your rooms?" the monk replied, turning toward the living quarters.

"Do you have a name?" Skorzeny asked, waving at his men to follow with Hitler and his doctor.

"I do," the monk said simply and kept walking.

***

"What sort of wretched place have you brought me to?" Hitler shouted. "Is it not enough that I have been shaken and beaten by intolerable rough mountain roads all day, fed nothing, and now expected to remain here *in a dungeon*? I am the Führer! The Führer! Do you not understand this?"

Hitler's ranting erupted almost as soon as Skorzeny led him into one of the windowless cells the abbey's monks used as sleeping quarters. The dismal room fell far below the standards to which the Führer had become accustomed. A simple wooden cross hung on otherwise bare stone walls. At the foot of the hard, narrow bed, a white enamel basin in a crude wooden stand contained water for washing. Nearby, a matching chamber pot awaited any nighttime personal emissions.

"My apologies, my Führer. Circumstances have forced us to accept unacceptable rooms for the night. We shall have better tomorrow," Skorzeny explained.

The heavy opioids that kept Hitler unconscious for the harrowing trip through the mountains had finally worn off. Now full of energy and unable to sleep, Hitler's tirade continued for several more minutes.

Skorzeny finally managed to divert the Führer's attention with a series of maps and explanations about the next part of their journey. With expertise honed through practice, Skorzeny showed Hitler several routes and timetables for their eventual arrival in the port city of Genoa. He asked Hitler his opinion on various alternatives, deftly guiding the ex-dictator to approve the correct route.

Meanwhile, Hitler's bodyguards and personal doctor slept soundly in rooms identical to Hitler's. But at the end of the hall, the blind monk sat fully awake and listening. He couldn't see. But he knew who now rested in God's holy house.

The devil himself.

CHAPTER THIRTY-SEVEN

Near Innichen, Italy

"Sir! Lieutenant!"

Jacobson slowly became aware of someone shaking his shoulder. As his eyes fought their way open, he also became conscious of a pleasant warmth huddled against his left side. Every fiber of his being resisted being pulled away from that warmth and into the cold morning.

"Okay. Okay," Jacobson said, his voice low and hoarse from sleeping outside. "What time is it?"

"Zero-five-thirty, sir," Pernell replied.

With his head clearing quickly, Jacobson remembered ordering the truck to stop along the road late the night before. Battling their way through the mountain pass and racing west late into the night had exhausted Jacobson and his team. They had been on the road for days with little sleep, and he had needed everyone, including himself, to be on their game.

He didn't mind that Rachel must have found a comfortable spot next to him sometime during the night.

Rachel sat up abruptly, obviously surprised and embarrassed at finding herself snuggled against Jacobson's side.

"I am sorry," she said. "I…"

It took a moment to realize how upset the Jewish girl had become after finding herself sleeping beside a man. He immediately tried to put her at ease.

"It got cold last night. That's all."

Rachel pulled her jacket tightly around herself and stood.

"In the camps, our only source of warmth came from each other," Rachel explained, looking at the ground.

Jacobson could see Rachel's growing discomfort. He walked over and, without touching her, said quietly, "Hey, I was cold too. I think we can both be forgiven for trying to stay warm. Maybe we should just forget about it. Anyway, I saw Pernell huddled up pretty close to Gosser."

Jacobson's joke made Rachel laugh.

"Alright, Cy. It is not like I did not enjoy your company," Rachel responded, catching Jacobson's eye. "What's that wonderful smell?"

Rachel walked away toward a glowing campfire at the side of the road, leaving Jacobson stunned and not a little excited about her last remark.

They found Pernell happily sitting by a small fire, munching on a slab of dark bread and sipping from a tin coffee cup.

"Gosser had us light a fire so he could cook breakfast. We got ham, eggs that somehow survived the crash, and some of that dark bread. Stuff Miss Rachel picked up back in Bad Ischl. He even made coffee. Best breakfast I ever had," Pernell explained.

"Hey, you want something to eat?" Jacobson asked Rachel.

"Yes. Thank you. But I shall skip the ham," Rachel responded.

"Why?" Jacobson asked.

Rachel looked at him quizzically. "Pork is not kosher, of course."

"Oh, yeah? Sorry, I don't know much about, uh, being Jewish."

Rachel gave a short laugh at Jacobson's discomfort. "Don't worry, Cy. I shall teach you someday. For now, let us eat."

***

Rachel watched Gosser fry two eggs in a cast-iron skillet over the open fire and slide the eggs between two slices of bread.

Handing the sandwich to Rachel, he said, "I washed the pan thoroughly after cooking the ham. I hope that's alright."

"It is perfect. Thank you," the Jewish girl replied.

Rachel decided that if Gosser wanted to make amends for his intolerable behavior at their first meeting, properly cooking her a meal didn't hurt.

After she ate, Rachel helped Gosser put out the fire and clean up. She noticed the hotel owner moved slowly, holding his hand over the bullet wound. She insisted that he allow her to change his bandages and check for infection.

Gosser didn't complain even when Rachel knew she had to be causing a substantial amount of pain.

"Thank you," Gosser said when she finished. "I meant it when I said you are quite skilled. You have done this before, have you not?"

"Yes. Many times," Rachel replied coldly. "The Nazis didn't provide medical care in the camps, so we had to learn to care for ourselves. Workers digging the tunnels suffered the worst. Almost every day, someone would return to the camp injured."

Rachel couldn't hide the pain and rage that came with remembering the horrific wounds inflicted on her people in the tunnels. Blasting accidents blew off limbs. Collapses and cave-ins crushed and trapped many workers. And, worst of all, the horrific wounds inflicted by guards as they brutally beat her people into submission. She recalled many nights spent hopelessly treating workers' injuries before the next day's work detail. If anyone failed to appear, the guards would come and drag the injured person to the pits. Despite her efforts, many simply surrendered to their fate and lay quietly through the night, waiting for death.

After a moment, Gosser spoke quietly. "Oh, my dear. I'm sorry. I had no idea you came from those horrible camps. We heard rumors, but nothing more. I grow more and more appalled at my behavior in Bad Ischl. I am a deeply flawed man, and I offer my formal and heartfelt apologies."

Over the years, Rachel came to blame all Germans and Austrians for the persecution of her people. They had, after all, allowed someone like Hitler to come to power. And she could not forgive or understand the wholesale abandonment of their morals. But as she looked at Gosser, she realized she couldn't despise every individual German and Austrian forever. Such rampant hatred would eventually tear her apart.

But she vowed to always remain vigilant. If such horrors could happen once, they could happen again.

"Let's not talk of such things," Rachel responded, her anger fading. "You may make what amends you can by helping us now."

"I gave my word to Lieutenant Jacobson. I offer the same to you. I shall do whatever is within my power to aid you in your quest and keep you safe," Gosser replied earnestly.

"Then everyone, including you, shall get the chance to see what your word is worth," Rachel responded, rising and walking away.

"Miss Cohen!" Gosser called after her. "Would you ask the lieutenant if he would have a word with me?"

***

Jacobson found Gosser packing away the remaining supplies and preparing to leave.

"You wanted to talk?" Jacobson asked.

"I have something to relate to you that may be of use," Gosser answered.

"Is this something you should have told me before now?" Jacobson demanded.

Gosser looked back at the bag he was packing. "Yes. And you will find this important."

"Then you better spit it out," Jacobson said, tamping down the anger growing in his belly.

Gosser took a deep breath before continuing. He knew that what he was about to reveal might cost him his life.

"Nine months ago, two men visited me at my hotel. They didn't reveal their identities, but I know they were Gestapo. You know of the Gestapo?"

Jacobson had heard of the German secret police and how they used terror and torture to get what they wanted.

Gosser nodded. "That is essentially correct. Everyone, myself included, knew a visit from the Gestapo meant certain death. Anyone targeted by them disappeared. And everyone heard stories about their, uh, methods. So, when they appeared at my door..."

Jacobson was becoming impatient. "Yes, yes. I understand. What happened? We don't have all day."

"Yes. Of course. These men proceeded to question me closely about my loyalty to the Nazis. They knew I regularly hosted high-ranking party members at my establishment, including, on one occasion, Herman Goring. At any moment, I feared they would accuse me of some disloyalty or treachery. But they didn't. After more than an hour, they had me take them on a tour of the hotel and grounds. Shortly afterward, they left."

Gosser continued, "I was relieved but confused. Two weeks to the day later, they returned. But instead of questioning me further, they handed me an envelope and told me to memorize the contents. They waited while I did so and then burned the envelope and single sheet of paper right in front of me."

Now intrigued, Jacobson asked, "And what was on the paper?"

"Ah, that's the strange part. Not much. Just two names. The first name was 'the Deacon.' The second was 'die Spinne,' which means 'the spider' in English.

"Continue," Jacobson said, taking a notebook out of his jacket pocket and jotting down the two names.

"Once the papers were destroyed, they told me to await a call from the Deacon. When and if the call came, I was to identify myself using the codeword 'die Spinne' and follow whatever instructions I was given as if ordered to do so by the Führer himself."

Jacobson studied the hotel owner carefully, but the story was almost too fantastic to be a lie.

"I take it this has something to do with Hitler being at your hotel?" Jacobson asked.

"Several days before he arrived, I received a call from someone calling himself 'the Deacon.' After I responded with the codeword, he ordered me to shut the hotel down and be prepared to receive important guests. He didn't say when they would arrive or identify who my guests were to be. Out of an abundance of caution, I dismissed the entire staff and made the preparations myself," Gosser explained. "I had heard the reports of Hitler's death. Never would I have imagined that the Führer would appear at my doorstep."

"Why didn't you tell me this before?"

Gosser shrugged in defeat. "Like the old saying in English, I was between a rock and a hard place."

Jacobson studied Gosser's face while he considered the revelation he had just heard. It made sense. If Hitler and other important Nazis planned to escape justice, they would need help.

His father used to complain about powerful men and corporations who corrupted politicians and judges, seeking unfair advantages and financial gain. *Why wouldn't it be the same for the Nazis?* Germany's vast war machine – its weapons, tanks, aircraft, fuel, and uniforms – must have cost billions to produce. As he sought political power, Hitler pushed for arming Germany to the teeth. Wouldn't the people who made and sold weapons of war have every reason to support him? And now, they would have every reason to actively work toward a resurgence of the Nazi nightmare.

The church? Powerful businesses? The Deacon? Jacobson's head swam in a soup of possibilities. But for now, he had to refocus on his mission to find and capture Adolf Hitler.

And they had all but lost the madman's trail.

CHAPTER THIRTY-EIGHT

While Pernell and Downtown took turns patrolling the area, Jacobson gathered Tucker, Rachel, and Gosser around the hood of the truck.

Unfolding a map, Jacobson said, "Okay, we are here, fifteen miles or so out of, uh, Innichen. We think they were headed in that direction twelve to eighteen hours ago. What's there?"

Gosser answered. "Innichen is well known for its excellent skiing. Although at this time of year, it would be less popular. I haven't been there in years. The war has been unkind to the tourist industry. But the town does have an ancient church, an abbey of monks, if I am not mistaken."

"That fella Smith did say churches might be helping Nazis escape. Maybe we should pay the monks a visit," Tucker suggested.

"That is not a bad idea. But every town in Italy has a church or convent or abbey. We can't search them all," Rachel observed.

Jacobson thought a moment and said, "I agree with you both. But Innichen would be a logical place for Hitler and this Colonel Skorzeny to stop for the night. Gosser, what else do you know about the church there?"

"Not much, I'm afraid. I recall a high tower overlooking the town and perhaps a stone wall around its exterior."

"So, they'll have a nice vantage point to see us coming?" Tucker asked.

"*If* I recall correctly," Gosser hedged.

"We'll check it out. But carefully," Jacobson decided. "Rachel? You want to go into town with me for a stroll?"

***

An hour later, Jacobson and Rachel walked arm-in-arm window shopping along the main street of Innichen and enjoying the bright spring morning. Their focus wasn't on the scant consumer goods displayed in the few open shops but on the belltower that seemed to watch their every move.

Finding a table at an outdoor café, Rachel ordered them both a strong cup of espresso.

"Did you see any movement in the tower?" Jacobson asked quietly, trying to avoid being heard and identified as an American.

"No," Rachel answered. "But the windows are dark slits. Good for looking out of, but hiding whoever is inside."

"We need to get closer," Jacobson said.

"How do we do that without being seen? They do not know what we look like, but I would wager they would get suspicious of anyone getting too close," Rachel responded. "Wait! I have an idea. I will ask them."

Rachel pointed at a group of children across the street.

"Kids?"

"Yes. They always know more than anyone thinks," Rachel said, rising from the table.

Jacobson watched as Rachel approached the five or six children arguing over some contrived game that involved throwing a rock into tin cans. It didn't take long for Rachel to join the fun. When she missed the can on her first several throws, the children clapped and laughed, obviously enjoying her lack of skill.

After another round or two of the game, Jacobson saw Rachel pointing to the abbey and asking a question. Most of the children didn't know anything, but one of the older boys pointed off to the west.

"I think we have our answer," Rachel reported after she returned to the table. "One of the boys saw two cars leave the abbey early this morning. He was surprised because the monks do not have a car and because the church gets few visitors, especially this time of the year. He suggested we talk to the caretaker, a blind monk."

The boy's story about two vehicles leaving the abbey matched what Downtown observed at the rockslide in the mountains, Gosser's description of Hitler's transportation, and the reconnaissance pilot's report. And it seemed to confirm that the church was providing aid to Nazis. Somehow, they had managed to reacquire the trail.

Jacobson wanted to take Rachel in his arms and kiss her right in the middle of the street. But he didn't.

"You are absolutely remarkable, Rachel Cohen," Jacobson exclaimed, his eyes locked on Rachel's.

Rachel's cheeks blushed.

"Should we not join the others and give chase?" Rachel suggested, pulling her gaze away.

"Oh. Well, yes. Of course," Jacobson responded after a long moment. "We'll meet up with the team. But after that, I think we need to talk with the blind monk. Several roads lead west. Maybe this monk knows which one they took."

"Or, perhaps, where Hitler will stop next," Rachel added.

CHAPTER THIRTY-NINE

Near Sabiona Monastery
Chiusa, Italy

Skorzeny had not been keen to inform Hitler that a monastery would serve as the next destination along their escape route. He could, at least, assure the dictator they would be hosted that night by none other than the Bishop of the Bolzano-Brixen diocese. But even promises of luxurious rooms and sumptuous meals did little to mollify Hitler.

"Did I not grant safety and enrichment to those robe-wearing hypocrites within the Third Reich? If not for me, the communists would have burned down all their precious churches! Under my leadership, *mine*, their ridiculous cult grew powerful, and their *Pope* grew fat. Now, when I ask for only decent accommodations in return, they offer me a cold cell and black bread as if I were no more than a convict. Their disrespect has not gone unnoticed! No! They shall reap what they have sown."

From the back seat, Hitler ranted and complained for nearly an hour, his temper exploding and dissipating and exploding again like fireworks in the night sky.

Before they arrived at Sabiona Monastery, Skorzeny decided to try to soothe Hitler's indignation by explaining how the church came to aid the Nazis.

"My Führer, our great benefactor, the Deacon, has strong connections to the church. Over the years, he donated great sums of money to bishops and cardinals whose beliefs aligned with the Nazi party. I understand that several prominent bishops bestowed the title 'Deacon' on him and that he took the title as his alias. The Deacon, working closely with those church officials, built 'die Spinne' to aid you and other members of the Nazi hierarchy wanting to relocate from Europe. Our enemies have no idea monasteries and other church properties now provide protection and refuge for our people as they move through Italy, Spain, and Norway. While dealing with these self-proclaimed holy men is distasteful, they are helping many of our people find safe passage to the Reich's new home in South America."

Hitler listened but continued to pout.

"They do no more than their duty," Hitler grumbled. "This bishop, whatever his name, walks a fine line with me. You shall ensure he keeps his promises, Colonel."

The fifty-mile drive from Innichen took most of the day, primarily due to Skorzeny's insistence that they avoid towns and villages. As evening approached, the SS colonel stopped the cars on a hill overlooking the picturesque town of Chiusa.

The Isarco River shimmered brightly as it flowed through the center of town. On the far side of the river, the last rays of daylight fell directly on the massive white walls of the famous Sabiona Monastery. Perched above the town on a high, craggy outcropping of rock, many generations of locals and tourists alike had marveled at the beautiful structure and its tall towers. But Skorzeny knew the monastery had always been more than a home for peaceful and studious monks.

Built like a castle, the monastery provided the church with a base for its military and a safe refuge from invaders. The SS colonel studied the monastery's defensive position with a practiced eye. Steep rock cliffs below the monastery protected it on three sides, while neatly arranged vineyards spilled down the hill and along the single-lane road that provided the only access to the monastery. And from its lofty vantage point, the church could see and control everything that happened in the valley below.

Where some saw the monastery's beauty, Skorzeny admired how it projected power over the entire region.

Ignoring the natural beauty before him, Skorzeny raised his field binoculars and identified the single bridge they needed to cross over the Isarco. Following the road from the bridge up the high rock bluff, Skorzeny watched as lights appeared along the monastery's walls and flooded the white-sided buildings as if the monks planned to throw a party.

A welcoming party.

Skorzeny knew that Hitler wanted to proceed as quickly as possible, but he needed proper reconnaissance before driving the Führer through town and over the bridge. Skorzeny sent two of his men ahead in the second car. The SS colonel followed in Hitler's vehicle only after he confirmed the first car's passage had attracted no unwanted attention.

***

The short drive through town, over the bridge, and up the steep grade to the monastery took only a few minutes. Skorzeny stopped the car in front of the monastery's massive front door, jumped out, and stood at attention while holding Hitler's door open. Three priests waited patiently on granite steps, flaccid white faces displaying insincere grins. The SS colonel detested soft men like these, who lived off the work of others. And he knew these priests held no actual loyalty to Hitler or the Reich. No, their hospitality had been purchased – by the Deacon.

Unlike the oppressiveness of Innichen Abbey, Sabiona Monastery looked like a grand castle of old. It reminded Skorzeny of the fairy-tale-like castle of Neuschwanstein in the Bavarian Alps. One would never guess that many generations of monks, not royalty, had lived and died within its walls.

One holy man, dressed in long black robes trimmed in garish purple, stood between and ahead of the others. A formal cassock flowed off his shoulders, and an opulent gold cross hung prominently over an expansive belly. The Bishop of Bolzano-Brixen clearly dressed to make an impression. The other two younger priests, both slightly built and wearing simple black robes, stood at the ready.

Hitler took his time getting out of the car. Placing one foot at a time on the ground, the Führer stood and made a show of smoothing his camel-hair topcoat and putting his wool fedora on his head. Only then did he place both hands behind his back and walk toward his host.

Skorzeny, following close behind, made the introductions.

"Mein Führer, may I present His Most Reverent Excellency, The Bishop of Bolzano-Brixen, Antonio Calbiani."

"It is my great pleasure to welcome you to Sabiona, Herr Hitler," the bishop replied, offering his ring for Hitler to kiss.

Hitler didn't even look at the pudgy hand hanging awkwardly in the air. Instead, he fixed the bishop in a judgmental gaze until the other man lowered his arm. To his credit, the bishop's sloppy smile never faded.

With practiced diplomacy, Calbiani continued his welcoming speech.

"We are honored to be of service to the Führer of all Germany. I'm sure you would like to rest and refresh yourself before dinner. With your permission, my assistants will show the way to your rooms."

Hitler nodded but said nothing as he stepped around the bishop and followed the two priests who had scurried ahead to open the ornate front door.

Skorzeny remained standing next to the holy man as Hitler disappeared inside.

"Your Führer has no love for the church," the bishop commented, keeping most of the loathing he felt out of his voice.

"And the church has no love for him," Skorzeny countered.

The bishop grunted in agreement.

"Both things are true," the bishop replied. "Yet being useful to one another does not require love."

"No. But it does require the fulfillment of agreements."

"Yes, and before this night is done, I shall show you how well the church fulfills its agreements and much, much more."

CHAPTER FORTY

Calbiani presided over the intimate but spectacular dinner party like a medieval king. The bishop sat at the head of a long table set with candelabras, crystal stemware, and delicate china. Hitler was seated at the bishop's right hand. Skorzeny, dressed in his full SS officer's regalia, sat stiffly upright across from Hitler while keeping a vigilant eye out for any possible threat to the dictator.

Silent priests presented dish after dish of sumptuous delicacies while Calbiani maintained a continuous self-serving monologue about his service to the church and the Nazis.

As the flabby bishop stuffed his mouth and laughed at his own jokes, Skorzeny could barely maintain his composure. But across the table, Hitler sat comfortably, picked at his food, and absorbed Calbiani's clownish behavior without lifting an eyebrow. Skorzeny knew that Hitler had grown accustomed to dealing with all kinds of people, from world leaders to fawning sycophants. He possessed a talent for making them feel comfortable in his presence, regardless of his true feelings. However, it was a well-practiced and calculated performance meant only to extract whatever he wanted.

As the evening wore on and Calbiani consumed more and more wine, Hitler finally joined the one-sided conversation.

"Your Excellency," Hitler began, correctly addressing the Catholic Bishop. "I am impressed with your hospitality. I shall be sure to mention it to the Holy Father when next we meet." Nothing could have pleased the bishop more.

"Thank you, Chancellor," Calbiani gushed, using Hitler's political title. "It is my honor to be of service. I have instructed my staff to provide anything you desire."

"That is quite generous," Hitler replied. "But we will have to take your leave early tomorrow. Colonel Skorzeny informed me we are on a tight schedule and cannot linger here."

"I know of your time limitations, and I am pleased to be able to offer a solution that will relieve this concern," Calbiani said softly, leaning forward slightly as if to reveal a special present.

"Please continue," Hitler replied, showing no emotion at the bishop's intended surprise announcement.

"When we learned you would be accepting our humble assistance, I personally contacted the secretary for the Holy Father himself and made a rather bold request. I must say that in doing so, I overreached my authority. But I believed it necessary, and I very much hope you approve."

Skorzeny bristled at Calbiani's venal self-flattery.

Hitler cocked his head, intrigued.

"You see," the bishop continued, now nearly breathless to get out the news, "the Vatican maintains a private aircraft for use by the Holy Father. From time to time, the church utilizes this aircraft for humanitarian purposes. I requested that it be flown here on a special mission of mercy. In point of fact, I have arranged for you and your party to be transported anywhere you wish to go within Italy."

Skorzeny leaned forward and asked, "Why wasn't I informed of this earlier?"

Calbiani grinned at Skorzeny like a child who had just won a parent's approval over his less capable sibling.

"I only learned of the authorization shortly before dinner. My apologies if this causes you concern, Colonel," Calbiani replied with false modesty.

"Has this been approved by our friend?" Skorzeny asked.

"The Deacon is more than grateful. In fact, I am to assure you of the safety of this method of travel. As you may be aware, the Vatican enjoys diplomatic relations with all countries. The flight will be logged with the Americans as a humanitarian mission. The aircraft will not be challenged or molested in any way while in flight."

"Do you know our destination?"

"Indeed. I am told that you would like to visit the area around Genoa. More specifically, Italy's beautiful coast, which we call the Cinque Terre," Calbiani replied.

Skorzeny detested unexpected deviations from plans already in motion. But as a soldier, he knew that no battle plan ever survives the beginning of actual combat. He had already made innumerable alterations to their planned route, and a flight from the Tyrol region to Genoa would save them days of treacherous travel through enemy-controlled territory.

"Other than you and the Deacon, who else knows of this?" Skorzeny asked, his eyes boring into the Calbiani's pudgy face, looking for any hint of deception.

Hitler's safety depended on one thing above all others – secrecy. And except for one glaring exception, they had gotten lucky.

"Only my staff. More specifically, the two priests who met you at the door and served this outstanding meal," Calbiani answered confidently. "They have been at my side and loyal to me since they were mere altar boys. The Vatican and the Holy Father trust my judgment and asked no questions when I requested the use of the aircraft."

Calbiani sat back in his chair, folded his hands over his belly, and gave Skorzeny a smug grin.

"When?" Skorzeny wanted to know.

"Tomorrow morning. By nightfall, you shall be at my private villa in the hills above Monterosso on the Cinque Terre. The Deacon requested the use of the villa as it provides perfect access to ships or other craft navigating the Ligurian Sea. You are welcome there as long as necessary, and I shall even send my staff along to see to your every need."

Hitler listened intently as Calbiani and Skorzeny planned the next move in what had turned out to be a cat-and-mouse game with the Americans.

"I approve of this plan," Hitler announced, rising to his feet. "Colonel, you will oversee its proper implementation."

"Yes, Mein Führer," Skorzeny said, jumping to his feet and standing at attention.

Calbiani remained seated, drawing a scowl from Skorzeny.

Hitler turned to go but stopped and looked over his shoulder.

"Colonel, if the good bishop doesn't show proper respect, you may teach him some."

Calbiani looked up at the SS commando and found a hint of pleasure written on Skorzeny's face.

As quickly as he could manage, Calbiani rose to his feet, recognizing for the first time who actually held all the power in the room.

"My apologies, *Mein Führer*. Please have a restful night."

Hitler stood another moment with his back to the bishop, hands clasped behind his back. Calbiani stood motionless, sweat rolling down one cheek. When he saw Skorzeny's hand resting on the grip of his Luger, his knees began to shake uncontrollably.

"If *Herr* Calbiani keeps his promises, he may live to go on fleecing his flock. If you feel he has failed in any way, do as you think best," Hitler said, refusing to formally address the bishop.

Without another word, Hitler disappeared up a broad set of stairs.

Skorzeny put a hand on Calbiani's shoulder and leaned in, his face only inches from the bishop's. The odor of garlic on Calbiani's breath mingled with the scent of urine soaking the front of his purple robe. Some of the church's leaders had been valuable allies, but they also needed to understand who they truly served.

And it wasn't God.

"You are a lucky man," Skorzeny snarled in a low, threatening tone. "You and your staff are useful. Remain so."

***

After Skorzeny and Calbiani left the dining hall, a single apprentice nun appeared from deep in the monastery to clear the table. Sister Gianna's hand shook as she loaded a basket with dirty dishes. She moved quickly, wanting more than anything to disappear back into the kitchens. Crossing herself over and over, the young nun recited Psalm 140.

> *Deliver me, O Lord from evil men;*
> *Preserve me from violent men,*
> *Who plan evil things in their hearts;*

As Sister Gianna quietly prayed for protection, she also realized she couldn't let men like the bishop and Adolf Hitler corrupt her beloved church.

CHAPTER FORTY-ONE

Tucker drove the old truck through the wide-open gates of Innichen Abbey. As soon as the vehicle came to a stop, Pernell and Downtown jumped out with their weapons. Tucker and Jacobson followed, leaving Rachel and Gosser behind with strict orders to stay in the truck.

The four soldiers spread out, searching the abbey's grounds and outbuildings. Finding the area deserted, they met at the back entrance to the abbey itself. The solid, arch-shaped door of rough-hewn timber looked like it had been in place for centuries. Windowless stone walls rose above their heads, giving Jacobson the distinct impression they were standing at the front door of a prison.

Using hand signals, Tucker placed Downtown and Pernell on either side of the door. After inspecting the exterior of the doorway for booby traps, Jacobson nodded. Tucker grabbed the ancient iron handle and slowly pulled the door open, half-expecting a hand grenade to drop from the ceiling or a hail of gunfire to rip through the opening.

Nothing happened.

Jacobson stepped gingerly through the entrance, finding himself in a long, straight hallway dimly lit by a few flickering candles. He could see four doors placed in the walls on either side of the hallway – all tightly closed.

"Hello!" Jacobson called, peering into the darkness.

Motioning for the others to follow, Jacobson held his pistol to his eye as he stepped from one door to another, kicking each of them open in turn. A quick inspection of each room revealed only empty monks' quarters.

"Looks deserted, sir," Tucker observed.

"You guys spread out and take a look around. See if anyone's home," Jacobson ordered. "But be careful. Our Nazi friends have a nasty habit of leaving surprises behind."

While Tucker and the men searched the abbey, Jacobson made his way deeper into the building, finally arriving inside the abbey's sanctuary. The lieutenant lowered his weapon but kept his finger on the trigger.

Romanesque in style, high stone arches reached across the ceiling from either side. Windows placed between the arches filled the space with light. A full-sized sculpture of Jesus Christ hung above the altar. Behind the altar, a short staircase descended into what Jacobson correctly guessed to be the crypt.

"Hello! Is anyone here?"

He was about to rejoin his men when he heard a distinct tap, followed by another and another.

Looking around to see where the sound came from, Jacobson nearly jumped out of his skin when a cloaked figure seemed to rise from the crypt entrance.

On instinct, Jacobson dropped to one knee behind a pew and aimed his pistol at the slow-moving apparition. "Stop right there!" Jacobson called. "Identify yourself."

As the figure emerged, a voice responded: "This is a house of God, my young American friend. You should put away your weapon."

Jacobson watched a bony hand rise in the air while the other held tightly to a long white cane.

"Who are you?" Jacobson challenged.

The figure pushed the hood from his head and looked directly at Jacobson as if he could see. Blank, stark white eyeballs further unnerved the young officer. But the monk's kind expression and friendly manner made him lower his weapon and slide it back into its holster.

"I am Brother Tobias. Thank you for putting your sidearm away. Now, how may I be of service?"

"How did you know..." Jacobson began to say.

Brother Tobias gently cut off Jacobson's question with a smile and a wave of his hand.

"The blind are often underestimated. Praise God."

"What do you mean by that?" Jacobson asked, now intrigued.

"Do not feel bad. Humans rely on sight more than any other sense, and it is only natural to assume those who cannot see are helpless. I have found blindness allows me a different, but in some ways, fuller understanding of God's creation through the use of my other senses. For instance, I knew you to be an American even as your footsteps entered the church, and the first sound you uttered only confirmed that fact. You are both welcome and safe here, so please ask your companions to come out from behind the back row of pews."

Jacobson looked around, and to his surprise, Tucker and Pernell stepped into the open from the very spot the old monk identified. He didn't know they had found the sanctuary and placed themselves in a position to provide him with backup.

"You are anxious to ask me questions," Tobias stated. "But perhaps I can provide answers to some by relating to you what took place here only last night. Afterward, I would be honored if you would dine with me."

"Thank you," Jacobson replied. "May I bring in the rest of my group as well?"

Jacobson sent Pernell outside to take up guard duty with Downtown while Gosser and Rachel joined Jacobson, Tucker, and Brother Tobias in the church.

Tobias took a seat in the front pew and described a hurried call he had received the afternoon before from the Bishop of Bolzano-Brixen. The bishop had ordered him to open the abbey's gates and receive a German colonel who would be accompanying several highly important persons. The bishop also instructed him to provide the Germans with rooms, food, and anything else they needed. But he was not, under any circumstances, to ask their identities.

"I also found it curious that the bishop insisted I say 'die Spinne' to this German colonel. I did so, but I have no idea what meaning it holds," Tobias said.

Gosser and Jacobson exchanged a knowing look.

"Probably a code word of some kind," Jacobson said somewhat dismissively. "Please continue."

Tobias went on to tell Jacobson and the others how he had complied with the bishop's orders, despite being uncomfortable and confused by the presence of German soldiers after the end of the war. The soldiers had been brusque but generally well-behaved, and mostly ignored him.

But later in the night, Tobias had heard a commotion. One of the guests had thrown a heated tantrum at the German colonel. And that is when he became scared for his life.

"So, you recognized the voice?" Jacobson asked.

Brother Tobias's head dropped, and his hand squeezed the head of his cane.

"I did. We do not have a radio here, but I heard that voice many times while visiting the ill or doing the shopping in town. I'm sure it is familiar to everyone, but I recognize and remember people by their voices, not their faces. Voices are also my guide to a person's personality and, often, their soul."

"Who did you hear?" Rachel asked excitedly.

"Ah, a Daughter of Judah!" Tobias said with genuine excitement as soon as Rachel spoke. "I am glad, so glad, to hear your voice. I feared I might never hear a beautiful accent like yours again."

"Thank you, Tobias, but I, uh, we have to know. Was it Hitler?" Rachel pleaded.

Tobias straightened and turned to face the young Jew.

"Yes."

"Are you sure?" Jacobson asked.

Tobias stood, turned, and bowed at the altar.

"I *know* without a single doubt that Christ is the savior of the world."

Tobias turned back to Jacobson.

"And I *know* without a single doubt that Hitler, the slayer of the world, slept here last night."

Tobias's chilling words dispelled any lingering qualms Jacobson or Tucker still held about who they were chasing.

"If I can ask there, uh, Father, weren't you scared they might, well, do away with you to keep you from talking or something?" Tucker asked, hesitantly.

Brother Tobias's confident smile returned.

"Oh yes, Sergeant. But I had three things in my favor. First, I knew God would watch over me. Second, since I cannot see, the Germans did not believe I could hear. Finally, a secret tunnel under the crypt leads outside the walls. I simply followed the tunnel and emerged outside. Then, I waited in the field of a neighbor until I heard the Germans' cars leave early this morning."

"Can you tell us where they intended to go from here?" Jacobson asked.

"Or where they might stay next?" Gosser added.

"I overheard only that they planned to travel in the general direction of Bolzano. I listened as long as possible, but the conversation quieted after the Führer's outburst came to an end. With the greatest shame, I believe they will be given refuge in another monastery. I don't know which one. But I do have an idea who may."

"Please. Any information will help," Rachel prompted.

"Go to the Novacella Abbey near the town of Brixen. Ask to see an old winemaker there named Bertram Klaus. He knows everything that takes place in the entire diocese. Tell him I sent you. He is a hard-headed pig of a man, but he will help you if the request comes from me," Tobias said.

"How do you know him?" Rachel asked.

"He and I have the same mother. We are half-brothers. More importantly, he owes me a favor. If he does not believe you, tell him I said to be thankful for my aim. He'll understand."

"What does that mean?" Jacobson wanted to know.

"You'll have to ask him."

CHAPTER FORTY-TWO

"I have never seen such a beautiful and peaceful place," Rachel said as Tucker drove the truck onto the grounds of Novacella Abbey a few hours later.

Jacobson had to agree.

Unlike the heavy, almost bleak abbey in Innichen, Novacella's white stone walls gleamed brightly in the midday sun. Above their heads, a lone tower overlooked neat rows of grapevines that surrounded the abbey on all sides. Travelers from around the world considered Novacella the most beautiful and important abbey in all of northern Italy.

Since the original abbey's construction 800 years earlier, centuries of builders used Baroque, Rococo, and Gothic architectural styles to create a masterpiece. A round building resembling a miniature castle, seemingly out of place inside the courtyard, caught Jacobson's attention. Complete with high defensive walls and topped by crenulated battlements, Jacobson would later learn that the building had actually served to protect the monks from attack during the Middle Ages.

***

While Jacobson and Tucker went in search of Bertram Klaus, Brother Tobias's half-brother, Rachel found herself drawn to a well placed in the center of the courtyard and covered with an eight-sided gazebo. She walked slowly around the well, admiring murals of the seven wonders of the ancient world painted on each side of the structure.

She didn't notice Gosser walk up behind her.

"I see you have found the famous Well of Wonders," Gosser said, seeing Rachel looking quizzically at the eighth panel.

"I recognize the seven wonders painted on every other side, but why does this final panel depict Novacella? Did the artist consider this place the eighth wonder of the world?" Rachel asked.

"Yes, but not for the reason you may think. The story has been told that after painting the first seven panels, the artist couldn't decide what to do with the last one. So, he sat here worrying that the monks might not accept his work. At that moment, a beautiful young girl appeared to draw water for the vineyard workers. When the two found themselves together under this roof, they fell deeply and irrevocably in love. As a tribute to Novacella and what he believed to be a miraculous gift, he painted the abbey itself."

"And you believe this story?" Rachel asked, intrigued.

"Oh, I do, indeed," Gosser answered wistfully. "You see, I once fell in love right here, under this very roof."

"You have been here before, then?"

"Before the war, I came here quite often to buy wine. The vines surrounding the abbey create the best Sylvaner and Riesling in all of Italy. Anyway, I met someone here. We stayed together for years."

"Who was she?" Rachel asked.

"His name was Rolf. And he was uncommonly beautiful. I can only believe the magic of this place made him look twice at a man like me."

Rachel could see Gosser struggling to contain a flood of emotions. She didn't judge. After years in the camps, she understood that love was elusive and precious. In a way, she envied Gosser as he stood at the Well of Wonders, fighting back tears.

"Where is Rolf now?" Rachel asked gently.

"Our type of love has never been socially acceptable. But when the Nazis came, they tried to purge the entire country of people like us. One day, Rolf disappeared. Whether the Nazis took him away or he simply fled, I do not know," Gosser explained. "But I still hold a tiny spark of hope that he will return."

As Gosser walked back toward the truck, Rachel remained at the well, wondering if it actually did hold some kind of magic. She didn't know the answer, but she couldn't help looking around for Jacobson.

***

Across the courtyard, Jacobson and Tucker had their hands full. After some searching, they finally found Bertram Klaus lying on his back under a massive mechanical wine press. Jacobson could tell that whatever the winemaker was doing wasn't going well. Waves of profanity in several languages punctuated the loud clangs from a heavy hammer striking metal.

Jacobson and Tucker hadn't said a word when Klaus shouted, "Whoever you are, go away!"

Bang Bang

Jacobson and Tucker looked at each other, wondering how the winemaker knew they were even present.

"Herr Klaus, I'm Lieutenant Jacobson of the United States Army. May we have a word with you?" Jacobson called between blows of the hammer.

"You may *not!* Now, go away. I am busy."

Bang Bang Bang

"Herr Klaus, Brother Tobias sent us," Jacobson replied.

Bang Bang Bang Bang

"Brother Tobias is an ass. Leave!"

Bang Bang Bang

"He said the same of you! And he appears to be correct! He also said you owe him a favor and to be thankful for his aim," Jacobson shouted.

The banging stopped, replaced by a hearty laugh.

After a moment, Klaus pulled himself out from under the grape press and stood facing the two Americans.

"You don't look like soldiers," Klaus commented, looking at Jacobson and Tucker's civilian clothes. "What do you want?"

Jacobson explained how they were looking for Nazis trying to escape from Europe and related his conversation with Tobias, leaving out any mention of Hitler by name.

Klaus listened carefully as he wiped greasy hands on a greasier rag. A mop of thin blond hair sat atop a jowly face that now scowled down at Jacobson. Nearly as tall as Tucker, Klaus's heavy frame gave him the appearance of an old boxer. Thick forearms covered in graying hair and meaty, callused hands evidenced a life of heavy manual labor in the vineyards.

"And why should I help you?" Klaus snarled, unimpressed with Jacobson or his mission.

"I can pay," Jacobson offered.

"Money? What would I do with money? Buy a fancy car?" Klaus scoffed. "Keep your money."

Tucker watched as Jacobson struggled to extract information from Klaus. He knew men like Klaus from back home – hard, proud men who used their hands to farm, build, and make things. Men like that could not be bought. Their respect had to be earned.

"I got an idea," Tucker interrupted. "If we fix your press, you give us the information we need."

Klaus looked at Jacobson and Tucker and laughed.

"You have a bargain. Please, be my guest," Klaus said, sarcastically inviting them under the press with a slight bow and wave of his hand.

"Not us," Tucker responded. "But I have just the man for the job."

A few minutes later, Downtown ambled into the pressing room. After looking over the press to see how it worked, he disappeared under the heavy machine. "I'll need a wrench!" he called out a minute later.

Klaus slid an adjustable wrench to Downtown.

After ten minutes, the big Iowan emerged from under the machine holding its drive shaft.

"This is bent."

Taking the eight-pound sledgehammer from Klaus's hand, Downtown took the shaft to a nearby anvil and expertly pounded it back straight. As the other three men watched, the big Iowan dove back under the press and remounted the shaft. But he wasn't finished. Gears driving the shaft had seized, causing it to bend. Using a crowbar and a few well-placed hammer blows, Downtown freed the gear teeth, checked his work, and threw the power switch.

Klaus looked into the press and saw its heavy barrels rotating smoothly and quietly against each other.

"Nice work," Klaus said, offering his hand to Downtown.

"No problem. Grease those gears regularly, and you won't have that problem again," Downtown replied.

"Now, Herr Klaus, what do you know about Nazis trying to escape through this area?" Jacobson asked.

"You have kept your end of the bargain, and I shall keep mine. But nobody can know the information you will learn came from me," Klaus replied, looking Jacobson in the eye. "It would cost my life and my brother's."

"That dangerous?" Jacobson asked.

"Explosive. Meet me in the dining room in ten minutes."

CHAPTER FORTY-THREE

Jacobson found Rachel sitting under the gazebo at the Well of Wonders.

"We are going to meet with Herr Klaus. He has important information for us," Jacobson said, sounding more excited than he intended.

Rachel brightened as soon as Jacobson arrived. She couldn't help being attracted to his sometimes-boyish enthusiasm. And she also couldn't help looking at the painting over her head and wishing for a little magic to fall on the handsome young lieutenant.

"Alright," Rachel said with a quiet sigh.

"Are you okay?" Jacobson asked, seeing Rachel's odd mood.

"Yes, but I wish we did not have to leave this place today. It would be nice to stay for just a while," Rachel answered longingly.

"Yeah, it's great. Come on!" Jacobson urged, totally missing the fact that Rachel wanted him to sit with her for a moment under the magical gazebo.

***

Inside a deserted café that had attracted many tourists before the war, Klaus produced a bottle of wine and several glasses. Jacobson,

Tucker, Rachel, and Gosser took seats at a round wooden table while Klaus poured.

Handing a glass to Gosser, Klaus said, "I know you. You own a hotel near Bad Ischl. You have come here to buy wine."

Gosser had never met the gruff winemaker.

"True. Your wines are a great favorite with my guests," Gosser replied.

Klaus glared at Gosser, trying to remember more about the hotel owner.

"What are you doing with these Americans?" Klaus asked suspiciously.

"We needed a guide, and Herr Gosser offered to help," Jacobson responded quickly. Klaus, who was already paranoid about sharing his information, didn't need to know of Gosser's past service to the Germans.

"And the girl?" Klaus asked, turning his attention to Rachel.

Rachel answered before Jacobson had a chance to intervene.

"I am Jewish. Nazis killed my family. I will hunt them until the day I die," Rachel answered, looking Klaus in the eye.

"Ha!" Klaus laughed. "You have a lot of spirit for such a skinny little thing! I like that. Alright, I will tell you what I know."

Jacobson got out his notebook and said, "Maybe you could just tell us whatever you know about Nazis passing through this area and if anyone is helping them."

He intentionally omitted what Brother Tobias said about the church to see if the stories matched.

"Yes. The wine you have in front of you is some of our best. As Herr Gosser said, it is very popular and draws many people here. One of our frequent visitors is the bishop of this diocese, Antonio Calbiani. He comes for the wine, takes what he wants, and never pays. As you might expect, this has angered the monks here at the abbey. Calbiani is fat, corrupt, and, most of all, ambitious. He has the ear of the Pope himself and likes to boast about it."

After downing his wine in a single enormous gulp, Klaus continued.

"Soon after he came to power, Mussolini disbanded the local councils and threw out the elected politicians. Calbiani took the opportunity to fill the power vacuum created by the fascists. He used the influence of the church to convince the people to work with the Germans, and if his false religious arguments failed, Calbiani had the fascists remove any resistance. After Hitler came to power in Germany, Calbiani had to go further to prove his loyalty and maintain his gluttonous way of life. When the Nazis started removing Jews from the area, Calbiani helped, using his local knowledge and network of loyal priests to root out the last of the Jewish population."

Everyone at the table could see Rachel becoming incensed at Klaus's revelation.

"How did you come by that information?" Jacobson asked.

"Well, I didn't need spies to see what they were doing in plain sight," Klaus huffed.

"Okay, that's what happened before. What can you tell us about what is happening now?" Jacobson asked.

Klaus held up his hand.

"I'm getting to that. If you want to be successful, you must know why parts of the church are still cooperating with the Nazis. As it became clear that Germany would lose the war, Calbiani found yet another way to profit from the situation. He, along with several other bishops and cardinals, came together and offered to help the Nazis escape from Europe should that become necessary. They lusted after the gold, art, and other valuables that Hitler and top Nazis stole from countries they conquered and the people they sent to the camps. For a hefty price, they offered to provide safe houses throughout Italy. They also arranged for documents to be printed, changing the Nazis' identities that allowed for safe passage out of the country. In some cases, corrupted priests even re-baptized Nazis, giving them new legal names and identities."

Jacobson and the rest of his team sat for a moment, trying to come to terms with Klaus's incredible revelations. A corrupt bishop making some personal gains from the Nazi nightmare was bad enough. But a broad organization involving hundreds of conspirators across Europe sounded incredible. And nobody could have predicted an unholy alliance between the Catholic Church and the Nazis. While there had been scattered complaints that the church had not sufficiently objected to Nazi odious policies over the years, Jacobson now had confirmation that at least factions within the church were actively cooperating with Hitler and his henchmen.

"How big of an organization are you talking about?" Jacobson asked.

"Most of the bishops and cardinals from northern Italy, some in Austria, and the Balkans. And the Pope, of course."

"I have heard rumors like this," Gosser added. "How do you know this isn't just so much gossip?"

Glaring at the hotel owner, Klaus looked like he might take offense at Gosser's question. But he managed to keep his quick temper in check.

"Monks, Herr Gosser. Monks. The church supports some abbeys, but most provide for themselves. Here, the monks make wine. Their loyalty is to God alone, and they despise being used. Monks have a vast network of their own, and they happen to trust me," Klaus explained without any hint of boasting.

Jacobson immediately appreciated the value of this information. A network of informants would be essential if they had any chance of catching Hitler.

"Would they help us?" Jacobson asked.

"I think so, but let's ask. Brother Michael! Would you join us, please?" Klaus shouted.

Jacobson looked around but saw no one. Then, a wooden door set back in a shadowy corner of the café opened slowly, and a small, stooped monk stepped into the room.

Nobody said a word as Brother Michael shuffled across the stone floor, one foot dragging slightly. Dressed in a thick white robe synched together at the waist with a simple rope and a hood pulled over his head, the monk looked almost ghostlike as he approached.

When he arrived at the table, Brother Michael removed the hood, revealing a face bearing deep and unsettling burn scars across its entire right side.

"I am Brother Michael," the monk said in a voice coarse and low with disuse. "You seek Hitler. I know where he is. And I know where he is going next."

CHAPTER FORTY-FOUR

Jacobson's team sat in stunned silence. Brother Michael resembled a mystical druid soothsayer from ages long past. None of them would have been surprised if he produced a magic wand and conjured a crow from thin air.

"Brother Michael, sit and have some wine!" Klaus said loudly, breaking the spell.

Tucker jumped from his seat and pulled a chair up to the table next to Klaus. Nodding his thanks, Michael eased into the chair and filled an empty glass from one of the several unlabeled bottles. After taking several deep gulps, he wiped his lips on his sleeve.

"What can you tell us?" Rachel asked with youthful impatience.

Brother Michael gave Rachel a smile that appeared on only one side of his face.

"Many years have passed since I have had the pleasure of speaking to a beautiful young woman. Or speaking at all, for that matter," Michael replied, his voice just above a whisper. "I took a vow of silence some years ago. But in this matter, silence is not an option, and I'm sure God will grant me forgiveness for breaking that vow. Perhaps Herr Klaus will save me some words and tell you about me."

"If you are sure," Klaus said, again rather loudly.

Michael nodded.

"Brother Michael arrived at the abbey in 1918 as a young man. He came here to recover from chemical burns he suffered in the trenches at the hands of the Germans. Italy fought against Germany in that war. After recovering, he decided to stay and become a monk. Now, his ears make it difficult for him to hear, yet he knows everything going on in the diocese. Yesterday, he told me about a young apprentice nun with an incredible story."

Jacobson listened carefully as Klaus described a message from a nun who claimed to have cooked a meal for none other than Adolf Hitler at the Sabiona Monastery just the night before. She explained how, to her deep embarrassment, one of Bishop Calbiani's staff priests had been making sexual advances toward her. That night, when she had finished washing the dishes, that priest sought her out and boasted that he would be going to the bishop's villa the next day on the Vatican's aircraft. He would be serving the bishop's guests for several more days once they arrived.

Though ashamed, despite never breaking her vows, she sent a message on the next day's supply run to Novacella for her great-uncle – Brother Michael.

"I am shocked at such behavior, but judgment of that priest is for God alone. I shall pray for God to protect Gianna. She has performed a brave deed, but in doing so, has placed herself in grave danger," Brother Michael said with a touch of pride in his voice.

"Did the note say when the plane would leave?" Jacobson asked.

"It left this morning," Michael replied. "It is flying all the way across the country to the Cinque Terre in Liguria. Hitler will be at the bishop's villa in the hills above the town of Monterosso."

"Does she know how long they plan to stay there?" Rachel asked.

"No. Gianna's note only indicated a few days."

"I know Monterosso well," Gosser offered. "It's one of five villages that sit between the mountains and the coast of the Ligurian Sea. A villa in the mountains above would be the perfect place to hide. But you can't fly directly there. The nearest airfields are in Genoa or Pisa, I believe. From there, they would have to take a train or a boat. The area is beautiful but remote."

Jacobson dug through his bag and found a map. He and his team gathered around the table, finding Monterosso hundreds of miles to the southwest as the crow flies. But from Brixen, driving across the country would take days. Days they didn't have.

Rachel looked dejected. "We'll never make it."

"No. Not by car. We need a plane," Jacobson responded.

Klaus grunted loudly. "There are no airplanes for hire in the whole of the Tyrol region. Where will you find this non-existent airplane?"

Jacobson had to smile at Klaus's skepticism.

"General Eisenhower will get me any one I want," Jacobson responded.

CHAPTER FORTY-FIVE

"Where are we going?" Rachel asked as Jacobson's team climbed back into their battered farm truck late in the afternoon.

"Bolzano," Jacobson said, barely glancing away from his map. "There's an American airfield there."

Rachel leaned across Jacobson to get a closer look at the map.

"We will pass directly under the Sabiona Monastery on this route. Should we stop and see Brother Michael's nun on the way?" Rachel suggested.

"I thought about that, but time is of the essence now. And I bet this Bishop Calbiani would be less than pleased to see us. For all we know, Hitler could be boarding a ship tomorrow and sailing away forever."

The shadows from the mountains had already darkened the long valley as Tucker finally pulled alongside the makeshift security shack outside Bolzano's grass airfield. Total darkness would follow quickly. If Jacobson had any hope of commandeering an airplane, he had to move fast.

Earlier, he had changed back into his army uniform and had his men do the same. Convincing the commanding officer at the base to believe his story would be impossible if he still wore civilian attire. The bored private guarding the entrance gave the truck a suspicious look but waved Jacobson through, pointing to an old hangar that served as the airfield's headquarters. Across the grass runway, a row of P-51D Mustang fighters, their yellow noses pointing into the sky, and aluminum bodies glinting in the fading light, sat like a row of unwanted toys. As they pulled around the hangar, Jacobson could also see several small scout planes parked haphazardly in tall grass.

"I don't see any transports," Tucker commented as he parked the truck alongside the hangar.

"Yeah," Jacobson said, undeterred. "Have everyone walk around and see what they can find. We'll need a Douglas C-47 or even a bomber of some kind. You come with me."

Inside, Jacobson and Tucker found a few old wooden desks manned by a single sergeant who slowly lowered his copy of Stars and Stripes when he heard the door open.

"Attention!" Tucker shouted.

The startled enlisted man jumped to his feet. He didn't expect a combat soldier in worn fatigues, chewing a cigar, and carrying a Thompson to burst through the door.

"Who is in charge of this airfield, Sergeant?" Jacobson asked with as much authority as he could muster.

The sergeant looked at the young lieutenant standing in front of his desk.

Who is this guy?

"Answer up, soldier!" Tucker barked.

"Yes, sir. Sorry, sir. Captain Rathman, sir."

"I'm Lieutenant Jacobson. I need to see the captain immediately."

"I'm sorry, sir. The captain is in town tonight, along with most of the squadron. They stood us down a few days ago. There's nobody around but me, a couple of mechanics, and the duty officer, Lieutenant McAllister, I think."

"Where is McAllister then?" Jacobson demanded.

"Probably out in the hangar, sir. That way," the sergeant said, pointing at an interior door.

Jacobson nodded at Tucker, who followed him through the door.

They found themselves in a vast hangar looking at the side of a large white Italian aircraft. The boxy fuselage with a single wing mounted over the body was an old design from the 1930s. One engine hung below each wing with a third mounted in the long snout-like nose.

Jacobson and Tucker walked closer, examining the strange aircraft.

"That's the ugliest dang monstrosity I ever saw," Tucker commented. "No wonder the Italian air force got blown out of the sky so easy."

Suddenly, a voice came from somewhere inside the plane.

"She's ugly as hell but tough as nails."

"Lieutenant McAllister?" Jacobson called.

A moment later, a man in grease-covered overalls jumped out of the side door, wiping his hands on a rag.

"I'm Cy Jacobson. Beautiful plane," Jacobson said, offering his hand.

"I'm McAllister. Y'all need to get your stories straight. What can I do for you boys?" he said in a Tennessee accent.

"Yeah, I suppose you're right. What kind of plane is this?" Jacobson asked.

"She's a Caproni 133, built back in '36 as a private cargo hauler. I found her sitting right here when we took over this airfield."

Jacobson briefly explained their mission, leaving out any reference to Hitler.

"So, you're out here chasing Nazis? That's the craziest story I've heard in a while!" McAllister laughed.

Jacobson pulled his orders from his briefcase and handed them to McAllister. When he finished reading, the pilot gave a low, long whistle.

"You boys sure have friends in high places. So, now I'll ask for real. What can I do for you?"

"Let me ask you two questions," Jacobson said, walking over and looking inside the plane. "Are you a pilot? And, can this thing fly?"

McAllister gave him a toothy grin. "Don't let this get-up fool you. I just like working on planes. I usually fly one of those P-51s outside. As for this, yep, she'll take you wherever you want to go. In fact, I'd fly her all the way back to the States if I could."

Jacobson pulled a map from his briefcase and pointed at the coast on the opposite side of the country. "I need to get here."

"When?"

"Now."

McAllister walked to the door and looked into the sky.

"Sorry, Lieutenant. It's already too dark. I might also point out that flying around in an Italian plane would make us a juicy target. Nobody is supposed to be flying anywhere in Italian airspace without authorization. Can you call someone before we leave and make sure we don't get our asses shot off by our own guys?"

"Yeah. Good call. I'll take care of it. We leave as soon as it's light."

McAllister agreed. "Okay, but this ain't no passenger plane. I hope you don't mind a rough ride."

CHAPTER FORTY-SIX

The next morning

The inside of the transport buzzed, rattled, and shook as air currents tossed the strange-looking airplane all over the sky.

"Sorry about the ride, folks!" McAllister shouted over his shoulder from the cockpit. "We'll be out of this turbulence in a few minutes."

Jacobson's team sat on the bare wood floor of the empty cargo area, holding on to straps mounted along the fuselage. Rachel kept a death grip on Jacobson's arm and buried her face in his shoulder. Gosser sat by himself, trying not to scream whenever the plane suddenly felt like it was falling away from under him. Tucker, Pernell, and Downtown wedged themselves between the aluminum ribs of the airframe and fell fast asleep. A rough plane ride didn't compare to an artillery barrage.

"I do not believe I like flying!" Rachel shouted over the din from the engines as the plane suddenly lurched upward.

"I've only flown once or twice. But it was never like this," Jacobson replied, trying to sound brave and reassuring but mostly failing. "It will get better soon."

As if on cue, the turbulence stopped. Compared to the carnival ride they endured moments before, the ride now felt like a new Cadillac gliding along smooth concrete.

"You okay over there, Gosser?" Jacobson asked.

"Harrowing. Just harrowing," Gosser commented. "I've never experienced anything like that. God willing, I shall not again."

The hotel owner's obvious distress quieted Rachel's self-consciousness about her own reaction to flying.

"I am sorry I held on to you so tightly," she said, a little embarrassed as she released her grip on Jacobson's arm.

"I'm not. In fact, there may be more bumps. Better leave your hand there just in case."

Rachel wrapped her arm back under Jacobson's. Even while riding in an airplane that she firmly believed would plummet into the earth at any moment, she realized she hadn't felt so safe and secure since the days before the Nazis dragged her into a concentration camp.

Gosser saw the couple across the plane talking intimately with one another, their heads nearly touching. For some reason, they reminded him of the time before the war. A time when people could be happy. When people allowed each other to be happy. Jacobson and Rachel's obvious feelings gave him hope that one day he might rediscover that kind of joy in his own life.

"Hey, Jacobson!" McAllister called from the cockpit. "It's about an hour to the coast. You want to tell me exactly where you want to go?"

Jacobson reluctantly unwound his arm from Rachel, climbed up into the co-pilot's seat, and unfolded his now-tattered map.

"I don't have information about all the available airfields, but the airport at La Spezia looks like as close as we can get to our destination," Jacobson said, pointing to the Italian city forty miles south of Monterosso.

McAllister took the map and scanned the area.

"Take the wheel a second while I look at my charts. That map is for you infantry guys. Mine are for pilots," McAllister said, letting go of the yoke and searching around his seat.

"I don't know how to fly," Jacobson objected, grabbing the large wheel in front of him.

"Just hold the damn thing still for a minute," McAllister prompted, spreading his aerial charts out on his lap.

Jacobson sat as still as a statue, his hands not moving a millimeter. For several minutes, McAllister studied the detailed charts of western Italy while sweat formed on Jacobson's forehead. Once, McAllister looked up, pulled back on the yoke a bit, and looked back at his charts. Finally, the pilot pointed to a tiny airfield only six miles down the coast from Monterosso.

"I can get us in here. It's short, rough, and probably hasn't been used since the start of the war. La Spezia is too close to the Allied airbase at Rosignano for an Italian-made plane. The war may be over, but even with whoever you talked to paving the way for us, I don't want to tempt some cowboy pilot trying to make a name for himself."

Jacobson glanced at the map and quickly turned back to look out the front windscreen.

"Sounds perfect," Jacobson agreed quickly. "Uh, would you mind taking over now before we crash and die horrible deaths?"

McAllister laughed out loud and looked at the instruments. "You did great. Kept us straight and almost level. Not bad."

Jacobson gratefully let go of the yoke, and McAllister swung the plane onto a new heading.

"Why don't y'all get a few minutes of shuteye?" McAllister suggested. "Looks like a heavy day for you. Say, who are you chasing anyway? With all the authority you have in that briefcase, y'all must be going after Adolf Hitler himself."

"As a matter of fact, it is," Jacobson responded, trying his best to sound sarcastic.

McAllister laughed out loud. "Alright then, don't tell me!"

CHAPTER FORTY-SEVEN

Near Monterosso, Italy

High above the quaint seaside town of Monterosso, Skorzeny enjoyed a view of the bright blue Ligurian Sea glinting and flashing in the morning sun from the balcony of Bishop Calbiani's luxury villa. Steep mountainsides framed the breathtaking scenery before him while a refreshing breeze gently rose up from the deep valley below. Waterfalls along the small river flowing through the valley added pleasant background music to the relaxing vista. The opulent villa provided a much-needed respite after his team's traumatic flight out of Berlin and harrowing escape through the Alps.

Skorzeny approved of their current location. A single-lane, steep dirt track up to the villa provided near-perfect privacy. The bishop had assured Skorzeny that, other than the little-used road to town, only a few old goat trails led anywhere close to the property. Skorzeny's professional evaluation told him it would take a dedicated team of well-trained commandos, like his own unit, to successfully assault their current position.

But the SS Colonel refused to let his guard down. Immediately upon arrival, Skorzeny deployed his two remaining SS soldiers into the heavily wooded area surrounding the house to locate any weak points in the natural defenses.

"A lovely view, is it not, Otto?" Hitler said, strolling up behind the SS Colonel.

Skorzeny spun around and snapped to attention. He had not heard Hitler approach.

"Yes, Mein Führer," Skorzeny barked formally.

"Otto, Otto. Be at ease. Let us enjoy this place while we are able," Hitler said, walking past Skorzeny to the railing. "This view reminds me somewhat of my Eagles Nest above Berchtesgaden. As you know, it was my habit to go there when I needed rest or when a celebration was in order. Today, this place shall serve both purposes as well. Do you agree?"

Skorzeny never totally relaxed in Hitler's presence, but he turned to look at the view alongside the German dictator. "I do, Mein Führer. But I look forward to tomorrow when you shall be in the care of your best U-boat captain and safely on your way to Argentina."

"Yes, I do as well. Let us review our plan once again, shall we?" Hitler replied.

"Of course, Mein Führer," Skorzeny began. "Tomorrow, a few minutes before dawn, we shall take the cars back down the mountain. Once at the shore, we shall drive a short distance along the beach to its southern tip. U-boat 110, commanded by Oberleutnant Schäffer, will be waiting at the end of an ancient stone jetty. I believe you decorated Schäffer on several occasions."

"Yes, I recall. Do you approve of this plan, my boy?" Hitler asked, a rare hint of anxiety in his voice.

"I do, Mein Führer," Skorzeny replied with confidence. "The flight arranged by Bishop Calbiani has put us out of reach of any pursuers. Herr Deacon has communicated that U-110 will be at the rendezvous point on time. Many fine people and organizations have aided us with this journey, and many more are awaiting your orders to begin building the Fourth Reich. The voyage to Argentina will take several weeks, but I am assured that preparations for your arrival are complete. At your word, forces across every continent will be set in motion that shall ensure the survival and expansion of National Socialist policies."

"Yet, I am also beset with traitors and those that wish only to use me for selfish reasons."

Skorzeny could see Hitler struggling with self-doubt. Only those closest to the Führer ever caught a glimpse of the man's human side.

"Mein Führer, there shall always be those who doubt your strength and challenge your leadership. And, there shall always be some that attach themselves to you, like the sucking remora fish on a mighty shark. But such scum pale in comparison to those who see your vision and stand by your side. Many of the world's wealthiest men, huge companies, and corporations have already offered their long-term support. You have friends and allies not only in the motherland but in Great Britain, the United States, and many other countries. I believe that today, even as the Fourth Reich is in its infancy and its leaders are being hunted, its true size is far greater than anyone could imagine. The world has not yet witnessed its glory, but the Fourth Reich already exists and awaits your leadership."

Hitler grasped the railing with both hands and gazed over the sea toward the distant horizon. Tendrils of his hair blew back in the ocean breeze, and the sun lit his face in golden light. Skorzeny could see him swell with deep determination as if summoning the Fourth Reich's rebirth through sheer force of will.

Hitler had suffered greatly and grown old. But with a new challenge ahead, his strength seemed to be returning quickly. Skorzeny knew that the Nazis would rise again. And this time, they would wage a new kind of war altogether. Ruthless politicians would replace soldiers, and propaganda would take the place of bullets and bombs.

Skorzeny had seen this coming. Powerful men pulled strings from behind desks and inside boardrooms, asserting control over governments and entire economies while maximizing profits. Even as the German army rolled over much of Europe in the early days of the war, the multinational companies that provided the Third Reich with everything from cigarettes to bombers had already won. Now, those same companies, and others like them around the globe, owned or controlled most of the wealth in the world.

But to keep it, they needed Hitler. Or a man just like him.

Full resurrection may take decades, but fascism will dominate the world.

CHAPTER FORTY-EIGHT

As the lumbering aircraft approached the Italian coast, McAllister picked out the tiny airfield carved into a plateau high in the mountains. With tall trees on all sides, it appeared he would be attempting to land in a shoebox.

"This is going to be bumpy! Hold on!" McAllister yelled over screaming engines and howling wind.

Banking the big Caproni into a tight turn, he knew he had only one chance to line up his plane on the short landing field. And he had to be perfect. If he missed to the left or right and a wing clipped the trees, the plane would spin into the forest. And if that weren't enough, he had to come in low and drop the aircraft onto the ground as soon as his nose passed over the rough runway or risk tearing the plane apart at the other end.

Other pilots, perhaps more reasonable pilots, would have refused to even attempt the landing. But not McAllister. He had been a bush pilot in Alaska before the war, delivering supplies to frozen outposts and flying rescue crews onto steep glaciers. And he loved a challenge.

The plane vibrated badly as huge flaps lowered into position. McAllister added power, keeping the plane just above stall speed. Trees flashed by under the heavy fixed landing gear. Ahead, the airfield grew larger and larger in the windscreen. When the last tree passed below, McAllister cut the throttles.

The plane practically fell onto the ground, bounced once, and settled. When McAllister turned the propellers into reverse, his passengers smashed together in a heap against the forward bulkhead.

The master pilot gently and expertly applied the brakes as the plane skidded across the slick grass field. He almost warned his passengers to brace for a collision, but the tires finally found enough grip to slow the plane's headlong plunge toward the woods, coming to a stop with only ten yards to spare.

McAllister wiped a bead of sweat off his forehead and turned his aircraft around to face in the opposite direction.

"Sorry about that, folks," he called back from the cockpit. "You've arrived at the sunny Italian coast. And thanks for flying McAllister Airlines."

"Jeez, I want my money back," Pernell declared, rubbing the back of his head.

"Is anyone injured?" Jacobson asked while they all found their feet again.

After everyone checked in unhurt, he added, "Okay, grab your gear. Let's get moving."

***

Outside the plane, Jacobson stopped to shake McAllister's hand.

"Y'all know where you're going from here?" the pilot asked. "In Tennessee, this is what we would call the backwoods."

"Yeah, we'll be fine. Tucker grew up in the woods, and the coast is only a couple of miles from here. I can't thank you enough for the lift," Jacobson replied.

"I thought I recognized a familiar twang in the sergeant's voice. Those orders you've got didn't leave me any choice. But to be honest, I would have flown you over here anyway just to get my beautiful bird up in the air. That's thanks enough. I only wish I could afford to ship her home," McAllister said, wistfully patting the side of the plane.

Jacobson quickly reached deep into his briefcase.

"Here, this should cover it," he said, handing McAllister two heavy gold coins.

The pilot turned the gold over and over in his hand, his eyes almost as wide as the coins he held.

"Good god! Are you foolin' me, Cy?" McAllister blurted.

Jacobson knew they would never have caught up to Hitler without McAllister's help and expertise. And Agent Smith had told him to spend the money as he saw fit.

"Those are yours. We'll call it traveling expenses," Jacobson replied.

"You want me to hang around in case you need a ride back? I mean, it's the least I could do," McAllister offered.

"Thanks, but I don't know how long we'll be here," Jacobson answered, turning back to his team.

***

They all watched from the edge of the forest as McAllister gunned the plane's engines and sped down the field. As the ungainly bird lurched into the air, one of the wheels snapped the top off a dead tree, making the entire team flinch in unison. But as he turned the plane away, McAllister wagged the wings in a final goodbye.

"Pernell, unpack that radio. Let's see if we can get a signal up here," Jacobson ordered.

A minute later, Pernell unfolded the antenna and cranked power into the radio.

"All set, Lieutenant."

Jacobson took the microphone. "Orion 6 to Smith. Come in, please."

Smith answered almost at once. "Smith to Orion 6. Report."

"We are in Liguria, near the town of Monterosso on the Italian west coast. We have reliable information that our primary target is near the town in a villa owned by Bishop Antonio Calbiani. The target plans to leave the country by boat or submarine in the next twenty-four to forty-eight hours. We request reinforcements. Over."

"We are checking for assets close to your location now, Orion 6. How credible is your information? Over."

"One hundred percent. Over."

Jacobson held his breath, waiting for Smith's reply. He had seen the ferocity of the men defending Adolf Hitler, and he had no way of knowing how many of those SS guards he still had at his side. While the lieutenant deeply admired the fighting skill of Tucker and his men, like any good commander, he didn't want a fair fight. He wanted all the help he could get.

"Smith to Orion 6. There is no backup available for you at this time. Over."

Without keying the mic, Jacobson barked, "Damnit!"

"Orion 6 to Smith. Our information is solid. I am with two eye-witnesses right now. I say again. We require backup. Over."

"Orion 6. Your message is understood. Be advised, we are in contact with two other teams that report they are close to capturing our primary target. One of those teams reports having visual contact with the subject as we speak, and, like you, they want reinforcements. Repeat. No reinforcements are available at this time. Over."

"Orion 6 to Smith. Sir...."

Before Jacobson could argue further, Smith cut back in.

"Orion 6. You are on your own. Good hunting. Smith out."

Jacobson had to restrain himself from tearing the microphone out of the radio console and throwing it over the mountainside. Instead, he handed the headphones and mic back to Pernell and wiped the sweat off the back of his neck with a handkerchief before turning to address the team he had come to trust and rely on fully.

"Okay. We're it. I wish we could wait to make our final move until more help arrives, but we can't," Jacobson stated with calm authority.

The news about reinforcements didn't surprise Tucker, Pernell, and Downtown. They had seen enough war to know the score. The people in charge almost never granted such requests. But in the last few days, Jacobson had more than earned their respect. They would follow him into hell if necessary.

"Which way do we need to go, sir?" Tucker asked.

"Down. Toward the sea."

"What are we looking for on the coast?" Gosser wanted to know.

Jacobson unfolded his map and laid it on the ground.

"Yeah. Let's take a breath. Gather around. We are here," Jacobson said, pointing to their location two miles inland. "Monterosso is here on the coast, about six miles north. First, we have to get off this mountain and down to the beach. From there, we'll need a road to town or a boat to take us there by sea. Sergeant, please have your men take the lead."

"You heard the lieutenant, Pernell. Find us a way to the ocean," Tucker ordered.

Jacobson's team plunged into the forest of the Italian coast. Overhead, a thick canopy of branches and leaves blotted out most of the sunlight. The lack of a trail forced them to pick one uncertain path after another. Massive boulders jutting from the mountainside slowed their progress, and they had to double back more than once when they encountered high cliffs or steep ravines.

Finally, after two hours of making little progress and sweating in the gloomy, dank forest, Pernell held a fist over his head and dropped to one knee. Jacobson motioned for everyone to get down and keep quiet.

While Pernell kept watch, Downtown crouched low and quietly made his way back to Jacobson.

"Looks like a local coming up a trail leading a couple of donkeys. He's just a kid. Maybe ten or eleven. Not much of a threat. You want us to stop him?" Downtown asked in a low voice.

"Two American soldiers stepping out of the woods might scare him away," Jacobson replied, thinking out loud.

Rachel put a hand on Jacobson's shoulder. "Let me talk to him. Downtown and Pernell can keep an eye on me."

Jacobson didn't like the idea of sending Rachel ahead on her own, but as usual, she was right. The unexpected appearance of a girl on the trail wouldn't be nearly as frightening as two combat soldiers.

"Okay. See if you can find out where the trail leads and how we can get to Monterosso," Jacobson agreed quietly.

Rachel straightened her dress and walked casually out onto the trail, looking all around as if lost. After a moment, she noticed that the boy had stopped the donkeys and was eyeing her with fear and suspicion.

"Buongiorno!" Rachel called. "Good morning!"

Seeing nobody else around, the boy yanked on the ropes around his donkeys' necks and trod slowly up the path toward Rachel while keeping one wary eye on the woods. The boy had probably been warned that robbers or other outlaws often hid out in the forest and to beware of traps.

"Buongiorno, Signorina," the boy said, politely doffing his old wool cap without offering a smile.

"Perhaps you can help me," Rachel said in Italian. "Is this the trail to Monterosso?"

"Monterosso? No. No. This trail goes to my family's farm below. From there, it leads only to the shore. Monterosso is on the other side of the mountain. There is no trail from this side."

Rachel planted herself on the ground and started to cry.

"My boyfriend brought me into the mountains for a picnic, but we got in a fight. I refused to leave with him, and I have been walking around all night trying to find my way home," Rachel explained as sadly as possible.

The ruse worked.

The boy responded quickly. "Do not worry, Signorina. It is not impossible to get to Monterosso. Just follow the path past my family's house. Keep going until you find a small beach. My uncle has a fishing boat that can take you to Monterosso. Tell him you met me. My name is Lorenzo. Lorenzo Pagolo. My Uncle is Stefano. He takes passengers sometimes for a little extra money."

Rachel stood and wiped her eyes. "You are my hero, Lorenzo! Grazia! Grazia!"

She bent and kissed Lorenzo on both cheeks, making the boy blush.

After saying their goodbyes, Lorenzo and his donkeys continued their slow climb up the mountain. When he had disappeared around a corner, Rachel waved the others forward and told them what she had learned.

"Perfect!" Jacobson exclaimed. "Now all we have to do is find this Stefano. I hope he's home."

"I hope he has something to eat," Downtown muttered.

***

While still on the trail, Gosser suggested a cover story to explain how they came to be standing on a nearly deserted beach after trekking out of the mountains.

"A fabrication is best when it contains a partial truth. Tell the fisherman you were sent into this area to arrest an Austrian collaborator hiding from the authorities. I am your prisoner, and you need a way to transport me to Pisa or Genoa," Gosser suggested.

"What about me?" Rachel asked.

"The lieutenant can say he simply found you with me. He doesn't know who you are, but he couldn't leave you behind," Gosser offered.

"It ain't a great story, but I can't think of a better one either," Tucker added.

Stefano's house turned out to be a two-room shack built directly on the beach but set back from the water. A long, open fishing boat with chipped bright blue paint and loaded with fishing nets bobbed in the water just offshore. A single long rope tied to a heavy boulder kept the boat from floating away.

Stefano couldn't have been more surprised to find four American soldiers, a Jewish girl, and a nervous Austrian standing in his doorway. He stepped from the shack dressed in thick, tattered overalls. Forearms that looked like they were stuffed with steel cables protruded from the rolled-up sleeves of a stained blue shirt. He looked at the group through dark eyes from which deep lines reached back toward his ears – a testament to a life spent squinting in the bright Mediterranean sun.

With Rachel translating, Jacobson explained their situation as Gosser suggested.

"He doesn't believe a word you said and wants us to go away," Rachel explained.

"Did you tell him we could pay?" Jacobson asked.

"Of course. But he doesn't like Americans or Austrians or Jews."

Jacobson had anticipated some resistance, but not quite this much. Luckily, he had come prepared. He reached into his pocket and took out a gold coin.

"Let's see if he likes this," Jacobson said, holding the coin between his thumb and forefinger so it glinted in the sun.

Stefano took the coin and examined it closely.

"Due," Stefano said firmly, holding up two fingers.

Instead of negotiating, Jacobson said, "Tell him I'll give him another as soon as we get to Monterosso. Not before."

As soon as Rachel translated the offer, Stefano jumped off his low porch. "Si! Si! We go! We go!"

"Looks like we got a ride," Tucker said.

"Yeah. Great. But what will we find when we get there?" Pernell responded.

CHAPTER FORTY-NINE

The old outboard motor coughed to life only after Stefano spent several minutes cursing and smacking it with a hammer. The display of Italian temper and the reluctance of the engine to comply with Stefano's demands made Jacobson's entire team doubt whether they would ever see Monterosso without winding up in the sea.

"I hate boats," Downtown said as he watched Stefano struggle with the ancient motor. "I'd go see if I could help, but somehow I don't think the old boy would appreciate it."

"Why don't you like boats?" Pernell asked.

"Because the last one we were on sank. Or don't you remember?" Downtown responded.

"Our landing craft got hit way back on D-Day. Not exactly the boat's fault," Pernell chided.

"We got thrown into the channel. I almost drowned!"

While Pernell and Downtown continued bickering, the engine coughed to life, and Stefano untied the boat from its anchor rock.

"We go! We go!"

Jacobson hurried everyone into the boat, causing it to settle alarmingly low in the water.

"How far to Monterosso?" Jacobson asked Stefano, with Rachel interpreting.

Stefano looked at Jacobson and said, "Dieci kilometers. No problem! No problem!"

***

Fortunately for Jacobson and his team, the Ligurian Sea decided to grant them an easy passage. The boat sped across the deep blue, glassy water while the incredibly bright Mediterranean sun warmed the majestic coastline. High tree-covered mountains reached all the way to the water's edge, with tiny beaches interspersed in narrow valleys. The old engine hummed along happily, and Jacobson's anxiety melted away as Stefano expertly navigated around several massive boulders protruding from the water.

"It is beautiful here, is it not?" Rachel asked Jacobson. "I have heard of the Cinque Terre but never believed I would see it for myself."

"Cinque Terre? What does that mean?" Jacobson asked.

"It means 'five lands.' Monterosso is one of five villages built on the edge of the sea in the valleys between the mountains. Maybe we can come back when our work is done?" Rachel said suggestively, looking into the lieutenant's eyes.

Jacobson reached over and took Rachel's hand. "I'd like that very much."

Nobody in the boat noticed the affectionate exchange except Stefano.

"Ah, amore. Amore."

Jacobson looked back at the fisherman, who grinned and squinted ahead.

"What did he say?" Jacobson asked Rachel.

"I will tell you another time," Rachel replied, squeezing Jacobson's hand.

***

Twenty minutes later, the fishing boat swung around a point of land, allowing Jacobson's team their first view of Monterosso. A wide crescent beach stretched for almost a mile to the far north end of the town. Brightly colored fishing boats lined the shore in front of a row of tiny shops and cafés. Inland from the beach area, rustic buildings and houses painted yellow, orange, and pink clung to the steep slopes above the ocean. Jacobson marveled for a moment at the charming little village perched precariously between the mountains and the sea. But his thoughts quickly returned to their deadly serious mission.

Even as Stefano grounded the boat on the beach, Jacobson knew that somewhere in the mountains high above, Adolf Hitler and his SS guards could be watching them.

But it wasn't the mountains he should have been worried about.

CHAPTER FIFTY

Two young boys knelt on the warm sand of Monterosso's beach, intensely scanning the ocean. They barely blinked, each determined to be the first to spot any strangers arriving in their town by boat. Earlier that day, a priest had approached them as they kicked a half-deflated old soccer ball to each other near the beachside shops and offered a twenty lire coin to whoever first reported seeing soldiers, especially Americans, to him in a nearby café.

Neither Carlo nor Dino had ever held a twenty lire coin, much less owned so much money. So, both twelve-year-olds readily agreed, thrilled at the prospect of witnessing real American soldiers and winning a veritable fortune.

Carlo was the first to see Stefano's blue fishing boat appear from around the point. But his friend, Dino, had better eyesight.

"That's old Stefano's boat! And he has passengers!" Dino cried, squinting into the bright sun. "American soldiers!"

"You don't know that they are Americans," Carlo objected.

"Fine. You stay here, and I'll get the lire," Dino countered, jumping to his feet.

"Not if I pound your head into the sand!" Carlo shouted, grabbing Dino by the collar of his blue striped shirt.

Dino slapped Carlo's hand away, and the two pushed and shoved each other in a rowdy scuffle. By the time their tempers cooled enough to look around, the boat had already grounded itself near the water's edge. As they watched, four soldiers, a dark-haired girl, and a short, balding man climbed from the boat.

"I saw them first!" Carlo announced, suddenly kicking Dino's feet out from under him.

As Dino struggled to get up, Carlo sprinted away, his feet throwing up little bursts of sand.

Less than a minute later, Carlo held the shiny coin, and one of Bishop Calbiani's loyal priests knew all about Jacobson's arrival.

***

Colonel Skorzeny slammed the receiver of the telephone onto the table. The antiquated phone system barely allowed him to understand the priest's report, but the message had been clear enough. Four American soldiers, along with two civilians, had entered Monterosso.

And Skorzeny knew who they were.

Anger rose in the SS officer's throat, making him want to lash out at the first person he saw. How could Jacobson have followed them here? He had left the Americans stranded back in the mountains of Austria! They could not have known his route from that point. And his decision to come to this particular spot on the nearly-empty coast of Italy had only been made hours before they departed from Sabiona Monastery. Skorzeny could think of only one explanation.

Someone betrayed them.

After taking a deep breath to calm his nerves, Skorzeny retrieved the handset.

"What are your instructions, Colonel?" the priest asked.

"Leave them alone. Keep them under surveillance, but do not approach. I'll deal with the Americans personally."

CHAPTER FIFTY-ONE

"Dang, we stick out like a sore thumb in these uniforms," Tucker commented as they walked along the sidewalk next to the cafés and shops near the beach.

"I don't think we'd pass for Italians even if we were back in civilian clothes," Jacobson responded, looking up at the tall red-headed sergeant.

"Maybe not, sir. But these folks are looking at us like we came from Mars or something."

"I know. We won't be here long. We just need directions to Bishop Calbiani's villa, and we'll be on our way. Maybe we could calm some nerves and get some cooperation if we find the mayor or whatever of this place and give him an explanation about why we're here," Jacobson suggested.

Gosser overheard the conversation.

"That is an excellent idea. We might tell him we are scouting for places American officers can rest and recuperate. Promise them substantial business, and you shall have all the information you need. I could act as your consultant."

Jacobson gave the plan some thought. "I like it."

"And I can be your translator," Rachel added.

"Alright then, let's go find the mayor," Jacobson agreed. "But stay alert. The Nazis will have people watching the town. I don't want any surprises."

***

Skorzeny and his two men wasted no time descending from the villa to Monterosso. The SS Colonel had to admit that Jacobson had shown remarkable cunning and tenaciousness in tracking him to Monterosso. The American lieutenant had proved himself even more dangerous than he first suspected. Now he had no choice but to deal with the Americans' sudden and unexpected appearance. Skorzeny knew he could easily ambush Jacobson in town, but his first and most important task was to hand Hitler over to the U-Boat captain waiting somewhere offshore. A firefight in the streets would only draw unnecessary attention from the locals and whatever police presence existed, jeopardizing the secrecy of Hitler's presence.

Skorzeny needed a way to delay Jacobson for another 18 hours – just long enough for Hitler to slip away early the next morning.

Dressed in civilian clothes, Skorzeny and his men found Calbiani's priest still sitting at the café near the water.

"Where are the Americans now?" Skorzeny asked.

"I will know shortly," the priest replied.

Skorzeny shot an intense glare at the other man. "You don't know?"

The priest seemed to melt under the SS commando's gaze. "I...I didn't think it would be wise for me to follow the Americans in my cassock. I am not a spy. I sent Carlo and Dino. I'm sure they will return here momentarily. I promised them each a lira to keep an eye on the strangers."

"And who are Carlo and Dino?" Skorzeny growled.

Just as the priest began to explain, Dino appeared, removed his cap, and walked quickly to the priest's table. He looked at the huge SS officer and the scar on his face. For a moment, the boy looked like he might run away in fright.

"All is well, Dino. This man is a friend," the priest said. "Now, where are the strangers?"

The priest's assurances calmed the boy enough to report what he knew.

"They went to see the mayor, Father," Dino responded, obviously still nervous. "Carlo is across the street watching what they do next."

"How many Americans did you see?" Skorzeny asked, trying not to frighten the child further.

Dino glanced at the priest, who nodded that he should answer.

"We saw four soldiers. I guess they were Americans. And they had a girl and an older man with them," Dino replied, not taking his eyes off the floor.

"Did you hear anything they said?" Skorzeny asked.

"Yes," Dino responded warily. "But I do not know what they said. They spoke only English."

"Where is the mayor's office?" Skorzeny asked the priest. "Perhaps I shall pay him a visit as well."

CHAPTER FIFTY-TWO

The mayor of Monterosso nearly panicked when his secretary announced that several American soldiers were in the office and wanted to see him.

What could Americans want with a small, out-of-the-way village such as this?

The war had not touched this part of Italy. No soldiers had ever been stationed in Monterosso. And, the people knew little to nothing of the politics in Rome, Mussolini's crimes, or fascism. More importantly, he had been elected to office almost fifteen years before the country fell under the dictator's spell. Whatever the Americans wanted, it couldn't involve him.

Despite his fears, he had no choice. He must deal with them.

After straightening his tie and pulling on the near-threadbare suit coat he kept in his office for visitors, the mayor opened the door. He was surprised to find a lieutenant dressed in a new uniform, accompanied by three obviously battle-hardened soldiers, a Jewish girl, and a fidgeting Austrian. He politely invited them into his office, but only the lieutenant, the girl, and the Austrian entered. The other soldiers remained in the outer office, gratefully sipping on tiny cups of espresso offered by his secretary.

"Good afternoon, I am Mayor de Marco. How may I be of service?" he asked in Italian since he knew no English whatsoever.

With Rachel interpreting, Jacobson introduced himself and the others.

"Thank you for seeing us, Mayor de Marco. I am Lieutenant Jacobson, and this is Herr Gosser, my destinations consultant," Jacobson began. "I hope our arrival here has caused no trouble."

Relieved at Jacobson's friendly manner, the mayor instantly became the consummate politician and smiled broadly. "Of course not. All are welcome here in Monterosso! I hope you find our town appealing."

"In fact, we do, Mr. Mayor. Very much so. I have been tasked with looking for quiet locations for members of our officer corps to rest and recuperate while stationed here in Italy. After being in Monterosso for only a short time, I think your town could be perfect for us."

The prospect of American officers coming to Monterosso seemed implausible to the mayor, at least at first. But he quickly recognized the opportunity this lieutenant had just presented. His rather poor little town could benefit a great deal from the money a steady flow of American officers would bring. And, if they enjoyed their visits, perhaps word would spread, and Monterosso would become a tourist destination. If so, he would get all the credit.

"I see," de Marco replied, trying to conceal his excitement. "This is quite interesting. We have several local inns, restaurants, and cafés. But the beauty of our land and ocean are our greatest asset."

"Of course. But I worry about your isolation here," Jacobson responded. "It is quite lovely, but the trip here from Genoa was not easy."

The mayor knew this would be a concern. The town's location had always made vacationers reluctant to make the trip, despite its stunning landscape, warm waters, and friendly people.

"Yes. Our little town is secluded. But that is also part of its charm. We have several notable people who come here regularly. Some have even built villas in the hills," de Marco explained.

"Oh? Would you mind sharing who they might be?" Jacobson asked smoothly.

"Well, everyone knows that the Bishop of Bolzano-Brixen himself owns a truly magnificent villa in the hills just a few kilometers from here," the mayor said proudly.

"Yes, Lieutenant," Gosser agreed. "This is true. I believe the villa sits to the north of town."

Gosser's ploy worked.

"No, no. The villa is built on the mountain to the south and east of here, on the road leading to the chapel of Madonna di Soviore. The bishop regularly comes into town to enjoy the fresh fish and other delicacies of the sea. The road to the bishop's residence begins at the end of Via Roma, only one kilometer from here."

"Thank you, Mr. Mayor," Jacobson said formally, rising from his seat. "My team will spend the afternoon in town, inspect the local establishments, and perhaps partake in some of your delicacies if that would be acceptable to you."

"Of course. Of course!" the mayor gushed, already imagining rich American officers lavishly spending their dollars. "I would be pleased to give you a personal tour of our beautiful village if you like."

Jacobson didn't need the overly effusive man interfering in his operation.

"Thank you, Mr. Mayor. You are too kind. But I'd prefer to take in the sights for myself and discuss everything with my consultant. I'm sure you understand."

"Yes. Yes. Please, make yourselves at home. I am available to you any time."

***

Skorzeny and his two remaining commandos didn't know the layout of Monterosso. They enlisted the priest to guide them through the narrow winding streets to the somewhat dilapidated building that served as the tiny town's government offices. Dino tagged along at the rear of the group, hoping to witness something exciting – or earn more easy money.

The Germans cautiously approached the mayor's office, stopping two blocks away in case the Americans posted men outside to keep watch. The steep cobblestone street in front of the government offices ran from the beach directly up through the center of town.

Skorzeny sent Dino to find Carlo.

When Carlo joined them, Skorzeny asked, "Are they still inside?"

With the priest translating, Carlo confirmed that the Americans had not reappeared.

"Mr. Priest," Skorzeny said, "I have a job for these boys. You will explain it to them. They will each earn a silver coin."

The priest listened carefully before explaining Skorzeny's offer to Carlo and Dino. With eyes as wide as dinner plates at the prospect of getting their hands on a genuine silver coin, the boys agreed to do as Skorzeny wanted.

Skorzeny sent the priest scurrying back to the café near the beach and waited for Jacobson to emerge from the government building. As a military man, he couldn't help thinking about how easy it would be to trap the Americans in a deadly crossfire and end Jacobson's dogged pursuit right then and there. But that would attract unwanted attention to his operation. Instead, the SS Colonel had something less direct but much more diabolical in mind.

CHAPTER FIFTY-THREE

After Tucker sent Pernell and Downtown to either end of the block as lookouts, Jacobson and the rest of his team stepped into the bright afternoon sunshine and paused to discuss their next move.

"I'm open to suggestions," Jacobson said to Tucker, Gosser, and Rachel. "How do we pry Hitler out of a secluded mountain villa?"

Tucker stuck a half-smoked cigar in his mouth and scratched at the stubble on his chin before answering.

"That ain't going to be easy. We don't know how many guards he has up there. And by now, I doubt we have the element of surprise on our side. On top of that, it looks like there's only one little road to the place. A direct assault would be suicide."

Gosser added, "These little towns along the coast all have paths and trails that lead into the mountains, much like the path where we encountered Lorenzo. They are narrow, steep, and difficult. One man with a rifle could stop anyone from approaching the house. But we don't know if such a trail even exists."

"Can we climb the mountain on either side of the road?" Jacobson offered.

"Not if the terrain is anything like what we encountered this morning," Tucker responded. "Even if we found our way through these dense forests, we wouldn't be in any shape to attack a well-defended strong point."

Jacobson nodded his agreement.

"Alternatives?"

"Ambush," Tucker offered almost immediately. "Hitler has to use the same road to get back to the beach or wherever he wants to go next. So, we just find us a natural chokepoint and bag him whenever he shows his ugly face."

"May I make a suggestion?" Gosser asked. "Perhaps we can entice Hitler to abandon his hiding place. If we convince them we will soon receive reinforcements, perhaps they will move Hitler more quickly than they would otherwise."

"Gosser, you are one crafty SOB, but that might put Rachel in more danger. I expect they will try to get Hitler out to sea somehow, but we don't know when. Most likely in the next day. We will have to be ready to ambush him in some kind of trap or something near the foot of the mountains. Probably by the coast," Jacobson said.

"I can't think of anything better," Tucker agreed. "Luckily, we got a guy with us who can build anything."

The three men discussed several options, trying to flesh out the quickly evolving plan.

They didn't see Rachel wander away.

***

Rachel didn't try to assist Jacobson, Tucker, and Gosser with military tactics. Instead, she sat down on the stoop in front of the government building and enjoyed being outside in the sunshine of the Italian coast. They had been chasing Hitler for days, and she hadn't taken a moment to just revel in her newfound freedom from the hideous Nazi prison camp.

At that moment, she couldn't have been happier. She vowed to never take the simple joy of being free for granted. But she would never forget or forgive how the German people so readily embraced the fear-mongering Nazi propaganda. And she silently promised herself to somehow, someday, hold the Nazis accountable for the deaths of her family and her people.

Rachel forced the dark thoughts from her mind and refocused on where she was at that moment – and the presence of a man she had to admit she had fallen in love with. She let herself imagine building a life with Lieutenant Cy Jacobson, maybe even in America. Rachel shook her head and told herself to stop daydreaming like a little girl. But she couldn't. She didn't want to stop.

Two boys playing catch with a red rubber ball farther up the street interrupted Rachel's musings. She watched the ball fly through the air, and the boys argue over who could throw it the farthest. The quaint, everyday scene brought a smile to her face.

Suddenly, one of the boys threw the ball hard against the wall of a building, causing it to bounce away in her direction. As it did, the boys shouted at her in Italian.

"Signora! Signora! Per favore!"

They wanted her to grab the ball before it rolled all the way to the bottom of the hill.

Rachel jumped to her feet and snatched the ball off the ground just as it was about to bounce by.

The boys waved and smiled as Rachel walked up the hill. Just as she got close enough to toss the ball back, both boys gestured for her to follow them and ran off down a side street.

Thinking they wanted her to somehow participate in their game, Rachel followed them to the corner. But when she arrived, the boys had disappeared. Confused, Rachel took one step down the street.

Just past the corner, a massive arm wrapped around her waist. Before she could scream, a hand clamped down over her mouth. In seconds, someone lifted her off the ground and carried her into a nearby building.

***

"Hey, Sarge!" Pernell shouted from up the street.

"What?" Tucker called back, irritated at the interruption.

"You seen Miss Rachel anywhere?"

Jacobson took notice as soon as Pernell asked about Rachel. He turned around and tried to figure out where she could have gone.

Not yet worried, Jacobson called back. "She's not down here. Take a look around. She couldn't have gone far."

Pernell walked farther up the road, checking several intersections and peering into a few shop windows.

"She's not here, Lieutenant!"

"Tucker, help Pernell. I'll join Downtown," Jacobson ordered, a little exasperated at Rachel for wandering off. "Gosser, stay here in case she comes back."

As the minutes ticked by, their search grew increasingly intense. They knocked on doors, checked inside any open businesses, and called her name in the streets. After twenty minutes, Jacobson called the remaining team back together.

"Damnit!" Jacobson spat. "What the hell is going on?"

"Yeah, I got a bad feeling," Tucker added.

Jacobson's stomach churned with guilt. He knew Hitler's men probably knew that he and his team had entered the town. The Germans had attempted to stop them twice before, and he should have taken more precautions. The SS could be anywhere. Now, Rachel had gone missing.

As they discussed what to do next, Gosser pointed to a man with a short gray beard slowly coming down the hill using a long walking stick. The newcomer wore a tattered suit jacket and a pair of work pants that bore more patches than original material. When he saw the Americans, he gave a slow wave. He wanted to talk.

Jacobson approached the aging gentleman, who looked to be about seventy.

"Yes?" Jacobson asked in English.

The older man looked at the American through dark brown eyes that still flashed with life. He said nothing. Instead, he pulled a single sheet of paper out of his jacket pocket and handed it to Jacobson.

Jacobson unfolded the paper and read the few lines written by hand in English. As he did, his brow knitted together, and his mouth tightened into a thin line.

"Who gave this to you?" Jacobson demanded.

The older man looked back at him, obviously not understanding the language yet clearly grasping the meaning of Jacobson's question.

"Uomo tedesco," the Italian said slowly. "Uomo tedesco."

Apparently frustrated by Jacobson's failure to understand his words, the messenger did something that confused the lieutenant even more. He ran one finger down his face from his left ear to his jawline.

Jacobson scowled and tried to figure out how to get more information from him. A moment later, Gosser appeared at his shoulder.

"He said a German man gave him the paper," Gosser offered.

"Really? See what else you can find out," Jacobson said.

Gosser asked the gentleman a few questions in broken, imperfect Italian.

"His name is Giovanni. A German approached him a few minutes ago and gave him a few lire to hand you that note. Of greater interest, that man was none other than our friend SS Colonel Otto Skorzeny," Gosser explained.

"How does he know it was Skorzeny?" Jacobson asked skeptically.

"He doesn't. But he showed us that he had seen Skorzeny's famous scar," Gosser explained, imitating Giovanni by tracing a line from his ear to his chin.

"Thank him for his help and send him on his way," Jacobson ordered, becoming increasingly furious with himself.

As Jacobson turned back to Tucker, he read the note again.

We have your little Jewess. Leave Monterosso or she dies. You have one hour. We are watching.

CHAPTER FIFTY-FOUR

Stiff, rough hemp ropes bit painfully into Rachel's wrists and ankles. She could smell horses and taste grease from the filthy rag stuffed in her mouth, but the coarse canvas bag over her head prevented her from seeing anything. After several minutes of lying awkwardly on a dirt floor, two men snatched her off the ground, dragged her outside, and tossed her into the trunk of a car. Rachel's whole body flinched when the lid slammed shut. She couldn't help thinking it sounded like the lid to her coffin.

After the car started moving, Rachel could tell they were driving through town over relatively smooth streets. But shortly, the road became rutted, bumpy, and steep. As the vehicle charged over what felt like a huge crater, her head smashed against the metal interior, and she had to fight to remain conscious. Rachel lost track of time as she bounced painfully against the top and sides of the trunk. When they finally came to a stop, her captors cut the ropes on her ankles and marched her into another building, probably a shed, and chained her to a pole. As a trickle of blood ran down her face, the realization of what had just happened fell on her all at once. She didn't know exactly where she was, but she had a good idea – the bishop's villa. And the young Jewish girl knew who was nearby.

Terror engulfed Rachel's entire being. She had lived with near-constant fear in the camps for years. During that awful time, anyone could become the Nazi's next victim. But this was different. This time, the Nazis chose her.

She tried to force herself to calm down. But the brief glimpse of the huge SS officer she had last seen in the Messerschmitt tunnels as the Germans evacuated shook her to the core. She remembered when his blue eyes fell on her that day. *Did he remember her?*

It didn't matter.

She was going to die.

The dirty canvas bag hid the tears that streamed down her cheeks, and her entire body trembled uncontrollably. Every horror-filled memory from the concentration camps came flooding back, descending like a black curtain across her mind, chasing away every bit of joy she had found since leaving Gusen. She tried not to feel sorry for herself. Her fate would be no worse than the thousands of other Jews the Germans murdered. But she had tasted freedom and, incredibly, a chance at love. And that made her seizure by the Nazis all the more bitter.

Rachel tried without success to pull herself together and control the fear that raced out of control. Then, Jacobson popped into her mind. She hadn't known the American lieutenant for very long, but she had complete faith that he would never abandon her. Cy would come for her. Rachel grabbed onto that one tiny thread of hope, held it close, and found strength.

Calm down.

Breathe.

Survive.

***

Jacobson rubbed his temples and tried to think. He had antici-pated a brutal struggle to get his hands on Adolf Hitler. And with Tucker, Pernell, and Downtown, they had a fighting chance to bring him to justice. But now he faced an impossible choice.

If he didn't leave Monterosso and abandon his pursuit of Hitler, Rachel would die. The death of one more Jew would mean nothing to the Nazis, but she meant everything to him. He was in love with the girl he found starving in the concentration camp. He had known it from the first moment he saw her, but never dared admit it to himself – much less tell her how he felt.

On the other hand, he had a mission to accomplish. Maybe the most important mission in the world.

And time was running out. He needed a third option.

Ten minutes later, Jacobson gathered his remaining team. Tucker, Downtown, Pernell, and Gosser listened carefully while he laid out his idea. In the end, they all agreed that Jacobson's plan came with enormous risk. But they also knew it was their only hope of capturing Hitler and keeping Rachel alive.

CHAPTER FIFTY-FIVE

The phone in Bishop Calbiani's villa rang only once before Skorzeny snatched up the handset.

"Report."

"Four Americans and the Austrian are boarding a fishing boat," the priest in Monterosso conveyed from the seaside café.

"Describe what you see," Skorzeny ordered.

"Three enlisted men and one officer – all wearing uniforms. The Austrian is a short, fat, inept man. They had to pull him over the side of the boat. One of the local fishermen is piloting them across the surf and out to sea as we speak."

Skorzeny wasn't satisfied. "Are they the same men that arrived this morning? Be sure of your answer before you respond, priest."

The priest thumbed nervously through a set of rosary beads with one sweaty hand while holding the receiver to his ear with the other.

"Yes, Colonel. They are the same men."

"You do not fill me with confidence, *holy man*. How can you be sure?" Skorzeny challenged. "Your life depends on the clarity of your eyesight."

"I watched them arrive. Also, it is not difficult to tell Americans from local Italians. Americans are brash and overconfident. They walk with sinful pride in their step. The men in the boat are, indeed, the Americans who came ashore this morning," the priest said, literally praying he sounded more confident than he felt.

"Very well. Do not move from your position until I order you to do so. Call immediately if they return."

The priest held the phone to his ear even after he heard the 'click' of the line disconnecting. After a few moments, he gingerly replaced the heavy black handset.

"I did as you asked. Colonel Skorzeny believes you have left Monterosso," the priest said, looking into the barrel of a pistol aimed at his head.

"Good, Father. You did real good," Pernell said from the floor at the priest's feet.

"Are you Catholic, my son?" the priest asked Pernell as the American stood.

"As a matter of fact, I am," Pernell replied. "So, you know, this really should bother me a little."

The priest's eyes opened wide just before Pernell stood and slammed his pistol into the side of the priest's head, knocking him out cold.

"Bless me, Father, for I have sinned," Pernell said, crossing himself. "But not near as much as you."

CHAPTER FIFTY-SIX

After confirming the Americans' departure, Skorzeny found Hitler pacing back and forth across the broad terrace in front of Bishop Calbiani's villa. The setting sun shot rays of light into the valley that danced through the new green foliage of the densely packed trees. But although nature provided a spectacular light show, the SS Colonel could tell that Hitler saw only darkness. When the dictator brooded this heavily, he became obstinate and demanding. The conversation he needed to have with him would not be pleasant.

"My Führer," Skorzeny said, formally announcing himself with a click of his heels. "May we speak for a moment about the arrival of the U-boat in the morning and a change we need to make to our short trip to the shore?"

Hitler stopped pacing and shot a sideways glare at the tall SS officer.

"You have explained all this before. Why must you continuously bother me with details? Details. Details. Details. Why must *I* always be the one to make sure the tiniest piece of every plan is in place? It is your responsibility to ensure my safety! Yours!" Hitler ranted, pointing a finger at Skorzeny's face. "If you cannot manage this simple task, I'll find another more competent officer. I have had enough of your prattling and sniveling!"

Skorzeny stood at attention as Hitler yelled and screamed obscenities, bits of spittle hitting him in the face. He had endured the other man's maniacal behavior before, excusing the Führer's outbursts as an outlet of sorts for the incredible stress the leader of the Third Reich withstood over many years. Skorzeny maintained his silence now only through steel-like discipline.

Hitler's ranting continued. He accused Skorzeny of betrayal and treason for the inhumane treatment he claimed to have suffered since leaving his bunker in Berlin. He berated Skorzeny unmercifully, ignoring the SS Colonel's heroic performance of his duties during the war and on the current mission.

"You have failed! Failed!" Hitler screamed into Skorzeny's face. "I will be captured and tortured by the detestable Americans and then handed over to be torn apart by the filthy communist Russian horde. And it is your fault! Yours! Get out of my sight. You shall face charges of treason by the Fourth Reich."

Setting aside his brilliant military exploits during the war, the SS colonel had just successfully transported the highest value and most recognizable target in the world across three occupied countries while pursued by a determined enemy and under constant threat of capture. Nobody, no matter how loyal, can withstand baseless accusations and threats from the person to whom they swore allegiance. Loyalty must flow in both directions.

Making sure they were alone, the highly decorated SS colonel looked directly into Hitler's eyes and saw only madness. Perhaps he should have seen Hitler's break with reality coming. During the past few weeks, he witnessed the man's psyche flipping between manic happiness and mirth to hysterical paranoia. Now he saw the truth. The once all-powerful leader of the German people had become nothing more than a crazy old man, so steeped in his own insane megalomania he could no longer make rational decisions.

Hitler took a step backward under the intensity of Skorzeny's gaze. But his frenzied complaints and denunciations of Skorzeny didn't stop. He had lost control of himself.

In a flash, Skorzeny grabbed the lapels of Hitler's coat in an iron grip. Anger, mixed with deep disappointment, flowed like a hot river through his veins. He had to restrain himself from smashing his fist into Hitler's face.

Aghast at the SS Colonel's sudden, violent action, Hitler fell silent. His watery, bloodshot eyes now conveyed shock and growing fear.

"How...how dare you," Hitler managed.

"How dare I?" Skorzeny snarled. "I dare as I always have. I dare in defense of the fatherland. I dare in the name of the German people. I dare to preserve National Socialism. And, I dare so that I may complete my mission."

"But... but your oath to me...." Hitler stammered.

Skorzeny pulled Hitler's face close to his own. "My oath to you is and always has been secondary to my oath to my country and the Nazi cause. My orders are to deliver you to the U-boat for transportation out of Europe. You may rest assured, *Adolf*, I will carry out my orders."

"You serve *me!*" Hitler screamed.

Skorzeny released his right hand from Hitler's coat and slapped the ex-dictator's face so sharply that the black fedora flew from his head.

"No. You put me under the command of the Deacon. I serve him now. Germany once worshipped you as a god. No longer. Now you are nothing more than a familiar face plastered on a puppet to be used as the new leaders of the struggle for National Socialism deem appropriate. You still retain at least that much value. But make no mistake. Your life is no longer necessary for us to regenerate and grow strong once again. So, if you wish to live, you will remain silent. You will not question my orders again. Do you understand?"

The last embers of defiance faded in Hitler's eyes, and he nodded slowly.

"Do not test me, old man," Skorzeny warned, his hand raised in the air to strike again if Hitler protested in any way.

Hitler's shoulders slumped in resignation as he reached to retrieve his hat.

"May I retire now?" Hitler asked pitifully.

"Go. Speak to no one. If you do..."

"Yes. Yes. I know," Hitler replied quietly as he staggered back toward the door.

Skorzeny watched the broken, dispirited man disappear inside the villa. Turning back to look over the balcony, he removed his black SS hat and ran one shaking hand through his hair. He had just abandoned his personal oath to the Führer, an act he never thought possible.

But he had not and would not walk away from his duty. He would get Hitler safely on board the U-Boat tomorrow morning.

Jacobson be damned.

CHAPTER FIFTY-SEVEN

"Lieutenant? Who were those guys in the boat with Gosser?" Downtown asked.

Jacobson took another sip of water from a ceramic jug and poked at the small campfire Tucker started deep in the woods above town.

"You remember that old character that handed me the note? Well, I had Gosser find him and explain how the Nazis took Rachel. The gentleman took offense at being used like that. As it turns out, he is extremely respected around here, and he persuaded several of his fishermen friends to put on our uniforms and get in the boat with him."

"So that's how we got lucky enough to have civilian clothes that smell like fish," Downtown said, sniffing at the sleeve of a well-worn shirt. "How did you know the priest would be watching the beach?"

Jacobson let a small smile appear on his face.

"Someone had to be watching the beach to see if we left town. Tucker thought the best bet would be one of Bishop Calbiani's priests. He was right," Jacobson replied.

"What happened to the guy?" Downtown asked. "Pernell kill him or something?"

"That's enough questions, Downtown," Tucker barked.

"It's okay, Sergeant," Jacobson said. "No. Pernell just knocked him out and tied him up in the storeroom of the café. He'll be fine."

"Should have taken out the son-of-a-bitch. Nothing makes me madder than an evil person pretending to be a man of God," Downtown said under his breath.

Jacobson nodded. "Yeah. I've been a Catholic all my life. Most priests and nuns are what they say and try to do good. But I've seen way too many willing to hit kids and do other, well, nasty stuff."

"What about Gosser? You think we'll see him again?" Tucker asked.

"I told him to stay with the other men in the boat at the next town up the coast for the night. Since no roads connect the two towns directly, we can't be sure the Nazis won't have someone else watching that beach for new arrivals or reinforcements. But I'm sure he'll find a way to get back here to claim his reward," Jacobson replied with little emotion.

Tucker could see Jacobson still struggling with losing Rachel. The lieutenant was taking a big risk trying to pull the wool over the Germans' eyes. Rachel's life, and those of the entire team, rested on his lieutenant's every decision. Not for the first time, Tucker patted himself on the back for not accepting a battlefield commission and all the headaches that came with being in command.

At that moment, Pernell appeared in the firelight.

"I checked halfway up to the villa. No sign of sentries or patrols," he reported.

"Okay, Downtown, your turn. How do we stop a car or cars without making it look obvious?" Tucker asked.

"Well, a tree across the road would stop them, but that would only give away our ambush point. We don't have a saw anyhow," Downtown responded, pondering the question out loud.

"Even if they believe we actually left town, the Germans aren't going to take any chances. They'll be hell-bent on getting out of the woods and onto the beach. And, they'll be well-prepared for an ambush while the cars are still passing through the trees," Jacobson remarked.

"I bet they run patrols along either side of the road inside the forest to flush out anyone waiting to attack," Tucker added.

All four men considered their options.

"Hey, Lieutenant? Let's say they expect an ambush in the mountains. Once they reach the beach, I think they'll get cocky and let their guard down. Maybe we can hit them there," Pernell suggested.

"Well, I'll be damned, Pernell. That's not bad," Tucker commented with genuine admiration.

"Sounds risky," Jacobson said, carefully considering Pernell's idea. "We'd have to find a way to surprise them without the trees to give us cover. Not to mention, once they hit the beach, they are only a quarter of a mile from that big rock pier. I'd wager a month's pay a boat, probably a sub, will meet them there. We'd have only one chance to stop them."

"Oh, I can build something to stop any cars driving along that little sand track at the top of the beach," Downtown stated. "But I'd have to get started right now to get it done by morning. And I'll need Pernell's help."

"One other thing," Jacobson said. "They'll have Rachel with them as a hostage if she's still alive. Please look out for her."

"No problem, Lieutenant. We'll grab Hitler and get Miss Rachel back to boot," Tucker pronounced.

Jacobson wasn't so sure.

CHAPTER FIFTY-EIGHT

Frankfurt, Germany

The Deacon pressed a button on his intercom with manicured fingers.

"Herman. Please come in and provide me with an update."

Almost immediately, the frosted glass door to his office opened, and his personal assistant appeared carrying a shiny black leather folder. Herman ran a thin finger down the paper inside and looked at his boss.

"Subject B is currently awaiting transport at the U-boat base in Narvik, Norway. Subject C embarked on U-108 yesterday morning at 0500 local time. Unfortunately, Subject D's transport team dispatched him yesterday to preserve operational security."

The Deacon didn't react or have questions, so Herman continued his report.

"Subject E flew out of Barcelona, Spain, yesterday, and is now on the island of Las Palmas in the Canary Islands. Subject F arrived at the same location yesterday. I'm given to understand the two men were more than a little surprised when they met."

"I'm quite sure they were," the Deacon responded, amused. "It was a little naughty of me to have two of our subjects meet each other.

But I couldn't resist the temptation of seeing what would happen if they did."

"I'm told their reaction was just delicious," Herman cooed.

"Herman! Don't be gauche," the Deacon chided.

"My apologies, Herr Deacon," Herman replied with a slight bow. "Their next stop will be Buenos Aires, Argentina, via an Argentinian-flagged cargo vessel."

"Very well. Now, what of Subject A? You know how I worry about him," The Deacon said with a smirk.

"Of course, sir. Reports from Colonel Skorzeny have been infrequent at best. Although, Bishop Calbiani reported that Skorzeny successfully delivered Subject A to Calbiani's villa in Monterosso, Italy, 36 hours ago. We received one somewhat garbled call from a priest in Monterosso who confirmed Skorzeny would meet U-110 on the coast near the town tomorrow morning just after sunrise as planned," Herman reported.

"And this Lieutenant Jacobson? Is he still in pursuit?"

"There have been no reports about Jacobson or any other impending dangers to Subject A since he and Skorzeny's team boarded the flight arranged by Calbiani."

The Deacon placed his elbows on his desk and intertwined his fingers, as he often did when deep in thought.

"We won't have long to wait for good news, then. And, no matter how dogged this Jacobson may be, if he has indeed followed Subject A all the way to the coast, he will not survive a direct encounter with SS Colonel Otto Skorzeny."

CHAPTER FIFTY-NINE

As dawn approached the Italian coast, Jacobson awoke to Tucker shaking his shoulder. Shuddering in the cold spring air, Jacobson wished he could warm himself in front of the campfire from the night before.

"Sergeant? What time is it?" Jacobson asked, forcing himself into full consciousness.

"O330. Sunrise is in two hours, sir," Tucker responded. "If the Germans are moving Hitler today, they will leave just before dawn."

"Damnit, Sergeant. Why did you let me sleep so long?" Jacobson asked.

"Well, if I ain't mistaken, you want to capture none other than Adolf Hitler himself and rescue Miss Rachel at the very same time. You'll need to be sharp," Tucker answered. "Come on, sir. You need to get to the beach."

"Fine. Did you get any shuteye, Sergeant?"

"Aw, hell, sir. I haven't slept since I made friends with a fat red-headed barmaid back in England before D-day," Tucker laughed.

"Alright, let's go see what Downtown has come up with," Jacobson said, getting to his feet.

"I better stay here for security, if that's alright, sir," Tucker suggested. "I wouldn't want any Krauts sneaking up on you before everything is set."

"Alright, Sergeant. But get to the beach as soon as you think you can. We'll need you there when things get hot."

Jacobson jogged down to the beach. To his surprise, he found the entire area deserted. A light surf rolled in under a bright half-moon. But he saw no sign of Pernell or Downtown – or anything resembling a roadblock on the narrow sand track leading south toward the old pier. Several abandoned fishing boats rested upside down a third of the way to the water from the road. Nearby, fishing nets swayed gently back and forth in the light breeze on spindly sticks buried deep in the sand.

Confused, Jacobson looked around for any sign of his men. He didn't want to call out to them for fear of attracting attention.

He couldn't believe that Pernell and Downtown would simply disappear. They had been loyal and highly competent during the entire mission. They had to be around somewhere.

Jacobson took off at a run along the sand road, looking left and right.

What the hell is going on?

Suddenly, a body seemed to materialize from under the sand and stand up.

Startled, Jacobson stopped dead in his tracks.

"Don't go any farther, sir!" Downtown's voice shouted.

"What?" Jacobson responded. "Where did you come from?"

Before Downtown could answer, Pernell appeared on the other side of the road as if by magic.

"We got a trap dug into the beach right there, sir," Downtown said, pointing a few yards from where Jacobson stood gawking at both men.

"Jesus, guys, you surprised the crap out of me!" Jacobson managed to say.

"Yeah, well, you know, that's the whole point of an ambush," Pernell said proudly.

"Alright, show me," Jacobson said, profoundly impressed with what he had seen so far.

Downtown walked with the lieutenant along the road until they reached a small rock that Downtown used to mark the beginning of his trap.

"You see it?" Downtown asked.

"See what?" Jacobson asked, not perceiving anything out of the ordinary.

"Good. Looks like we got it right," Downtown said. "It took us all night, but me and Pernell managed to dig a trench right here all the way across the road. We had to pitch the sand out onto the beach so it wouldn't pile up."

"I sure don't see any trench," Jacobson responded, admiring his men's ingenuity. "How did you camouflage it so perfectly?"

Downtown explained what he had concocted. "Now, that part took a little doing. After we got the pit dug out, we pulled apart one of those old boats. I don't think anyone will mind. It was rotten and of no use anymore for fishing. But it fit our needs perfectly. We used the boards from the sides to make a little bridge over the ditch. We covered the boards with a couple of fishing nets. Finally, we carefully tossed sand over the nets until it perfectly matched the height of the rest of the road. The hardest part was making the surface look exactly right."

"So, when a car drives over the ditch, the rotten wood will cave in under it?" Jacobson asked.

"No doubt about it. Those old boards couldn't support the weight of a big dog, much less a car," Pernell added.

"And if there are two cars, and the second tries to go around, they won't get far. We picked a spot where the beach on either side of the road is too soft to drive over," Downtown explained.

"Excellent job, men. Just goddamned excellent! But you guys seemed to appear out of nowhere. How did you manage that?"

"That was all Pernell's idea," Downtown said, looking at the other soldier.

"Yeah, well, my family spent a lot of time on the beach at Coney Island. We used to play this game where we buried kids in the sand and tried to scare grown-ups as they walked by. We'll do the same thing here. If you do it right, nobody can see you even if they're standing right next to you," Pernell explained. "All you need to do is scoop out a shallow depression, climb in, and throw sand over yourself except for your nose and mouth."

"We thought about hiding under those boats until the cars passed by, but that wasn't the right place relative to the ditch trap. Too far from the road," Downtown explained.

Tucker appeared a minute later.

"I don't think we got much time left, Lieutenant. Dawn is in less than an hour. Downtown and Pernell get the ambush set?" the sergeant asked.

Jacobson quickly explained Downtown's trap and Pernell's idea about concealment in the sand.

"I don't much like all of us being buried up to our noses, but it will work for part of the ambush. Here's what I suggest," Tucker said, turning to Jacobson.

After discussing tactics for a few minutes, the four men took their positions.

CHAPTER SIXTY

"Doctor, get him in the car and make sure he remains silent," Skorzeny ordered.

"Of course, Colonel," Hitler's physician replied quickly. "He is heavily sedated and will remain compliant."

Skorzeny glared at the doctor.

"It is your responsibility if he becomes difficult."

"Yes, Colonel. I understand perfectly," the doctor replied sheepishly.

Skorzeny no longer found it necessary to fulfill Hitler's every demand. On the contrary, the SS Colonel now treated Hitler as little more than a package to be delivered.

"Sergeant Adler, get the girl and place her in the front seat of my vehicle. We may yet have use for her. If all goes as planned, you may have the pleasure of ridding the world of one more Jew when our task is complete," Skorzeny said to his senior non-commissioned officer.

The sergeant came to stiff attention. "Yes, sir! Thank you, sir."

"Is Sergeant Bentler still on patrol?" Skorzeny inquired, already knowing the answer.

The sergeant looked at his watch.

"He should be returning now, sir."

Fifteen seconds later, Bentler appeared from the woods.

"Report," Skorzeny barked.

"Per your orders, I reconnoitered both sides of our route from here to the beach. I saw no sign of the Americans. I did find where someone lit a small fire recently, but after searching the area thoroughly, I could find no evidence of who or when someone might have been present, sir," Bentler reported.

Skorzeny didn't like unknowns. He had to assume Jacobson and his men remained nearby.

"Sergeants, you will take the lead car. Shoot anyone who appears without hesitation. I foresee a trap. What is your weapons status?" Skorzeny asked.

"Sir, we both carry the StG 44 assault rifles provided by Bishop Calbiani with a hundred rounds of 8mm ammunition per weapon and our sidearms," Adler replied.

"Excellent. I shall have the same in the second vehicle. I would have preferred to have heavier weapons available, but such could not be arranged. Stay alert, men."

"Yes, sir!" the two sergeants replied in unison.

While the doctor led Hitler from the villa and placed him in the back seat of Skorzeny's car, the SS Colonel looked at his men with genuine affection. They had followed him into countless perilous, even suicidal, combat and commando operations. They had earned his respect.

"Hans. Ernst," Skorzeny began, using his men's first names. "This will be our last operation as proud German soldiers. God willing, we will survive to carry the Nazi cause forward in another place and at another time. We will not fail to complete this one last mission. Our goal seems simple enough, but I assure you it is not. The Americans have shown great tenacity, and we cannot assume they will not yet try to stop us. Our duty is clear. We must deliver our sacred charge, such as he is, to safety. *We will not fail.*"

The two SS sergeants stood at attention, thrust their chins forward, and puffed out their chests with pride.

"Yes, Colonel!"

Neither missed the fact that Skorzeny did not end his short pep talk with 'Heil Hitler.'

***

Rachel tried to keep her hands moving. After finding it impossible to escape the tight ropes and chains that bound her to the wooden pole, she concentrated on moving around enough to keep her hands from going numb from lack of circulation.

The initial terror had faded, slowly transforming into iron determination to survive. And if she got a chance, she would take what revenge she could against the vile Nazis. She even buoyed her spirits by fantasizing about attacking Hitler himself.

So, when she heard the door to the shed open, she didn't fear that death might be coming for her. Instead, she truly believed that this was the beginning of God's plan for her to avenge the Jewish people.

Rachel said nothing as rough hands pulled her to her feet and released the chain holding her fast against the support pillar. The canvas sack remained over her head as the guard led her outside and tossed her into the front seat of a car. With her hands still securely tied behind her, she had to lean forward awkwardly in her seat.

If she could have looked backward, she would have seen Adolf Hitler himself, wearing the same camel-hair overcoat and dark fedora she had seen back at the underground laboratory. She might also have noticed his glassy eyes and blank expression.

A moment later, she heard the driver's door open.

"Good morning, Jew," she heard Skorzeny say, mocking her predicament. "Welcome to the last few minutes of your life. Try to enjoy them."

Rachel said nothing. She refused to respond to ridiculous taunts from Nazis.

"Nothing to say this morning?" Skorzeny asked with mock interest. "Alright. But I think you would be interested to know who is riding behind you in the back seat."

Rachel remained silent.

"Huh," Skorzeny huffed. "A brave Jew. Excellent. Since you don't seem to care, I'll tell you that the Führer, Chancellor of Germany, and grand exterminator of Jews, like you, sits just over your left shoulder."

Rachel's low, menacing response wiped the leering grin off the SS Colonel's face.

"Good."

CHAPTER SIXTY-ONE

A few minutes later, Skorzeny braked hard into a tight right-hand curve. The steering wheel jerked in his hands as the tires bounced in and out of deep ruts in the dirt road. Ahead, he could see Bentler wrestling his vehicle around the next corner. Skorzeny accelerated, trying to keep up with the lead car. Although three highly trained and experienced SS troops comprised a formidable threat to any attacker, they couldn't risk becoming separated from each other.

Even though Bentler scouted the length of the road to the beach earlier that morning, Skorzeny ordered the two-car convoy to drive as quickly as possible. The trees and terrain alongside the rough, narrow track provided ample cover for an ambush, and speed would provide their best defense if the Americans were waiting in the forest. The SS colonel didn't anticipate an attack near the villa, but the chances of a surprise assault increased exponentially as they neared the beach.

Driving the dangerous road above 20 mph left no room for error. From time to time, a deep gorge appeared to the left of the road. A hundred feet below, a fast-running stream carried the last of the melted winter snow to the Ligurian Sea. Occasionally, brief, tantalizing views of bright blue ocean water appeared through the windshield.

***

With her hands tied behind her back and a bag over her head, the wild bumps, dips, and curves made Rachel's stomach churn into a ball of hot nausea. She fought the urge to vomit, drawing in one deep breath after another. On one tight curve, she slid across the seat, bumping into Skorzeny's arm.

Skorzeny growled with disgust and violently shoved Rachel away, causing her right shoulder to crash into the metal door handle. Her entire arm went numb for almost a minute before being replaced by a sharp, stinging pain. Though painful, she was relieved to find her arm and hand still worked so she could use a gun, knife, club, or even her bare hands...if she got the chance.

No. When I get the chance. God, please give me strength. Please.

***

As they approached the bottom of the mountain, the road leveled out. Soon, the rutted dirt path turned into a better-maintained gravel and seashell surface.

Skorzeny could see the ocean ahead, and as planned, Sergeant Bentler turned left onto the beach road and accelerated hard.

So far, there had been no sign of Jacobson or anyone else. As the SS officer turned to follow the lead car, he saw the old pier less than a half-mile ahead. And out to sea, he glimpsed the conning tower of a black U-boat slicing toward the rock pier.

Skorzeny allowed himself a rare moment of triumph. In just minutes, he would hand off Hitler to the U-Boat captain, marking the successful end to yet another near-impossible mission.

Suddenly, twenty yards ahead, Bentler and Adler's car slammed nose-first into Downtown's trap as if a giant invisible hand reached out and snatched them into the earth. The front of the vehicle disappeared, and the rear wheels left the ground, spinning uselessly in the air.

Skorzeny slammed on the brakes. But before his car could come to a stop, two figures rose from the beach on either side of the lead car and threw coverings off their weapons. As sand drained off the men, they unleashed a deadly rain of fire into the wrecked automobile.

Ambush!

Rounds from Pernell and Downtown's M-1 Garand rifles punctured the thin sheet metal of the car's doors as if they didn't exist. Trapped inside, Adler and Bentler died in a hailstorm of .30-06 bullets without firing a shot.

Then, the two Americans turned their rifles on Skorzeny.

***

Skorzeny threw his car into reverse and hit the gas, expecting shots from ahead to shatter the windshield at any moment. The rear tires spun wildly in the sand, but the car barely moved. Near panic, Skorzeny pressed the gas pedal into the floor. Nothing. They were stuck.

To make matters worse, he saw two more men approach from behind, weapons aimed at his head.

"Shiest!" Skorzeny shouted.

He was trapped. Surrounded.

But he had one last card to play.

Skorzeny reached over and snatched the canvas bag off Rachel's head. Grabbing her by the hair, he yanked her from the car with his Luger pressed into her temple.

CHAPTER SIXTY-TWO

"Stop!" Jacobson ordered. "Hold your fire!"

Tucker approached slowly with his submachine gun aimed at Skorzeny's skull. A moment later, Pernell and Downtown took up positions behind the desperate SS officer.

Jacobson glanced at Pernell and then at the car stuck in Downtown's trap.

Pernell got Jacobson's meaning and made a slashing motion across his throat. Everyone in that car was dead.

"Do you speak English?" Jacobson asked Skorzeny.

"Of course, Lieutenant Jacobson," Skorzeny responded, hoping to surprise the young officer by using his name. "I am glad we have a chance to meet. You are a determined man."

"Let the girl go. This is over," Jacobson said, ignoring Skorzeny's false politeness.

"Is it? If this little Jew is important to you, I think we are not finished. In case it is not obvious what I want, you will let me and my passengers walk to that pier, or I'll put a bullet in her head. If she means nothing to you, so be it."

Rachel looked at Jacobson without a hint of fear, turned her head, and spit in Skorzeny's face.

"Kill him, Cy."

Skorzeny didn't react to Rachel's act of bravado other than to tighten his grip on her hair and yank her head painfully backward.

"Uh, sir," Downtown called. "Look what I found in the back seat."

Jacobson took his eyes off the SS colonel only long enough to take in the astounding sight of Downtown dragging Adolf Hitler out of Skorzeny's car.

Skorzeny didn't even glance in Hitler's direction. "Well, Lieutenant? We have a boat to catch. I must insist on an answer. Now."

Jacobson glanced out to sea.

"I don't think you do, Colonel," Jacobson replied calmly, pointing toward the open water.

The sub, which just minutes before had been on course to dock at the pier, had turned away. As Skorzeny watched, plumes of compressed air erupted from under the black submarine. Almost immediately, the U-boat slipped under the water and disappeared.

"I guess somebody with a good set of binoculars saw you fail and decided to save their own ass," Jacobson commented.

"Cowards," Skorzeny snarled. "But our situation remains the same. Release the Führer to me and let us drive away. You have ten seconds to decide."

To emphasize his resolve, the SS Colonel pressed his Luger painfully under Rachel's jaw.

Jacobson looked into Rachel's eyes and found only defiance.

"Kill Hitler, Cy," she said again as loudly and clearly as possible.

Rachel's words pulled Hitler from his drug-induced stupor.

"No! No!" Hitler screamed in terror. "Otto, do something!"

Skorzeny turned to see Hitler kneeling on the ground with the barrel of Downtown's rifle pointed at his head. His personal loyalty to the man had faded, but his fanatic belief in the Nazi cause still burned brightly. To Skorzeny, the sight of Adolf Hitler with a gun to his head was the same as a gun to the head of Nazism itself.

Skorzeny struck with the speed and precision of a cobra. In a single smooth motion, he removed the gun from Rachel's neck, turned, and fired at Downtown.

The shot spun the big Iowan around, causing him to drop his rifle.

Skorzeny's unexpected attack came so fast that the Americans didn't have time to react. But Rachel did. As soon as Skorzeny removed the pistol from her head, she spun violently away and dropped to the ground.

In a last-ditch effort to save himself, Skorzeny swung his Luger toward Tucker.

Jacobson's pistol barked once, sending a .45 caliber round slamming into Skorzeny's chest. But the battle-hardened SS officer barely flinched. Almost inhuman strength and self-discipline kept him on his feet.

Skorzeny snarled like a wounded animal, and his eyes blazed with hatred. With one last mighty effort, he lifted his pistol toward Jacobson, intending to take revenge on the one enemy he could not defeat.

Tucker and Pernell fired simultaneously. The clatter of Tucker's submachine gun mixed with the deeper thumps of Pernell's rifle.

Blood erupted through Skorzeny's black uniform from nearly a dozen lethal wounds. The SS officer staggered backwards as if in slow motion, before finally toppling onto the sand.

"Check on Downtown!" Jacobson ordered before walking over to the barely breathing Skorzeny.

With his last breath, Skorzeny peered up at Jacobson and croaked, "Heil Hitler."

Jacobson aimed his pistol at Skorzeny's forehead and fired.

"Fuck you."

CHAPTER SIXTY-THREE

Rachel flew into Jacobson's arms seconds after he delivered the final kill shot.

"Are you okay?" Jacobson asked, holding Rachel tightly. "God, I thought I'd lost you."

"I am fine, Cy," Rachel assured him. "You saved me. Thank you. Are you okay?"

"I am now. I am now," Jacobson said, looking into Rachel's spectacular dark eyes and stroking her hair like the most precious thing in the whole world.

After a long moment, Rachel reluctantly pulled herself out of Jacobson's arms. "Go check on Downtown, Lieutenant."

Jacobson found Tucker already at Downtown's side, pressing a field dressing into a wound in the soldier's shoulder.

"How is he?" Jacobson asked.

"Downtown's tougher than an overcooked steak. Looks like a through and through. He'll be fine," Tucker reported, just before noticing Pernell appear to check on his friend.

"I told you to keep an eye on Hitler," Tucker barked.

"I got him and that weaselly doctor I found in the car tied up tight right over there," Pernell said, pointing to where Hitler and his physician sat in the sand, their tied hands behind their backs and leaning against the rear bumper of the car. "They ain't going anywhere."

Suddenly, deep thudding explosions from out to sea drew everyone's attention.

"What's going on?" Pernell asked.

Jacobson stood and found the source of the sounds. A half-mile offshore, tall geysers of water erupted into the air. Seconds later, more rumbling explosions washed over the beach, just as a giant seaplane turned and climbed away from where it had just dropped a salvo of depth charges.

"Looks like the Navy found the U-boat," Jacobson concluded.

"Yeah, but what are they doing now?" Tucker asked.

As they watched, the big high-winged plane turned back toward shore, descended, and settled into the water, high rooster tails of spray flying into the air behind the massive aircraft.

Jacobson looked around. "Where's Rachel? She should see this."

***

While the men focused on Downtown's injury and the depth charge attack, Rachel turned back to Skorzeny's body. She stood over the corpse, coldly examining the lifeless remains of Germany's most renowned soldier and the embodiment of the Nazi's mythical 'master race.' Against all odds, she had escaped his grasp. But no smile of relief or satisfaction crossed her face.

She wasn't finished.

Kneeling, Rachel ignored the blood and gore as she unbuttoned Skorzeny's black tunic. Almost immediately, she found what she wanted.

Checking to be sure that Jacobson, Tucker, and Pernell's attention remained on Downtown, she crawled around the body with her prize, staying out of the men's line of sight. Rachel didn't like avoiding Jacobson, but she couldn't chance him stopping her from what she had to do next.

A few seconds later, she knelt directly in front of Adolf Hitler.

With his hands tied tightly behind his back, the once all-powerful dictator appeared to be asleep or unconscious, his chin resting on his chest. Hitler's doctor had watched her approach and opened his mouth to cry out when Rachel put a finger to her lips and showed him Skorzeny's ornate SS dagger.

"Make a sound and die," she whispered in German.

The doctor's eyes grew wide with terror, but he kept his mouth shut.

A second later, Rachel grabbed Hitler's coat and tried to shake him awake.

It took several attempts, but Hitler finally opened his eyes, only to find himself staring at the face of a young Jewish girl. Then he saw the SS dagger flash in the bright morning sun.

"What do you want of me, Jew?" Hitler managed to say, his eyes locked on the highly polished steel blade only inches from his face.

Even as the hate-filled words left his mouth, the dark terror Rachel suffered at the hands of the Nazis drained away as if she suddenly woke up from a horrible dream.

"I want many things. I want you to look at me. Look into my eyes. See the soul of my family and of every Jew you murdered. And I want you to know you failed. We survive."

Hitler grimaced with disgust, obviously nauseated by a Jew's close presence.

Seeing Hitler's reaction, Rachel brought her face to within two inches of Hitler's famous mustache. Her eyes blazed with righteous contempt.

"I want you to look upon the face of vengeance, smell its breath, touch its skin," Rachel snarled, grabbing the dictator's neck in her left hand.

Hitler tried to move away, violently twisting his head from side to side.

"And, I want you to know that you die by the very weapon upon which the SS swore to protect you."

Hitler's eyes grew wide with fear, and his mouth opened to call out for help.

But before any sound could escape, Rachel plunged the SS dagger into Hitler's chest with every ounce of strength she could muster. The blade stuck for a moment on a rib, but the young Jewish girl wouldn't be satisfied until she pierced Hitler's heart. She grasped the dagger with both hands and, using the weight of her body, forced the blade deeper and deeper.

Hitler's mouth opened in a silent scream. His body stiffened and arched upward in pain.

Rachel ignored the hot blood that spilled over her hands and pushed the blade deeper still. Little by little, the razor-sharp dagger disappeared until only its swastika-emblazoned hilt remained visible.

Finally, blood seeped from the monster's mouth, his eyes stopped moving, and his head flopped sideways onto his shoulder.

Wiping her hands on Hitler's coat, the Jewish girl who spent years in Nazi prison camps and watched hundreds and hundreds of innocent people die knew that she had done what she was always meant to do.

Rachel stood slowly, leaving the dagger protruding from Hitler's chest.

Still staring at the corpse of Germany's 'Führer,' she felt a hand rest softly on her shoulder. Turning, she found Jacobson looking into her eyes.

"You said you would kill him," Jacobson said gently.

"And I did," Rachel replied without a trace of pride.

"Yeah, you sure as hell did."

CHAPTER SIXTY-FOUR

Jacobson and his team watched the massive Catalina flying boat come to a stop thirty yards beyond the shoreline. A few seconds later, a side door flew open, and a crew member threw an anchor into the water. Another sailor launched an inflatable boat and jumped inside, followed by a short, slightly built, balding man wearing a civilian suit. A small outboard engine coughed to life, and the boat headed directly toward Jacobson.

"That's incredible!" Rachel commented in awe. "I knew flying boats existed, but I had no idea they could be so large."

"They use them for all kinds of things," Jacobson said. "That one has depth charges mounted under the wings."

As the inflatable boat approached, Jacobson recognized the civilian on board. Mr. Smith, the peculiar bespeckled OSS officer, gave a short wave as the craft bumped over the low surf and landed directly on the beach.

Smith jumped out of the boat in a few inches of water and walked directly to Jacobson.

"It is good to see you again, Lieutenant. Please report what happened here," Smith said, not introducing himself to anyone else.

"Yes, sir. But I have an injured man. Do you have a medic with you?" Jacobson asked, first making sure Downtown would receive proper care.

After Smith ordered the sailor manning the inflatable to transport a medic to shore, Jacobson began his report.

"If you'll come with me, I'll explain as we examine the evidence."

Still tending to Downtown's injury, Tucker and Pernell watched from where they were. Rachel joined the combat soldiers, knowing that Jacobson would let her know if he needed her.

Jacobson first led Smith to Skorzeny's body.

"Well, I wasn't expecting to see SS Colonel Otto Skorzeny here," Smith said with genuine surprise. "You managed to kill the most accomplished and skilled SS officer of the entire Third Reich. I must say I'm impressed."

"It was a team effort."

Smith looked over his glasses at Jacobson. "Modesty, Lieutenant?"

"No, sir. Truth."

"Very well. Now, the most important question. Where is Adolf Hitler?" Smith asked with no more emotion than if he had asked Jacobson to pass the salt.

"Over there," Jacobson replied, pointing to where Hitler's body remained slumped under the bumper of his car.

"Please rejoin your team, Lieutenant," Smith ordered. "I don't want to be disturbed."

For the next half-hour, Jacobson and his team watched as Smith studied the body. He retrieved several photos from a briefcase and carefully compared them to the corpse's face. Using a set of calipers, Smith measured the body's forehead, the distance between the eyes, the width of the mouth, and several other dimensions, making precisely written notes in a small notebook. Finally, he laid the body out on the ground and measured the corpse's overall height and the length of its arms, legs, and fingers. He even removed its shoes and checked the size of the feet. He ignored the SS dagger still protruding from the body's chest.

While the medic tended to Downtown, Tucker asked, "What's that fella doing, sir?"

"I can't be sure, but I'd say he's making sure that's really Hitler," Jacobson suggested.

"Aw, come on, sir," Pernell scoffed. "That's Adolf himself. That's plain as day to see."

"Apparently, it's not that easy," Jacobson replied, keenly interested in Smith's comprehensive examination.

When he finished with the body, Smith pulled the doctor to his feet, and a quiet conversation ensued. Smith asked questions, and the doctor answered. Jacobson couldn't hear what they said, but he guessed Smith was questioning the doctor about Hitler's medical condition.

After almost an hour, Smith walked over and pulled Jacobson well out of earshot of the others.

"Okay, Lieutenant. I know you have questions. Now is your chance to ask them. Then I will have a few of my own."

"My first question is obvious. You were trying to confirm that man is, indeed, Adolf Hitler. Is that Hitler?"

"What I am about to tell you is top secret and the truth," Smith began, looking into Jacobson's eyes. "You will not repeat it. Not to your team. Not to anyone. Ever. The answer to your question is yes. That is indeed the body of Adolf Hitler, former Chancellor of Germany, Führer of the Nazi party, and war criminal."

Jacobson wasn't surprised. He believed all along Hitler had been his target.

"I'm not sure I follow, sir. Hitler is dead. His body is in the sand right over there. Why is it critical that simple fact remains a secret?" Jacobson wanted to know. "If no one else, my men and Miss Cohen have a right to know what they accomplished."

Smith understood Jacobson's concerns.

"Yes, well, the world has already been told Hitler killed himself in his bunker. The Allies have been promoting that version of his death for nearly a month. We risk a backlash from the press and the public, and it might even give aid and comfort to Japan if we change the narrative now and admit we were wrong. Also, the Russians have already gloated about finding and identifying the body. We will shortly begin negotiations on how to rebuild Europe. A revelation like this could begin a controversy with the Soviets we don't need," Smith explained.

"At least tell me what I *can* tell my team," Jacobson urged. "They think they caught and killed the most wanted man on earth. And they did. They deserve an explanation."

Smith agreed. "I commend your loyalty. Yes, they do deserve an answer. And I have one. Partially based on the truth. Do you recall how I told you the OSS had several other teams like yours working on credible reports that Hitler survived the fall of Berlin?"

"Of course," Jacobson said.

"And how, as your investigation progressed, I informed you that other teams reported they were also in pursuit of Hitler?"

Jacobson nodded thoughtfully.

"Well, the reason I couldn't send you more men or come myself is that another team killed an imposter posing as Adolf Hitler only two days ago in the Netherlands. And not just a look-a-like. The Nazis, or someone helping them, must have scoured Europe and possibly Russia and North America looking for Hitler doppelgangers."

"Doppelgangers, sir?" Jacobson asked, never having heard the term.

"A doppelganger is an exact replica of another human being or someone that looks so much like someone else they are nearly indistinguishable from each other," Smith explained.

"Oh, my God! That's incredible! Did you examine the imposter from several days ago?" Jacobson asked.

"I did. And I almost bought the hoax. But you were so sure you were actually following Hitler, I decided to make sure. It took me nearly a day to find all the information I needed about the real man, but after I did, I was able to conclusively prove the man killed in the Netherlands was, as you said, an imposter," Smith replied. "Thus, my detailed examination of the body today."

"So, whoever was helping Hitler escape used that imposter as a decoy," Jacobson concluded.

Smith hesitated a moment before responding.

"I'm about to reveal another secret. Same conditions. We don't think the Nazis planned to use him as a simple decoy. We believe that whoever devised this plot had more than one doppelganger ready to evacuate Europe. They would act as decoys for the escape of Hitler himself, but could also take his place if needed."

Jacobson finally understood.

"And you believe the Nazis, or whoever took these extraordinary measures, wanted to be sure the real Hitler, or someone able to successfully pose as him, could lead a new Nazi party? And, you also believe that one or more successfully escaped."

Smith nodded. "We don't know how many. But yes, I'm afraid so."

Jacobson hadn't experienced the full devastation of World War II. Still, he had seen a Nazi concentration camp, inspected one of their near-futuristic underground technical facilities, and, most importantly, seen what the Nazis had done to Rachel and her people.

"So, my team will think they caught and killed an imposter," Jacobson repeated. "I know it's necessary, but..."

Smith interrupted. "Don't worry, Lieutenant. Their accomplishment will not go unrecognized. I will recommend, and they will all receive, promotions, full retirement benefits, a Silver Star, and an immediate flight back to the United States. Also, I provided you with a small fortune in gold coins and cash. If you haven't disbursed those funds, you can tell me you used it for bribes and such, if you get my meaning. I'll leave any reward you care to disburse to your men to your good judgment."

"I think that will work out just fine. Thank you, sir," Jacobson replied with a smile.

"Good, now I have a question. Who stuck that SS dagger into Hitler's chest? I noticed Skorzeny's was missing from his body, but I know he did not kill the Führer."

Jacobson had come to trust Smith, but hesitated to answer.

"I don't want anyone to get in trouble."

"I'm a Jew, Lieutenant. I'd like to shake his hand."

"Her hand," Jacobson corrected.

"The girl? Rachel Cohen? How did she manage to do that?" Smith asked, a bit astonished.

Jacobson just looked at the OSS officer.

"Oh, I see. Hitler killed thousands, maybe even millions, in cold blood. He deserved no better. She's Jewish, correct?"

"Yes. As I wrote in my first report about the tunnels, she identified Hitler and stuck to her story while helping me gather the evidence of his presence in Gusen. She is determined, brilliant, speaks several languages, and is the most courageous person I have ever met. I am not overstating anything when I say this mission would not have begun, much less succeeded, without her."

Smith smiled. "And you have fallen for her if I'm not mistaken."

Jacobson couldn't deny his feelings. "I guess so."

"Please ask her to join us, Lieutenant."

Rachel walked over hesitantly, thinking she would be admonished, or worse, for killing Hitler as she did. She was wrong.

"Miss Cohen, my name is Smith. It is not my real name. I, too, am a Jew. It may go against tradition, but it would be my greatest honor to shake your hand."

Rachel was taken aback by Smith's words and looked to Jacobson for help.

Jacobson smiled and nodded.

Rachel stuck out her hand, and Smith took it, bowing gallantly.

"You are truly the Queen Esther of our time, Miss Cohen," Smith pronounced with great deference.

Rachel blushed with embarrassment, like the eighteen-year-old girl she was, at being compared to the queen credited with saving the Jewish nation during the height of the Persian Empire.

"Thank you, sir," she managed to say.

Smith reached around his neck, unclasped a small necklace, and pressed it into Rachel's hand. At the end of a thin silver chain, a brilliant Star of David glinted in the morning light.

"This I received from my mother when I entered the military years ago. Please take it as a tangible reminder of what you have done for me, my family, and all Jewish people," Smith said.

A single tear ran down Rachel's cheek. She didn't know how to respond.

"She deserves to know the truth," Jacobson urged.

"Yes. I agree," Smith answered without hesitation.

Smith repeated what he told Jacobson about the man Rachel killed and the existence of imposters. When he finished, Rachel swore to never reveal the truth.

"Now I have one last question," Smith said. "The OSS needs men and women like you two. Lieutenant, I would like to bring you back to Washington to join my office. We will be pursuing Nazi criminals for many years, and I could use your help."

"I'd be honored," Jacobson replied. "But..."

"Yes. Yes," Smith interrupted. "I know. You won't come without Ms. Cohen at your side. Correct?"

"Uh, uh," Jacobson stammered, looking at Rachel. "Yes?"

Rachel took Jacobson's hand and looked up into his eyes.

"Yes."

EPILOGUE

Frankfurt, Germany

Herman knocked on the Deacon's office door.

"Enter."

The Deacon stood behind his desk, pouring over blueprints. He didn't acknowledge Herman's presence for almost a minute as he scanned page after page of plans for a massive dam project to be built in northern Argentina.

Finally setting the blueprints aside, he asked, "You have news?"

"I'm afraid so, Herr Deacon. And it is not what we hoped," Herman replied.

"Well, perhaps I should decide whether it is good or bad. Please proceed."

Herman opened his leather binder and read from the report he had received just minutes before.

"This is from sources loyal to Bishop Calbiani familiar with events of this morning in Monterroso, Italy. I shall read it verbatim."

It is my duty to report that American aircraft attacked and destroyed U-boat 110 off the coast of Italy near the town of Monterosso at approximately 0600 this morning. Immediately afterward, the same aircraft landed in the sea offshore. Several American soldiers dressed as civilians and one Jewish female boarded the aircraft a short time later. They retrieved two bodies known to be those of SS Colonel Otto Skorzeny and the Führer, Adolf Hitler. Examination of the area took place as soon as practicable. Two vehicles owned by Bishop Calbiani and provided for the use of the Führer were found destroyed, along with the bodies of two non-commissioned SS officers. A third body, that of the Führer's personal doctor, was also discovered, the victim of an apparent suicide (although the precise cause of death cannot be confirmed). Evidence at the scene suggests that the Führer and his party were ambushed and overcome by American forces led by Lieutenant Cy Jacobson. End Message.'

The Deacon took a seat in his office chair and intertwined his fingers over his desk.

"I see. So, the Führer is dead."

"Yes, Herr Deacon," Herman replied tentatively.

Herman waited nervously for the Deacon's reaction. It was not what he expected.

The Deacon cocked his head and opened his hands in resignation.

"Well, *que sera sera,* as the Spanish say. What will be will be. That crazed fool made me wealthy beyond my wildest dreams. If he hadn't stupidly delayed leaving Berlin until the last possible moment, he might have successfully escaped to Argentina."

"May I ask a question, Herr Deacon?"

"Of course, my dear Herman. What is it? You appear concerned," the Deacon replied.

"Will the loss of Adolf Hitler hinder your plans for South America?"

The Deacon laughed out loud.

"Herman! You know as well as I that we have more than enough Adolf Hitlers. And each looks more authentic than the original.

Plus, they shall be much more compliant and effective than the sick old man who turned Berlin, and the entire country, into a burning wreck. Fear not, Herman. The Nazis will reappear again – to our great profit. Perhaps not wearing those ridiculous black uniforms and flying those silly red swastika flags. But we shall make sure they rise again."

"Nothing makes men like us more money than political chaos and war."